THE
DESERT LAKE
MYSTERY

THE DESERT LAKE MYSTERY

Kay Cleaver Strahan

COACHWHIP PUBLICATIONS
GREENVILLE, OHIO

The Desert Lake Mystery, by Kay Cleaver Strahan
© 2024 Coachwhip Publications edition

First published 1936
Kay Cleaver Strahan, 1888-1941
CoachwhipBooks.com

ISBN 1-61646-587-5
ISBN-13 978-1-61646-587-2

1

I had dark forebodings. I had evil premonitions. Naturally, Adam Oakman being the high type of man he was, and his visitors being his relatives, mannerly and well educated, I didn't predict anything so uncouth as murders and dead bodies disappearing like the morning dew all over the place. But I had forebodings, just the same, and the difference between mine and most forebodings was that I stated mine far in advance.

It was early June, hot as hades in a skillet here in southern Nevada, so I decided to drive out to Adam's house and cool off. He called his place "Hay Patch" because he wanted to make it sound humble. The house was built acres deep in palm groves and for size it compared well with a couple of battleships.

Nothing, not even the dog, was stirring around the place when I got there. But, since Adam and I have never stood on ceremony since we were kids together in the first grade, I went right in through the big hall to the front parlor and was blinking the sun out of my eyes when I heard a murmuring voice remark, "My heart was once a vagabond."

"No?" I said, trying to be surprised politely and seeing for sure that what I thought I saw was Reggie Duefife, curled up as much as an unwieldly fat man can curl on one of the sofas, sucking a lead pencil.

"Oh, my, Jeff!" he said. "You startled me. What rhymes with vagabond?"

"Drag a pond," I said.

"Mercy, no!" he said. "I'm writing poetry. My heart was once a vagabond—"

"Try calling it something else," I suggested. "An internal organ."

He flitted his hands nervously and straightened his glasses. There was always something about the way those glasses pinched close together on his little fat nose that reminded me of the double *oo* in *cootie*.

"Organ rhymes with Morgan," I told him. "Either J. P., or 'Morgan, Morgan the raider and Morgan's terrible men.'"

"Perfectly absurd," he said very fretfully. He talked like that. He called his socks his "hosiery," and overeating "dietary indiscretions." Adam said that if Reggie undertook to eat a bunch of grapes he'd hire somebody to spit the seeds out for him. But Adam wronged him there. Reggie never was lazy when it came to eating. He bought all the ladies' magazines and, after he went to Memaloose Lake, he'd cut the pretty pictures of food out of them and pin them around to decorate his cottage. His mamma, Mrs. Ivy Duefife, who thought the world of him, said that he was a culinary genius, the lad only twenty-five years old and able to read a recipe and tell in a flash whether or not it would be tasty. It was Reggie himself who found the recipe for the frozen pudding named "Pineapple Supreme" that figured later in the horrible tragedies at Memaloose Lake.

Leaving Reggie, then, saying only, "Good-by, Reggie," I went along hunting for Adam and was very abashed and bothered when I parted the curtains to the back parlor and saw the crippled boy named Terwilliger Young but, luckily, called "Twill" for short, holding Adam's daughter, Betty-Jean, in his lap and kissing her ungrudgingly.

Adam liked Twill—everybody did—but I knew that he'd raise thunder about having him for a son-in-law. I knew, too, that a few weeks ago Adam had sent a cable to his foster son, Kent, down in South America telling him to come straight home. And I was certain that the old dizzard was getting Kent here to try to make a match between Kent and Betty-Jean, for the purpose of saving himself the trouble of dividing up his fortune instead of leaving it in a lump sum as he'd always planned.

I wouldn't call this an evil foreboding, but I was worried all right when I knocked on the library door. Rosemary Young opened it and I stopped worrying.

Rosemary was this Twill Young's sister. The first evening I met her a young author fellow, a widower named St. Dennis O'Dell who has lived in these parts off and on for the past fifteen years, was out at Hay Patch too, calling on the new arrivals. We left together and I asked him what he thought of Rosemary Young.

He got very dreamy and answered, "Is there a Rosemary?"

O'Dell's daughter, Brigid, a saucy, red-haired, seventeen-year-old trick who was with us, said, "You mean she is too lovely to be true, St. Dennis?"

I said, "She's the prettiest girl I ever saw," but he snapped me up.

"She is not at all pretty," he said. "She is— Let me see. A picture Shelley painted. A sonnet Giotto wrote. How's that, Brigid?"

"Rotten," she answered. "Because it is forced. Untrue. Rosemary is real, healthy, vital—"

O'Dell groaned. "Charming, I suppose? Adorable?" He hated being criticized.

"Yes, she is," Brigid stood up for herself. "And beautiful. But why do you suppose Mayor Oakman dislikes her?"

"He can't dominate her," O'Dell said. "He forced her to play bridge this evening. In some way, by being so gay and amusing I believe, we all felt that the victory was hers and not Adam Oakman's. Also—she won. If those two ever came to a genuine conflict, she'd win. He senses her superiority and hates it. Her strength is the force of natural things: flowing water, growing seeds. Oakman's strength is money, and a sledge hammer."

"A sledge hammer can smash a seed," I said.

"Not if it can't find the seed."

Brigid said, "She isn't remote. And she doesn't seem in the least mysterious."

"A quality of the miraculous," O'Dell said.

You might think that all this, as described by the O'Dells (though I'll admit that they had a reputation around here for being probably crazy), would abash an old desert rat like me at every meeting with her. I never felt more at home with anybody in my life than I did with Rosemary Young.

"Hello, Jeff!" she said. "Come in. I'm glad to see you." And I knew she meant it and was just on the point of accepting her invitation when I saw Mrs. Ivy Duefife— Reggie's mamma—in there; so I backed out, making excuses.

At first glance, because Mrs. Duefife was so large, loppy and kind of always at loose ends like a load of hay, you'd probably have thought that she belonged to the home-staying type of womanhood. That is, if she hadn't already begun telling you about her successes in public life on the platform. She was a great talker. But I always had a feeling that she was just repeating passages, absent-mindedly, from her public speeches. After you got used to it you didn't care so much; but, at first, to have her break a silence by beginning out of a clear sky, "Let us be frank. We know that race suicide is now the rule, rather than the exception," was very embarrassing. Her voice was queer, too. It was the kind of voice you'd expect to hear saying words like, "Victory!" or, "Hark!" or, "Beware!" or, at least, "Amen." Though when she said only a few words they were, generally, "Reggie, dearest, don't blow your nose." (Reggie was always blowing his nose. He said it was because he had sinus trouble. His mamma said he had sinus trouble because he blew his nose. I never learned the facts of the matter.)

Outside the kitchen door I found Twill's little dog that he'd picked up in an Indian town and named *De Profundis*—"Funny" for short—drooping with that long lonesome look that dogs put on when there has been trouble; and, sure enough, in the kitchen Jeremiah, Adam's old French cook, was on another rampage.

"Well, well, Jeremiah," I said, as cheery as I could with him looking so downcast, "how in the world are you?"

He snatched his white cap off and slung it on the floor like it had bit his head. "The boss says I have a yellow streak," he told me and burst out bawling.

Jeremiah's custom of bursting out crying and sobbing was the most embarrassing habit I ever saw in any man, foreign or native. Adam, after thirty years, could cope with it. I never could. But I tried.

"So has a rainbow," I said. "I'll bet he was complimenting you. Honest."

"I am not a rainbow," he said. "But if I was I'd be quitting anyway, because I'm not six men, nor eight, nor ten, nor—" He went right on, sobbing and counting by two until I stopped him at thirty-six by asking gently where in hades Adam was.

"Ants," Jeremiah answered, pointing outdoors and hiccupping pitifully.

Seeing Adam, the cause of all this sorrow, sitting out
in the sizzling hot sun, comfortable and patient as an old
slipper, watching one of his anthills made me mad all over.

"Hello, Mayor," I said.

"Hello, Sheriff," he said.

Adam was a senator from this state for as long as he
wanted to be. Since then he's been mayor of Ferras. I've
been sheriff of Oakman County since his senator days, so
why calling each other by our titles should mean cussing
each other out, I don't know. But it does.

He kept on rubbering at his ants. Ants have been a life-
long hobby of his. There's a saying out here that whenever
Mayor Oakman moves from one anthill to another he's
made a million dollars.

"'They aren't beautiful,'" he said, pretty soon, "'and
certainly they aren't funny.' I read that in a book about
ants the other day. The same man wrote, 'Guest ants are
harmless. Their greatest pleasure consists in riding pick-
a-back.'"

"So Jeremiah's quitting?" I said.

Adam stood up, shook down his overalls and buttoned
his undershirt. His worst enemy—and he has plenty—
couldn't accuse him of often being dudish in private. "So
Jeremiah is not quitting," he said. "Do you remember that
automobile park at Memaloose Lake?"

"Why?" I said, hating to admit remembering it.

A few years ago there'd been trouble about whether the
new highway was going straight from Sackawash to Mesquite Forks, passing the puddle called Memaloose Lake, or
whether it should detour, far, through Ferras. Adam had
large interests in Ferras. The highway detoured. A young
wise guy from L. A. was left stranded with the deluxe auto
park he'd had foresight to build on the lake. Adam, who
sometimes gets sentimental, took the place off his hands
so the young fellow didn't lose a dollar, and put up a

twelve-foot fence all around it to keep stray tourists out and allow the trees planted on the place to grow in peace. Adam said that trees took so long to grow that folks loved chopping them down, but that if he could prevent them doing so Memaloose Camp would soon be a paradise on earth.

Maybe. In the meantime the trees all died and the place with its dazzling, flat-roofed white stucco buildings, its network of cement roads and walks made from the white granite off of old Tumboldt Mountain, glittering stark and desert bare under the blinding sun, was fit for nothing but an eyesore. Adam liked the lake. What I thought was that in any other county such a thing would have got discouraged and dried up long ago. But Memaloose held out, sprawling in the heat, reflecting the calico hills humped yonder beyond it, mocking the thirsty stunted sagebrush that struggled down through the rocks in mangy patches to its rim.

"I've decided," Adam said, answering my question, "that it would be a pleasant change to take my guests over there for the summer. There is plenty of room. Eighteen furnished cottages and the big community house. I'll provide everything but service. Jeremiah needs a rest, as do the other servants. They'll stay here at Hay Patch."

"You and Betty-Jean going too?" I asked.

He had a strong streak of politeness that I always forgot between times. "Certainly. I shall suggest it as a vacation for us all. There is an interesting anthill by the gate. Some work will be good for Betty-Jean and all of us."

Then and there I began expressing my forebodings, explaining to him that his taste for the blazing sun without a sprig of shade was shared by none and was healthful for few.

He wouldn't listen. He honestly liked Memaloose so well that if it had been in another county he'd have thought it was all right. Besides that, he liked the idea of a social experiment—or so he said—with its possibilities for developments.

"You bet," I told him. "For developing sunstrokes, suicides, blindness and maniacs. It is no place for white folks," I told him. "Even the Indians were on to it, and down on it when they named the lake 'Memaloose.'" Memaloose being, as everybody knows, the Indian word for death.

2

Our chatting had brought us to the kitchen door, and the next thing I knew I heard Kent's nice voice saying, "Hello! Hello, Dad! Hello, Jeff!" And, sure enough, here he was at home, all the way from South America.

Adam was so tickled that if Jeremiah and I hadn't been there I'll bet he would have kissed the boy besides hugging him. "Good to see you, son," he kept saying; and then, out of a clear sky, "Married? Paying alimony?"

"Neither," Kent said. "I thought you sent for me to attend your wedding."

That gave us reasons for laughing heartily as we sat down to the ice cream that Jeremiah was dishing up for us with tears of joy.

"Broke?" was Adam's next question.

"Broke?" Kent stalled, knowing as well as I knew that Adam hoped he was stony. "I tell you what, Dad. You grubstake me and I'll strike out and find us a gold mine."

Adam was so pleased he couldn't begin to hide it. "What do you want with a gold mine?" he asked. "I thought glass-sand was your hobby."

It might have been, all right. Three years ago Kent had located the largest glass-sand properties in the world right here in Oakman County where Adam had been sitting on them for years watching ants. And the best of it was that the boy went ahead on his own hook and sold them to a certain automobile manufacturer for a cool million. It was Kent's first year out of mining school. Adam had taken him into partnership, so they whacked even; but Adam was sore to the bone and big bones at that.

The kid had beat him at his own game and was sitting pretty in the king-row able to jump either way out from under Adam's thumb where he'd been ever since Adam had adopted him right after the Pink Purse Mine disaster. Kent's father, Van Zandt Kent, was one of Adam's and my best friends. He got killed that night, helping with the rescue work. Maybe Van wasn't as careful as he could have been. Kent's mamma had died only a couple of days before that.

Boylike, when Kent collected his money he wanted to travel. Adam had traveled so he saw no use in Kent's doing so. He was so vexed when Kent left for his trip that he wouldn't even write to him. Kent sent telegrams from here and there, but Adam wouldn't answer them; so that's how the two had got out of touch.

"Glass-sand isn't bad," Kent answered Adam's remark. "But I've heard that gold mines were all the fashion lately."

"I'm sick of them, myself," Adam said, and went forgetting how he'd promised me that when Kent came whimpering home, fleeced of his last cent, he'd never do another thing for him, "but if you want one I expect you should have it. We'll see. Now I have a surprise for you. You thought you were joking when you spoke of my being married. Well, I was married, son, more years ago than you are old."

One of the many most astounding things about Adam is that he never knows he makes talk. That marriage of his, by this time, was a part of the folklore of the state, like the Tonopah death, or Mrs. Bower's fortune-telling. All there was to it, though, was that Adam came home from Washington, D. C., one spring, aged forty, with a pretty little eighteen-year-old girl for a wife. He parked her in Hay Patch and went right off on a prospecting trip. "Inopportune" is the word O'Dell used for that trip of Adam's. Adam explained it by saying that a grown man couldn't sit around the house all summer with a girl. When he came home in the fall he found a note for him right where it belonged on the pincushion.

If any of this was news to Kent so was the Revolutionary War. I doubted that Adam had other news for him, either, since Kent had ridden out from Ferras with Joe Laud who is as gossipy as a rocking chair. But Kent never said a word and Adam went on, telling about his daughter and his visitors.

Chances are if Adam's wife, Elizabeth, had lived he never would have heard about his daughter, Betty-Jean. But his wife had died three years ago and late last winter Adam got a letter from a Judge Shively down in Pasadena, California, telling him the facts. The Judge said that he himself was getting old and was straightening out his affairs; so he thought, now, it was his duty to inform Adam that he had a daughter, Betty-Jean Oakman, born April 25, 1912, in his, Judge Shively's, home as the enclosed copy of the birth certificate would show.

He apologized for not letting Adam in on the secret sooner by saying that when Elizabeth had come to his home, instead of returning to her own people who had opposed her marriage, she had exacted solemn promises from Mrs. Shively and himself that they would never let Adam know he had a child. Betty-Jean, he said, had grown up in their household and flowered into a beautiful young woman of whom he was as fond as he was of his own son. Mrs. Shively had passed on, recently, and since his own days were numbered he wanted Betty-Jean to have a father.

What crazed Adam was that that doll-faced wife of his had known that the meanest revenge she could take on

him was to have a child of his living in the world and not
tell him about it. Next to ants, children were always his
favorite hobby.

St. Dennis O'Dell looked the Judge up in *Who's Who,*
and he sounded fine with college degrees, one son, two
clubs and a nice religion after his name. So we advised
Adam to go right down and see his daughter.

"What daughter?" Did we mean a couple of slickers
who were playing him for a sucker? While he was in this
mood he wrote a letter to the Judge, and the old gentleman
answered ending the affair and being most respectfully
his.

How the old fox finally managed to get Betty-Jean to
come to him, instead of his going to her, I don't know. But
she came in March, and she struck me as being a pretty
little blonde with dimples and a small voice always saying,
"Yes, indeed," and, "Thank you very much."

O'Dell said she was a pleasantly commonplace, excellently reared young woman. Brigid O'Dell said that she
was God's perfect gift to parents.

"Depending on the parents," O'Dell objected. "She
bores me irreparably. She has been boring me all my life."

When I mentioned that he'd just met her, Brigid who
is nice that way, explained. "He means all the 'dear, sweet
girls.' The sort who still think that calling a Ford car a
'Lizzie' is a splendid joke."

"Our handsome Mayor," O'Dell said, referring to Adam
who, folks say, looks like Ramsay MacDonald, "will be off
on another prospecting trip one of these days."

At his age Adam's prospecting trips were pretty well
over. But, a month later, he invited Mrs. Duefife and Reggie to come to Hay Patch, sending them the money for
their tickets, when he got her letter from New York asking
for a loan. Mrs. Duefife was Adam's half-sister, divorced
for years from Mr. Duefife.

Rosemary and Twill Young were the children of his other half-sister. She had died when they were little tykes. Their father fell out of a high window in 1929. Since then, Mrs. Duefife said, they had been having a terrific struggle to exist, but she didn't think the poor things would come to Nevada for a visit, proud and sensitive as they were. Adam wrote to them, anyway, including the wherewithal, and they must have hopped the first train out of New York.

Since Adam had always had it in for his stepmother's branch of the family, claiming that she'd hounded his father to the grave though she died years before the old gentleman did, I thought Adam wouldn't have taken such a sudden interest in all these kinfolks of his if things had been more stimulating at Hay Patch that spring. His excuse was that Betty-Jean needed young company.

As I said, I'll bet none of this was surprising news to Kent, though Adam's version of it may have been. It was to me.

The surprise came later when we three walked out to see Kent's horse, Acrasia, and saw her from a distance, loping around the pasture as gentle as a cradle, with something white on her back. To date, as far as any of us had known, Kent was the sole mortal who had sat Acrasia longer than one second flat and lived.

By the time we got to the fence Rosemary was climbing it with a bridle in her hands, and Acrasia without a sign of a saddle was nosing up to the rails and munching suspiciously.

Rosemary was wearing a pair of Twill's white pants, but kind of grimy, and held up by a belt that shirred them in big wads below her waist, and a shirt with a patch on it. Costumed, in fact, something like a scarecrow without its hat and looking, no matter what O'Dell said, prettier than dawn on the quiet deserts. Her brown hair had come loose from the dignified way she fixed it and was fluffing around her face to her shoulders; and her eyes, which I'd thought were brown, turned out to be a queer soft shade of purple.

"Hello?" she said, questioning a little, smiling and wiping the sugar off her hand to her shirt-front.

Adam never opened his mouth. Kent had his open just enough to look gawky. I was never a hand for etiquette, so I kind of fumbled saving the situation. "Kent," I said, "meet Kent. Rosemary, this is Rosemary."

"Rosemary," Kent said, sounding a little silly and doing the first fresh thing I ever saw the boy do with a lady. He put his hands round her waist and jumped her down off the fence.

Then and there I noticed a peculiar thing. There was something alike about Kent and Rosemary. Now Kent being an upstanding, sunburned blond, good-looking though not resembling, I'm pretty certain, the Vikings of old as Mrs. Duefife accused him later, it stands to reason that he and Rosemary didn't look alike. No, and they didn't act or talk alike. I figured a lot over it on my way home and the best I could do was to say that they jibed, like a question and its right answer.

Since it was only twenty miles out of my way, I went around past the O'Dells' place to give them the news.

O'Dell said, "That bag of candy was symbolical."

He had said that before, talking about the bag of candy Adam had given to Kent when he was a curly-haired three-year-old getting underfoot the night of the mine disaster. The baby ate it and threw it right up.

"Beginning with that evening," O'Dell went on, "Kent has consistently refused to swallow the unsavory stuffs that Oakman has forced on him. Schopenhauer, Nietzsche—when the boy was seeking at seventeen. A capital offense, if I had my way—"

I interrupted, knowing how hot O'Dell always got on the subject: "Adam may have made mistakes but he wanted Kent to be a good mining man and he is."

"Wrong. Kent is a good mining man, but Oakman wanted him to be the traditional mule that strays away to the outcropping ledge so that its owner finds the mine with the mule. Now he has picked the boy's wife for him. We'll wait and see. But I'll tell you one thing, Jeff. You didn't fumble your introductions. That was the wisdom in you, man—your deep soul speaking in spite of you."

I never did know whether O'Dell's talk was senseless or just sounded that way. But speaking of mules had put me in mind of Adam so I repeated another piece of news he'd told me that afternoon.

"Betty-Jean," I said, "is reforming Twill of all his bad habits."

Brigid said, "How nice for Betty-Jean. But I didn't know the sweet kid had any bad habits."

"He hasn't," I said. "Smoking, taking a drink once in a while. Adam wouldn't care. It made me kind of wonder if he was up to something. What he can't get in one way he usually gets in another. He's pretty slick," I said, half admiringly, maybe, "and slippery, the old codger."

"So's a wet fish," Brigid said.

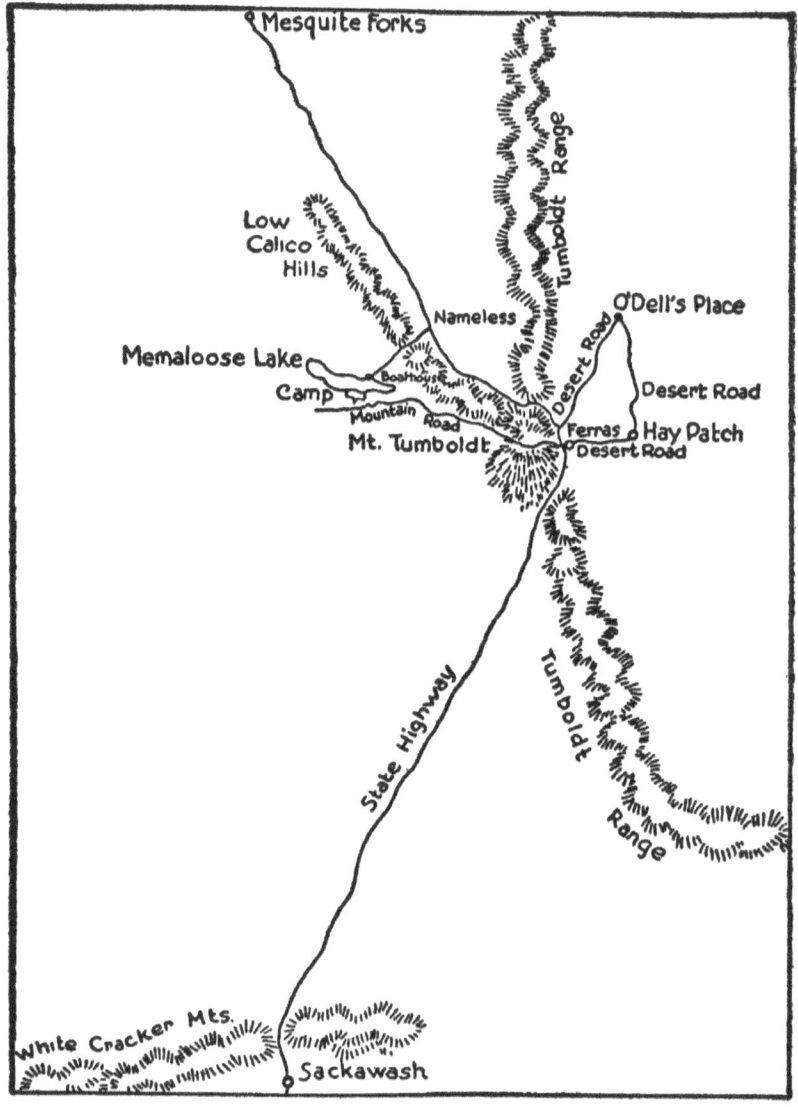

3

One of the more affronting aspects of the Memaloose murders was why the criminal should pick a day when I, Sheriff of Oakman County, was present in person on the place. What made it worse was that I'd been up around Tahoe, chasing some bootlegging Indians for a couple of weeks giving any criminal a good chance to take advantage of my absence instead of my presence.

The morning after I got back I met Joe Laud in at Slim's eating breakfast. As soon as he got through with his wisecracking about Indians always escaping up Tahoe way—though he had his mouth full of my Tahoe trout right then—he began on the news.

Seemed that old Judge Shively had been over at Memaloose for three days now. Joe had it sized up, wrong as usual, that Kent had got sweet on Betty-Jean and Adam had sent for the Judge to help him put a stop to it.

Changing the subject, I asked Joe how the Labor Day barbecue that Adam had held at Memaloose had panned out.

Joe said, "Something awful. They had fireworks. Mrs. Duefife made a speech," and added: "Something awful."

"How are all the other folks over there?" I asked.

"Hot," Joe said. "And going crazy. All but the pup. Oakman has gone already. I drove Brigid O'Dell over there last week. The O'Dells' car is up for overhauling and her papa had to take a flying trip back East. Oakman said to me, 'Joe,' he said, 'male ants, after marriage, are brainless. The only comfort is that, being too idiotic to feed themselves, they soon die.' Was he insulting my ex-wife, or what did he want to say such a thing to me for?"

I turned that off by saying that it was hot enough here and now to bring on a thunderstorm during the day.

"Not a chance," Joe said, wrong as usual. "Ellie won't need to sweep out under your bed today."

I don't know that I'm scared of thunderstorms, but I don't like them. So, that afternoon when I was having a little snooze in my room at the Ferras Hotel and was waked by the thunder I got up and went directly downstairs.

The poolroom was chuck-full of the boys who acted like they had never seen a man in his socks before. I guess they wouldn't have let up on me yet if Kent hadn't been there playing stud. He dropped out for a couple of rounds and rescued me.

Seemed that I'd slept through the worst of the storm when there had been a cloudburst. Kent thought the folks at Memaloose would be worrying for fear he'd been caught in it on the south slope of Tumboldt Mountain. If he had, nine chances out of ten he'd have been killed so they likely were bothered all right. The phone wires were down so he couldn't call them.

He said he could borrow a horse or walk the nine miles over there, but he hoped that when the storm cleared they'd find the road wasn't washed out so bad but what the boys could fix it in a few hours and he could drive the car back. Judge Shively was planning to leave for home on Number 24 at eleven that night, and Kent wanted the old gentleman to get off on account of the heat affecting him pretty seriously—chills, cramps and so on.

I never thought much of Adam's driving, but Adam did and I knew he wouldn't let anybody but himself drive his car around Tumboldt at night. So I wondered to myself whether the Judge wouldn't rather put up with a few more nice chills in this weather than wind up at the bottom of one of Tumboldt's hairpin curves.

Kent, who always was kind of a mind reader, said, "I won't bring the car unless the road is safe for Dad to drive at night," and went on asking me a favor, he said. Would I mind riding my nag, Dollar, over to Memaloose and telling the folks he was O. K. and would be over pretty quick? Betty-Jean, he said, was giving a send-off dinner for the Judge at eight that evening, and he gave me the bottle of sherry that he'd come for and that she'd be fretting about not having to use in her cooking.

"You'll stay for dinner, of course, Jeff," he said. "Betty-Jean would have invited you if she'd known you were back from Tahoe."

I'd eaten Betty-Jean's dinners and, knowing that they were the best ever served in the state of Nevada, I accepted with pleasure. I was glad to accommodate him by riding to Memaloose; but I had a few little things to attend to first. So, by the time I got there the sun was out drying things up so fast you could hear the murmuring sounds they made getting shed of the damp.

I dismounted and opened the Memaloose gate, all plastered up the same way the road had been with wild western hospitality ("Private Property." "Keep Out." "No Trespassing."), and there, leading Acrasia, was Rosemary.

She was wearing a big, black rubber slicker of Adam's that fitted her like the cage fits the canary bird. I knew the minute I looked at her pretty pointed face so white that it made her eyes twice as big as usual and darker, where she was going and what she was dreading.

"Kent's fine," I said, as fast as I could. "I just left him at the Ferras Hotel playing poker."

For a minute I thought she was going to break down and cry from the sudden good news; but, by the time I got to her, she was smiling and thanking me and explaining that she'd have started sooner for Tumboldt only that Twill wouldn't let her.

"He knew that Kent was too wise to come home when a storm was threatening," she said, defending Twill as she always did, "but we've all been worried. Aren't the deserts glorious after the storm?" she said next, and that she was going to take a quick canter out toward the White Cracker Mountains. And up she was, and off and away, sitting her horse as pretty as any buckaroo that ever pulled leather.

Along with everything else, she was a natural-born horsewoman, that girl, and meeting her made me feel good all over as usual. So, when I opened the kitchen door at the community house and Adam, who was in there rasped out at me, "You!" which I've thought was what folks said only to the villain, I did not take it kindly.

"Sorry to discover you, Mayor," I said, noting a guilty-looking sandwich in his hand. "I just dropped in to tell you that Kent is winning all the money in Ferras at a stud game over there. He'll be home pretty soon, but not driving the car. The cloudburst wasn't so bad, but there's one mean place where another hunk may slide later."

"I beg your pardon, Jeff," he said. "I thought you were Kent. Not that I was actually worried about the boy, but—" He went on then, inviting me to stay to dinner, to stay all night, to stay a week if I could; even going so far as to offer me his sandwich, which I refused.

He looked at his watch. "Four o'clock," he said, "and we aren't dining until eight, you know."

I'd had a smack at Slim's knowing, too, that it doesn't take long to get hungry after six in the evening; so I said that nothing on earth would make me spoil my appetite for one of Betty-Jean's dinners and added, only by way of making conversation, that I'd just met Rosemary out by the gate.

"Jeff," he said, "did you know that when a Miner Ant Queen gets into a Scamp Ant's nest she is the most lovable thing imaginable? She caresses the Scamp Ant Queen, dresses her hair for her, flatters her, until in the friendliest sort of way she—" He stopped and opened the back door. I should have known he was up to something, the old dizzard, remembering how he prides himself on his story-telling, but I didn't. "Saws her head off!" he shouted and banged the door, leaving me alone and more taken aback—to make a long story interesting by beginning at the end—than I was when I heard the gunshot three hours and a half later.

4

Brigid, Kent and I were on the front porch of the community house, all of us feeling upset because of a quarrel Adam and Kent had just had inside, when the shot cracked out.

"What's that?" Brigid and I said.

Kent's answer, "Must be a firecracker left over from Labor Day," was sensible, so we all went on down the steps. But before we'd turned east toward Brigid's cottage, which we were bent for, Adam came around the house from wherever he'd gone out of the back door after his quarrel with Kent, and joined us. We stopped a minute, just standing, and then Kent and Brigid strolled on ahead leaving me to trail after them with Adam.

It was about half-past seven and dark was dropping down so the place didn't look quite as hideous as usual. Everything was nice and still, too, except for our footsteps clapping so loud on the cement walk that they made me feel humiliated.

When we came to Rosemary's cottage (Adam's and Kent's quarrel had been about her), I noted that Kent slowed up, and I was hoping the boy wouldn't get Adam sore again by going in there, when I saw Rosemary come running out of Twill's cottage, which was just beyond hers, and heard the awful sound that she was making—too low for screaming but too loud for moaning, shaking itself out into the quiet, and drawing in, and shaking out in horror again.

By the time Adam and I got to her Kent had his arm around her and was begging, "No, no, dear. Don't say that. It isn't true."

"But it is true," she said, and I heard her teeth chattering. "I've killed Twill. I've shot him and killed him. I know I pointed the revolver at him and said that I'd kill him, but I didn't mean it. I didn't mean to. He said I didn't mean to. He knew it. He knew I loved him. Just before he died he said to tell you that he'd killed himself. But he didn't. I did. Kent, can you understand? I can't. But I shot Twill."

Adam started running up the walk to Twill's cottage. I went with him. The door was ajar and the electric light in the parlor ceiling was on showing us at a glance that Twill was not in there dead or alive. The wall bed had been let down and a pillow from it was on the floor between the parlor and the breakfast nook, dented down in as if somebody had just that minute got up from lying on it. In the dent and around it were spots red and wet with blood.

"Flesh wound," Adam said. "Twill isn't much hurt. Rosemary is hysterical." He stepped around the pillow and went striding through the breakfast nook into the kitchen, snapping on the lights. I went with him. I'll give a plan of the cottage here. We went through the kitchen, through the bedroom, through the bathroom, back into the parlor again. I had a crazy feeling that Twill was, maybe, keeping one stride ahead of us through the house; so I half expected to find him in the parlor when we went into it. But he wasn't there.

Rosemary was lying on the bed. Kent was sitting beside her. Brigid was standing by the window looking out with her mouth open. (She said, later, that her mouth opened like that when she saw Rosemary's arms and pretty white frock all smeared with blood, and that she couldn't make it stay closed for half an hour afterward.)

Adam spoke to Rosemary. "Twill isn't much hurt," he said. "He has stanched his own wound. Don't worry. He's all right."

"He died only a few minutes ago," she answered. "There, on that pillow. I held him in my arms. He said, 'Tell them suicide.' He couldn't hear what I said to him. He stopped breathing."

Kent turned to us. Some of the blood had got on his white shirt. "Can't you find him?" he asked, vexed.

I was picking up the small pearl-handled revolver. I broke it, snapped it shut and put it back where I'd found it on the bureau.

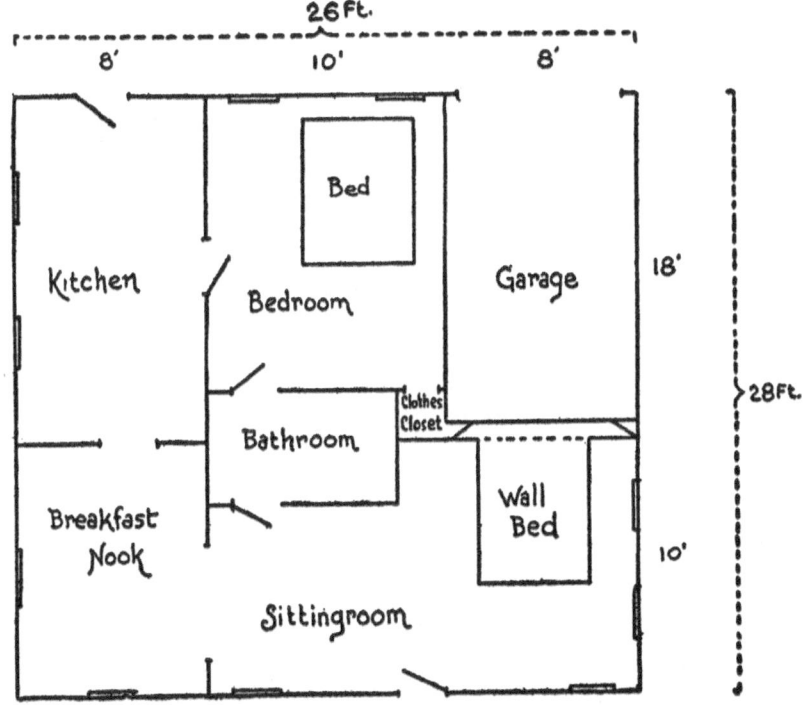

"He died so soon," Rosemary said. "I think it couldn't have hurt very much. It was below the little hollow in his throat, at the side. Rather far down. Would that hurt very much? Would it, Kent?"

"Please, sweet," Kent begged. "Look again. See that pillow over there? No one is on it. You didn't even wound Twill seriously. He has been able to get up and walk away."

"If it had hurt very much," she asked, "could he have spoken? Could he have thought for me and told me to say that it was suicide?"

"Darling, darling—" Kent begged and he sounded more pitiful, though that wasn't possible, than she did.

It seemed to me I'd better get out of there, so I went through the front door and Brigid came with me. I hadn't missed Adam in the house, but when Brigid and I got out in front, here he came hurrying, stumbling over the sagebrush from the back of the place. He had searched the cottage again, he said, beginning with the garage, looking into the clothes closet, under the bed in the bedroom, behind the curtains in the shower bath—all places that we'd overlooked the first time—but he hadn't found Twill.

"He must have gone to the community house," Adam said, still not too worried, though we were all walking mighty fast in that direction. "He probably went out the back way while we were in front with Rosemary. He'll be all right. I want to bring him back and show him to his sister. She's worse off than he is right now."

In spite of one confusing point, which I'll come to presently, that was what I thought. My idea was that Rosemary, in what Reggie afterward called "a mad moment of passion," had taken a shot at Twill and had been so scared when the gun went off that she'd gone out of her mind. This wasn't very sensible, but it seemed barely possible. The ghoulish removing of a dead body off the floor and out of the house in less than ten minutes' time didn't seem possible at all.

"I never dreamed that Rosemary had a temper like that," Adam went on, and I'm sorry to say he spoke admiringly, being like most of us the kind that likes his own faults in himself and others. "I thought she was wishy-washy. Weak as water. Deplorable, of course. Most regrettable. But— understandable. There have been several occasions in my own life when I've been glad afterward that I didn't happen to have a gun in my hands. Cactus Point—eh, Jeff?"

"Yes, you bet," I said. "The only trouble is that if she fired twice it wouldn't look so well."

"Twice!" Adam said. "What do you mean?"

I explained the confusing point. "That revolver she used had been shot twice."

"And did you discover for yourself, Sheriff," he asked, "or were you told that the past few minutes were the only ones in which a revolver could be discharged, here or elsewhere?"

We'd come to the community house. Brigid said, "Rosemary shot only once. We heard it right here on the porch. One shot," and stopped outside the screen door.

Adam and I went on into the big living room. Reggie was trudging around at a brisk gait for him, sweating and vexed.

"It's about time someone was coming to help us," he said. "You chaps take hold of these tables. They have to be pushed together for dinner—"

"Seen anything of Twill?" Adam interrupted, making it careless, and explaining when Reggie said he had not, and, "Why?"

"He was fooling with his revolver just now and it went off and nicked him a trifle. He's more scared than hurt, but he rushed outside and we thought he'd come here."

"Oh, my!" Reggie piped up. "But, for goodness' sakes! He didn't come here. Well, but then where did he come—go, I should say? Where is he? Where can he be?"

"He'll be about somewhere," Adam said, but he didn't sound so careless; and I made a big mistake by suggesting on our way to the kitchen that we'd better get a move on us, since the boy had been bleeding pretty bad and might have fainted.

I don't know yet how Reggie beat us to the kitchen where the two ladies were, but he did, shouting, "Mummy! Betty-Jean! Twill has shot himself. He's lost. Bleeding. Fainted—"

Adam said, "Shut up, you damn fool," and the way he said it, slow, not very loud, accenting the damn, sounded fine. But it was too late. Reggie had done his best to start a panic and for once, anyway, Reggie's best was as good as any man's.

5

Thinking back on it now, it seems to me that there was a long panicky spell of frenzied searching when we were all running like wild through the cottages and garages, stumbling over the sagebrush and rocks outside and shouting in the dark. Time doesn't flit by when you are hunting for somebody as we were hunting for Twill, thinking that every five minutes' delay in finding him might mean the difference between finding him alive or finding him dead.

The moon was in its last quarter and the outside lights were no good because someone had put small colored bulbs in all the sockets, strung high along the walks and driveways, trying to make the place look romantic, I guess. Before long Adam ordered Reggie to get a box of clear glass globes and exchange them for the colored ones. Reggie tried; but the one ladder on the place cracked under him like a nut at the second light. He wasn't hurt but the ladder was and so both he and it continued being useless from then on.

I'll give a map of the camp, offering it as one excuse for us going off half-cocked at first. The territory inside the fence was only five acres of flat, rocky sagebrush desert. We all kept thinking that Twill, a cripple and wounded besides, had left his cottage by the back door bent for the community house. So our plans were to work fast searching the cottages and the grounds between the community house and his place.

Two more excuses were Adam and Mrs. Duefife who both took full charge of everything from the minute Reggie sounded the alarm. Adam could issue orders a little louder than Mrs. Duefife could, but she could issue them lots faster and when it came to one countermanding the orders of the other I'd think it was about a draw.

Adam said, "Jeff, you go back to Twill's cottage and search it thoroughly again. Rosemary may have come to her senses enough to help us. If Kent's there tell him he is needed out here."

"No," Mrs. Duefife said. "Brigid you run to Twill's. I want Jeff to go through this cottage with Reggie."

The result of this particular matter was that when I got up from making an exhibition of myself by looking under the wall bed where Rosemary was lying with Kent sitting

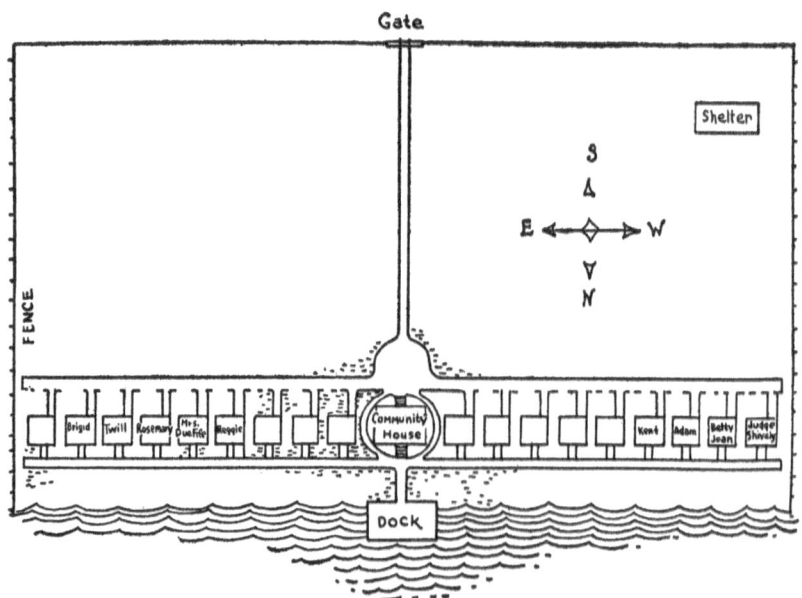

on it beside her, I saw Brigid standing with her freckle-colored eyes squinted up regarding what I thought was
me in a coldly speculative manner.

Rosemary was quiet now, but she looked so sad that I
didn't have the heart to tell Kent that his dad wanted him.
Brigid didn't either. She took hold of my arm and kind of
led me out of there to the front stoop.

"Wait, Jeff," she said, then. "I've something to tell you.
There's no hurry about finding Twill. He is dead.

"How do I know?" she answered, before I'd finished
asking the question. "I know Rosemary. She is not hysterical now. If she didn't know that Twill was dead would she
be lying in there, looking like Death with its eyes put out
and doing nothing? You know that if she thought that there
was a chance in a million of finding Twill hurt, wounded,
she'd be out hunting for him as long as she could walk,
and when she couldn't walk she'd crawl. You know that if
Rosemary had one ghastly sick hope that Twill might be
alive she wouldn't allow Kent to stay with her doing nothing. And Kent wouldn't stay, either. He knows, now, that
Twill is dead. If he didn't, he'd be hunting for him. He'd
know that finding Twill would be better for Rosemary than
staying with her. Kinder and wiser. Kent is lots of both."

I knew that what Brigid had said was good horse sense,
except for one thing, and I told her so. "The trouble is," I
said, next, "that if Rosemary did kill Twill, then some person must have come in the back door, during those three
or four minutes we stopped out in front, and carried his
body off."

Brigid asked, "After we heard the shot, was it ten minutes do you think before we went into the cottage and
found Twill's body gone?"

"Hardly that," I said. "But, anyway, Brigid, no one
would sneak in and steal Twill's dead body."

"Why not?" she said.

"Well," I said, "looking at it the other way: Why? What in thunder could anybody want with Twill's dead body?"

"I know," she said, "I'm just silly. But I'm nervous. Jeff, darling," she went on, smoothing my sleeve, "since St. Dennis isn't here will you take his place for me? Stand by me and be my friend? I'm young, Jeff. And so alone! And you're so good and wonderful."

"Brigid, honey," I answered, "there's been nothing your old Jeff wouldn't do for you, and you know it, since you were knee-high to a grasshopper."

"Promise, darling?" she coaxed. "Word of honor. Not Sheriff's word of honor. Brigid's wonderful friend's word of honor?"

"Promise on all my words of honor," I said.

"Fine!" she snapped, and went on very growling and menacing. "You've promised. Don't forget. If you don't help me I'll marry Joe Laud and St. Dennis will shoot you on sight in your shoes when he gets home for allowing it. The idea! He's forty years older than I am. Revolting. Stop fidgeting and listen.

"A person can't be tried for murder unless the body is found. Someone has had sense enough to help Rosemary. We must help too. The body is probably hidden in one of the farthest east cottages. If we can find it, you can take it on Dollar around Tumboldt as far as Dead Man's Hook. It won't be found for ages, if ever. It's a sheer drop—"

"Brigid," I had to interrupt, "you're as crazy as hades. I'm Sheriff of Oakman County. I can't go riding around Tumboldt disposing of dead bodies in the dark of the moon."

She said, "Well, I can. And I will," and began walking away from me very fast.

I went with her, hoping to talk her out of dastardly deeds and trying to think who on earth could or would steal Twill's body. There was no sense in my thinking of

Judge Shively just then; but I did, and was so surprised
at forgetting him and remembering him that I spoke his
name. "Judge Shively," I said.

"Yahweh!" she said, which is a cuss word for her. "No,"
she went on. "He's old and lame with rheumatism and
doesn't know Rosemary at all. He couldn't. But— Wait!"

She started on a dead run and didn't stop until she came
to Judge Shively's front door where she knocked hard. The
house was dark and had the feeling of nobody being at
home. We found both doors and all the windows locked.
She was all for breaking a window. I didn't like the idea.
Finally, against my better judgment, we compromised on
one of the small, high kitchen windows. I boosted her up to
it and she broke it with a rock, unlocked it and crawled in.

The understanding had been that she was to open a
door for me. She didn't. I got scared for her and began
hoo-hooing, soft at first but, when she didn't answer, quite
a bit louder.

She came to the window then and told me to go to the
front door. "I've found something in the bedroom," she
said, as she let me in. "Come on."

What I dreaded seeing in the bedroom I hardly know.
What I did see were some pillows and bedding strewn
around on the floor in front of the closet. I was relieved,
I guess, until Brigid stooped and began tossing them over
as ladies do when sorting the laundry. But instead of
counting, "Two sheets; two pillowslips; one towel," she
was saying, "See, there's blood on this. Blood on this.
This pillowslip is twisted and wrong side out. Blood on it.
Blood here—"

As fast as I could step around her and over the bedding
I went into the clothes closet behind her. Clothes were
hanging on a rod in there, and grips and things were on
the floor, and what with stumbling down and tangling up
I completely lost my patience.

"Stop swearing," she said, "and come out of there. Twill isn't there. I looked thoroughly while you were yelling outside. I found these bloodstained covers in there, but—Yahweh!" she said again. "They've been taken from the wall bed. Come, Jeff. Hurry."

I hurried. I let down the wall bed. It was heavy coming down. The covers had been taken off so that the body of a dead man could be strapped in their place and make room for the bed to shut back into the wall.

I see it in nightmares yet. But even so, I think I wouldn't have lost my senses as I did, in fact I know I wouldn't, if that man wearing striped pajamas had been any man I'd ever seen before, or even heard of in all my life.

I was rattled all right, and rattled bad. My only excuse is that all the folks on the place being good friends of mine, I got an idea that an utter stranger, even in the condition he was in, was more apt to have caused trouble than anybody else. And I knew right then that there was trouble and lots of it.

I guess I ought to stop here and explain that Brigid was a nice girl at heart and didn't mean to be flip at such a time. It was just a bad habit the child had fallen into, thinking and talking that way, from associating too long with her papa.

"Wait, Jeff," she said. "You're making a mistake. You can't do it, Jeff. You can't put it over. You can't arrest the victim." And then the poor kid bolted for the bathroom and I could hear her being awfully sick in there.

6

The next thing I heard was somebody coming up the front walk. I opened the door a crack and there was Adam. I wanted to save him from the shock I'd had, if I could, so I tried to tell him before I let him come in.

"Adam—" I began.

"You've found Twill?"

"No, but—"

"Why were you yelling, then?"

"I was not yelling," I said, forgetting about hoo-hooing.

"You were yelling. I heard you by the gate. What's the matter? What frightened you?"

"Nothing frightened me—"

"Your idea in yelling, then, was merely to frighten everyone else?"

I gave up. "I guess you'd better come in here," I said, and sat down in a chair by the door.

It was quite a few minutes before Adam said anything that would do to repeat. But I was relieved to find that he knew the poor young fellow. He was Clyde Shively, the old Judge's son, who had come to Memaloose just that afternoon.

As soon as Adam had settled down, some, he wanted to get the straps undone. He asked me to lend a hand. I'd heard of a convention about not touching the body before the coroner touched it; but it seemed the only decent thing to do, so we did it.

He turned the body over a little. "Shot in the back," he said. "By the Eternal, hell has certainly broken loose independently all over this place tonight!"

Brigid came in from the bathroom looking terrible and asking if Twill had been found.

Adam shook his head. "We all fear that the boy must have done away with himself in the lake immediately after he left the house."

Brigid should have said then what she said later, that Twill couldn't have drowned himself in the lake immediately after we found him gone from the cottage for the reason that she had watched the lake from that minute until the dark shut down. She said nothing because she could see no connection between finding this Clyde Shively murdered a quarter of a mile away from where Twill's body had been stolen; and she was bound and determined to help whoever was trying to help Rosemary. From first to last Brigid never changed her mind about trying to help Rosemary. This complicated things to some extent, I suppose; but I can't see that it did any real harm, or that any of the other murders would have been prevented if the kid had been less loyal.

I said nothing, either, when Adam mentioned the lake. But I thought that if someone had thrown Twill's body in the lake we'd find it the first thing in the morning. Memaloose wasn't more than eight feet deep at its deepest, and glass clear. Then I remembered that there wasn't a boat on the place. Adam had offered to buy one if the folks cared for boat riding, but nobody had so he'd let the matter drop. I was wondering about getting Sig Hansen's boat over from Nameless, when Adam took out his watch.

"It is nine-fifteen now. Rigor is practically complete. I'd say this man had been dead at least five hours. What do you think, Jeff?"

I said, "I think it is pretty much guesswork after a couple of hours, anyway."

"Yes, you're right," he agreed. "But we know that he was alive shortly after three o'clock this afternoon. The rain began at two-thirty. The telephone wires are up again, so I'll call the boys at Ferras presently. There is no particular hurry now. The killer has had hours to climb the fence, or break through it, and make his escape."

"The fence?" I asked, very much surprised.

"That sand and alkali strip outside the gate," Adam said, seemingly going off at a tangent, "takes impressions like soft putty when it is wet. No stranger has come into this camp or left it since the rain. Rosemary with Acrasia left and returned after the rain. You, Jeff, came in with Dollar after the rain. Kent came in, around a quarter to seven. The sand is still soft enough to take impressions. My own footprints show where I stepped out there just now."

Brigid is usually smart. It was the shock and all that made her ask, "But how can you be sure that the footprints are Rosemary's? How can you be sure of any of them, except your own?"

Adam got too patient. "Jeff saw Rosemary leave. I saw her return. She is here in camp now. Jeff came in. Kent came in. They are here now. One horse left and returned. Acrasia. She is here. Jeff led Dollar in. Dollar is here. Numerically my reasoning seems sound."

"I should think," Brigid argued, "that the horses' prints, at least, would be hard to distinguish—tracked over, all that."

"The sun hardened the prints made directly after the storm," Adam answered, no longer too patient but worse. "And, if you'll remember, the gate can't be opened or closed from horseback. I had my strong flashlight and I examined the sand very carefully. I was searching for prints that might be Twill's."

I spoke without thinking, which is always bad. "Twill couldn't have climbed the fence," I said.

"No," Brigid said, vexed about something. "He wasn't a vine. He was a cripple."

Adam put on his meanest formal manner. "May I suggest that attempted wit is misplaced just now?"

"You may, of course," Brigid answered, being the one person I've ever had the pleasure of knowing who could match manners with Adam at any minute. "If I was witty, I'm sorry. My only excuse is that St. Dennis once told me that when things get beyond the bearable I wouldn't sink if I'd stick up my nose. Unconsciously, I may have tried to do so."

Adam's own head, carrying his nose with it, went up like he'd been checkreined and he began walking busily around seemingly looking for something high and low. Just as I'd feared, he took it out on me, the next minute.

"Jeff," he said, "if you are sufficiently rested, I'd appreciate some help. If the killer has left anything behind him that might aid us in tracing him, I should like to find it now."

To this day I believe that Adam used that notion as a means of changing the subject. But it seemed pretty sensible at the time, so we three pitched right in and gave the house a good going over, finding nothing—as far as I knew that night—that could be called a clue or a trace.

"I am going to have another talk with Rosemary," Adam said very grimly, when Brigid, he and I finally rounded up in the kitchen again. "Two shots were fired from that revolver of hers. There is no gun here. I think she may know more than she has told us as yet. I'll want you to check up with me at the gate, Jeff. I'll telephone to the boys at Ferras—"

While he was talking he was also trying to open the kitchen door, which was locked and refused to budge, and this must have vexed him extra, for he added, "By the Eternal, I'll get the truth out of that girl!" and gave a mean rattle at the knob.

Brigid began, "You can't—"

"Why can't I, I'd like to know?" Adam asked, mad as hops.

"You can't open that door," she said, keeping her temper very slowly, "because it is locked and the key is gone."

(If she'd known it, she was talking like her papa often did, symbolically; but she didn't know it.)

"Where is the key?" Adam asked.

"I think that the murderer took it," she said. "I imagine that he locked the door after him and took the key away. Shall we use the front door?"

I guess that gave Adam an idea because, on the front stoop, he locked the door and put the key in his pocket. In the nick of time at that, for who should we meet right afterward, walking fast and looming large, but Reggie and Mrs. Duefife.

They and we said, "Any news of Twill?" and we and they said, "No."

Reggie spoke up quiveringly: "'What shall we do when hope is gone?'"

He was a great one for using poetry, so nobody paid any attention to him.

Adam asked sharply, "Where is Betty-Jean? I told her to stay with you."

"Poor, poor little Betty-Jean," Mrs. Duefife said.

"What's the matter with Betty-Jean?" Adam asked, sounding scared.

"Well, but of course," Mrs. Duefife began, drawing in her chin and meaning, I judged, something about Betty-Jean and Twill being sweethearts, but deciding she'd better not mention it further, she went on: "We left her in the community house. Such a dear girl. 'Just a cup of coffee,'

I warned her. 'Nothing else.' We had no dinner you know. But, 'Just a cup of coffee—'"

"And a few sandwiches," Reggie put in worriedly.

"The old Judge is with Betty-Jean, I suppose?" Adam asked.

"With her?" Mrs. Duefife sounded as if she couldn't believe her own ears. "With Betty-Jean?"

"Exactly," Adam said. "Judge Shively is in the community house with Betty-Jean, is he not?"

Mrs. Duefife seemed to take affront. "No, he is not. Certainly he is not," she answered.

"No? Where is he, then?"

"I don't know, I'm sure." Mrs. Duefife sounded as if Adam had asked her something very indelicate. "You just came from his cottage where, one should suppose, he probably could be found."

"He isn't there," Adam said and stopped. I admired him for it. I knew how he felt. Everybody who has ever not yielded to temptation has felt the same way—urgently disappointed.

I spoke up in a hurry before he might change his mind about taking the wind out of her sails. "Maybe he is in one of these cottages," I said. "Somebody has lighted all the lights in them."

We had been walking toward the community house and I'd noted that the cottages were showing up lighted, one by one.

"My son and I lighted those lights," Mrs. Duefife said. "We have gone systematically through each of these cottages. We have left no stone unturned, spared ourselves no effort—"

Brigid interrupted, talking too fast. "We know you have, haven't," she said. "We're sure you didn't—did. But wasn't Judge Shively in any of the houses? We thought he'd gone to the community house at dinner time. We thought— Hasn't anyone seen him, anywhere?"

It was Reggie's turn, again. "Oh, dear me!" he said, very twittery. "He is somewhere with Twill. He has found Twill and can't leave him. But, my goodness, why doesn't he call for help? Shouldn't you think he'd call for help? Or answer our calls? For mercy's sakes, why hasn't he answered our calls?"

I seem to remember that Mrs. Duefife spoke soothingly to Reggie, but I'm not sure. I know that Brigid and Adam said nothing. I know my own voice caught on me. I know why. We all were remembering what we'd left back there on that doggone dropping-down bed. We all were fearing that somewhere—maybe in another of those beds—we'd find the reason that the old gentleman hadn't called or answered our calls.

7

Why Brigid, Adam and I hadn't given our first thoughts to Judge Shively, while we were in his cottage, I'll never understand. I guess that we were too excited, thinking about losing Twill and finding a murdered man. But, though we did forget the old gentleman for a time, we certainly made up for it by remembering him from then on.

Our searching after that was entirely different from our first searching for Twill. Hope had been leading us then; hope every minute that we'd find him and not much hurt at that. We'd been mighty anxious, mighty worried; but all the time we'd kept our manners and acted pretty much like any group of polite people hunting for a friend, who had been hurt and was likely needing help, would act.

Fear led us now, holding on to our sweating hands. It was heavy in every one of those doggone dropping beds as we lowered it. It was empty in all those bare-roomed cottages and in all those hole-hollow garages. It was riding like witches on the backs of the two horses in the shelter. It made breathing hard. It beat on our hearts like drums. It tied our minds into tight knots in a jiffy and slowly picked them loose again and tied them over and twisted them down.

The only way I know to tell how bad it was, is to say that the time soon came when finding the old Judge murdered or finding Twill dead would have been a relief. How

we all knew then, as we knew when the lake had been gone
over foot by foot the next day, that we'd find neither body
in it, is a mystery. Premonitions, maybe. Or maybe we
didn't know. Maybe we felt that, if we did find the bodies in the lake, that Something that turns fear into grisly
terror would still be with us. The uncanny part, I mean.
The feeling that someone is shouting at you in a whisper,
or tapping you on the shoulder from across the road, or
watching your every move with blinded eyes.

It was bigger than that, though; worse, spreading out
more. It was like being on a hot dry desert and feeling
yourself getting soaked, cold, wet to the skin when there
wasn't a drop of rain. It was like seeing trees switching
back and forth with their leaves being torn off and scat-
tered, and the tumbleweed scooting and bouncing through
clouds of dust, when there wasn't a whisper of wind. It
was that blurred, empty, falling, out-of-focus feeling that
you get in bad dreams when you know things can't be what
they are and so must be what they aren't.

Confusing? You bet it was. Take how it seemed to me.
Take what I thought that I knew while Adam and I were
back at the gate checking up on his deductions concerning
the footprints in the stretch of alkali dust and sand just
outside the gate.

Merely believing my eyes, I thought that Adam was
right about the prints. My own with Dollar, and Rosemary's with Acrasia showed up as clear as the kid's fingers
on the new cake frosting. Kent's could be seen, where he'd
walked in. And Adam's, made not long since, were plain
enough for him to step back into them to prove it to me.
The gate opened in, and the cement road came right up
under its edge, so no tracks could show on that side. I
thought I knew then that Rosemary had gone and come,
that I had come in, and that Kent had, and that not another

soul had been through that gate since the rain, except
Adam, of course, investigating.

I thought I knew that the twelve-foot-high plank fence
was as well built as a man with Adam's money to squander
could have it built when he wanted to keep tourists out
and, also, prevent their tearing it down to build bonfires
with. I thought I knew that getting over that fence would
not be a matter of a flying leap. Most particularly not if
the leaper was carrying even one dead body in his arms. So
I thought I knew that if someone had got over the fence
he'd have had to use something to climb over it with—a
ladder, a board, or a pile of something. I thought that we
wouldn't have much trouble finding any of these, or else a
loosened plank where he might have crawled through.

Later, for a long time, Adam kept nailing his hopes to
that fence. Not a plank in it was found tampered with in
any way. Not a trace of anybody's getting over the fence
showed. And tracks or traces—holes where the ladder legs
or the edge of a board with a man's weight on it had sunk
in—would have been left even on that rocky desert. So
I don't know why Adam kept insisting that whoever had
murdered Clyde Shively had got over the fence and away.

I thought I was a lot smarter during the following days
when I agreed with the other folks that the killer had
swum the lake. It had a couple of yards of sandy shore
line but by morning there had been too much stepping
around on it, done by the folks who had tried peering
into the lake right off that night, to tell anything about
footprints found there. Where the fence ran down into
the lake, though, there weren't any prints at either end; so
we knew that nobody could have waded around the fence
and got back on the deserts again that way. He could have
avoided all nonsense about leaving footprints if he had
gone straight down the cement walk from the community

house to the dock and stepped off. But that wouldn't have been a very secret way of escaping. We all had to admit, of course, when Adam pinned us down to it, that thinking for a minute that Judge Shively, at his age, in poor health and stiff with rheumatism, had swum the lake for any reason was too ridiculous to be suggested.

But continuing with what I thought I knew out by the gate that Wednesday night. I thought I knew that Twill, dead or alive, was missing. I thought I knew that I, myself, had found Clyde Shively, shot in the back and strapped in the wall bed. I thought I knew that old Judge Shively could not be found high or low on the place.

Right here I'm bound to say for myself that even early that murderous night, with things in the fix they were in, I didn't even think that I thought what the lady detective, Lynn MacDonald, seemed to think when she first came down from 'Frisco. I didn't hear her, myself, and since Joe Laud told me maybe it was partly wrong. But Joe said that she asked whether we had asphalt pits or quicksands, or anything of their nature around about.

I suppose she thought of these because there is an asphalt pit near L. A. that swallows up everything whole that gets into it. There may be quicksands everywhere all around 'Frisco, for all I know. I never go over to California much. I hate their climate. But I knew then, just as I know now, positive and for certain, that we haven't and never will have any such freaks of nature in Oakman County. We have opal mines, marble quarries, petrified trees and other points of interest. But no asphalt pits. No quicksands. No place what-so-some-ever where alive or dead bodies could disappear. None.

Returning for the last time to the gate and Adam and me that night. I thought I knew that before we went to the gate Adam had phoned Joe Laud (I forgot to mention that Joe was coroner and undertaker) and told him to keep his mouth shut, round up Doc Sprague and my two deputies, Homer McLarty and Ernwright Wardner—Mac and Ernie to all—and ride over to Memaloose, pronto. I thought I knew that when we heard them coming, Adam took his flashlight and, stepping cautiously over the sand to miss all the other prints, went out to the road to head them off.

The trouble was that the boys get bored because there are practically no crimes in Nevada except, of course, away up around Reno where the outsiders come in to get divorces. So, while I wouldn't wish to say that the boys hoped something interestingly criminal had happened at Memaloose, the fact that Adam had phoned for the doctor, the coroner and undertaker and my two deputies must have whetted their curiosities, if not their hopes, very keen.

So up they came, riding like fury through the gate, destroying forever the footprints that Adam had set his heart on saving; to say nothing of all but destroying Adam who only escaped being ridden down by dint of lively jumping at the last.

Quite a bit of cussing went on for a few minutes while the boys were dismounting and claiming that they thought Adam had been waving and yelling to hurry them along and that they hadn't seen him anyhow. The cussing got worse, though more concentrated, when Adam found that Joe, instead of bringing Doc Sprague, had brought F. Gregory Taylor and James Kelly—the last named being better known as Rimrock Jim or just plain Rimrock.

Joe's explaining that Doc Sprague couldn't be reached, so he'd brought two fellows in his place, and Rimrock's humming the *Volga Boat Song* and disclosing at once that if he wasn't stewed he was simmering vehemently, did nothing toward making anything better.

"All right, Taylor," Adam said, "you're here. But if one word of this gets into your paper" (Taylor happened to be owner and editor of *The Ferras News*) "before I'm ready to have it there, I'll call my loan on your press and fixtures and cancel your lease so fast it will make your head swim. That mortgage was due three years ago and I haven't seen a cent of interest for five years."

"Threat, eh?" Taylor asked.

"No," Adam said. "Three threats. As for the rest of you boys, if anything I've said to Taylor should happen to fit your own affairs, think it over. Unless it is necessary I'm not going to smear the county with what's happened here to-night. You're here for business, not for gossip. Think it over."

(If Adam was unpopular, as some said, in his own coun-ty it was because he'd done too much for it. There was hardly a man-jack of us who wasn't under obligations to him in one way or another and, of course, being grateful year in and out gets irksome.)

Joe Laud asked, "Yes, but what has happened here to-night?"

And Rimrock stopped humming and spoke very spright-ly, "I've got no idea."

"Nor have I," Adam said. "But one man has been killed. It seems probable that another man has been killed and, possibly, a third man."

"Who umpired?" Rimrock wanted to know.

Adam began issuing orders. "Taylor," he said, "you take this souse and get him out of the way in one of the empty cottages. Keep him there. Understand? Joe, here's the key to the last cottage at the west end of the walk. You and Ernie and Mac go down there and look things over. The dead man is Clyde Shively, Judge Shively's son. See what you can make of it. Jeff and I will join you there presently. Wait for us."

Joe, Mac and Ernie set out right away. Taylor started leading Rimrock off, but they'd gone only a few yards when Rimrock halted in his tracks, insisting on reviewing his grammar.

"I kill," he said. "You kill. We kill. She kills. He kills. They kills—"

"Stop it," Taylor was scolding him. "Stop it, I say. This is definitely absurd." (Taylor ate crêpes Suzette up at Reno for supper about a year ago and he's been very sophisticated ever since.) "Come now, my man. Come, come!"

I had been shutting the gate. "Adam," I said, "it wouldn't be a bad idea to lock this gate, would it?"

"The padlock has been lost all summer," he said, as if that settled everything, and continued with deep injustice as we struck off shortcutting across the yard: "Why in hades did you allow me to send for these sons of sea-cooks? Couldn't you have kept your head for five minutes, even though I did lose mine?"

"I didn't allow you to send for them," I said.

"You did," he said. "They are here, aren't they? Hurry up, if you're coming with me."

"Where are you going?" I asked.

"I'm going to have another talk with Rosemary. Wait. What's that? Someone calling?"

We stopped to listen. Something must have vexed Rimrock, for he was shouting, "He was killed. She was killed. I or you can or may be killed."

8

When Adam and I reached Twill's cottage, where Rosemary was, we found Brigid sitting on the stoop. She got up and tried turning herself into a barricade; but, on account of her being built more like a stick of macaroni than anything else, all she could do was stop us for a minute while she said, "You cannot go in there and heckle Rosemary any more tonight. You sent word for her to stay in this cottage, Mayor Oakman, so she is here. But she is in the bedroom lying down. We've given her a bromide and we are hoping that she may sleep. Surely any further inhumanities that you and Jeff may have thought of can wait until morning."

Before Adam had stopped at the community house to phone to Ferras, he'd told me to go and fetch Kent and tell Rosemary to stay where she was because he was coming to have a talk with her. He didn't mean particularly for her to stay in Twill's cottage. He just wanted her stationary someplace. I'd done the errand and that was all I had done and I said so to Brigid then and there.

Adam didn't bother defending himself. He went right on into the house. I followed him.

Mrs. Duefife and Reggie were sitting in the parlor alone and doing nothing in that awful, finished way that folks have of doing nothing when there's been a death in the family. Somebody had pushed the wall bed back into place and got the bloodstained pillow out of sight. The room was hot and hushed and terribly tidy.

Mrs. Duefife put her head forward and whispered, "Any news?" stretching her lips wide for the "any" and puckering them like a whistle for "news." She was trying to whisper plainly, but it gave her a gruesome look of making faces.

"No good news," Adam answered.

"Don't, Reggie, dearest," Mrs. Duefife said, speaking louder. I knew that Reggie was preparing to blow his nose and I was only uninterested until something kind of tinkly dropped at my feet.

When I picked it up I saw it was a pair of spectacles that Reggie had flipped from his pocket when he'd pulled out his handkerchief, so I offered them to him. He cringed away, and kind of squeaked, "Those aren't mine."

Sure enough, they didn't look like his. His pinched onto his little fat nose. These were made of heavy glass and had gold rims and wires to curve around the ears.

Adam, who always was as curious as a cat, took them away from me. "These are Judge Shively's glasses," he said. "There is no mistaking the thick lenses. Where did you find them, Reggie?"

"I didn't find them," Reggie said. "I never saw them before in my life."

"You've seen them many times on the old Judge s nose," Adam said, but Reggie interrupted pitifully:

"I never saw the Judge's nose many times. I never even saw the Judge many times—just such a few times, such a few—"

"Never mind," Adam said. "Where did you find these glasses?"

"I didn't find them," Reggie said and repeated a little annoyingly, I'll admit, "I never saw them before in my life."

"Listen to me, Reggie." Adam was deceivingly kind and patient. "These are Judge Shively's glasses. His, you understand. The glasses he wore. He had only the one pair here with him. He couldn't see without them. Now the old gentleman is lost. His son has been found murdered—"

"I know all that. I know all that. I know all that," Reggie interrupted, adding, "I know all that."

For a few minutes then things were very embarrassing. Reggie held fast to the statement that he'd never seen the glasses before. Adam kept insisting that Reggie look at them, which Reggie simply and positively would not do, even going so far as to cover his eyes with his hands.

Betty-Jean and Kent came in from the outside while this was going on. Betty-Jean's pretty face was all blotched and bruised-looking from crying; and while Adam was telling them about Judge Shively's glasses she kept sniffing up and sniffing up. This seemed to make Adam nervous and finally he took his handkerchief out and offered it to her, saying:

"Here!"

I'd noted Mrs. Duefife watching him like a hawk, so I was abashed when she spoke to me in her "Victory!" tone of voice.

"You have no reason for watching Adam Oakman now, Jeff. Nothing will come from his pocket save his handkerchief. Reggie has taken his own handkerchief from his pocket hundreds of times this evening. Not until this last moment did the glasses appear. Consequently, we know that within the past few moments someone deliberately and maliciously concealed those glasses in my son's pocket."

Adam, it happened, was standing close to Reggie. He moved away now, not in a hurry but sort of carelessly, as if he'd had on his Sunday clothes and Reggie was bales of barbed wire.

Kent asked Mrs. Duefife whether Rosemary had gone to sleep, but Adam answered. "I hope not. If she has it will be necessary to wake her. I intend to talk with her right now."

Adam was much nearer to the bedroom door than Kent was, so Adam got there first. Brigid, who had edged in from the stoop, unnoticed, beat them both by a good six inches.

"You'll keep out of here," she said, and stamped her foot.

Adam made gestures more like Reggie's than his own, kind of paddling the air down fast with his hands. I guess it bewildered him that this redheaded kid should keep shooting up from underfoot. She looked cute, at that, with her nose stuck up, but she spoke very saucy.

"You wouldn't know about this, Mayor Oakman," she said, "but Rosemary is suffering. I'll not have her tortured any more tonight. If you try it, I'll tell straight out that I saw you slip those glasses into Reggie's pocket."

Mrs. Duefife said she had known it from the first. Adam didn't say anything. I was behind him, but there was that about the set of his neck and the bend of his legs that looked stricken speechless.

Rosemary opened the bedroom door and came into the parlor. She had taken off that terrible white dress and was wearing a lounging robe, soft-looking and that quiet greenish color of sweet grapes in the shade. Her hair was pretty the way it had been that day when she'd sat smiling on the fence after riding Acrasia, but her face was different. Brigid said afterward that everything was gone from it but beauty. Kent fetched her a chair and stood beside her.

"Rosemary," Adam said, and he was very nice until he got used to looking at her, "I am sorry that we must disturb you, but you will understand that it is necessary now for you to tell us the truth."

She said, "I have told you the truth. I shot Twill. He
died almost at once."

"You were quarreling, as usual, I suppose?" Adam was
getting meaner by the minute and, as I thought, getting
also unjust. Come to find out, the folks told me later
that Rosemary and Twill had quarreled sometimes, as folks
who have opposite natures but love each other enough to
bother are bound to quarrel.

Just then my attention was turned by the sight of Joe
Laud, Mac and Ernie who came crowding up to the open
door and froze there, half in and half out, at first sight
of Rosemary. They all stared at her and were very maud-
lin-looking.

Adam was asking, "Twill didn't like Kent, did he?"

Since up to that minute I'd never known that there had
been any hard feeling between Kent and Twill, both fine
young fellows, hearing this and Rosemary's answer, "It was
only that Twill didn't know Kent," was something of a
shock; though nothing, less than nothing, compared with
the shock I got in the next minute when Brigid sidled up
to me and said in a threatening low murmur, "If you don't
stop looking at that spot I'll send your right name to a
matrimonial bureau."

I'd been resting and almost at myself, but before Brigid
finished snarling I found that I was nothing but an object
polka-dotted with eyes that I didn't know what to do with.
I kind of felt like scratching them, only they didn't itch.
They were just lumping up all over me like checkers on a
checker-board.

If I'd known then that the spot she was referring to was
not a blood spot it might not have been so hard on me.
What got me down with the dog's plate was that I didn't
know where I'd been looking when she told me to stop it. I
couldn't look where I hadn't been looking when I'd no idea
where I had been looking. How I got into the breakfast

nook and found myself another chair with my eyes shut is a wonder to me. But I did, and began listening again in time to hear Rosemary saying:

"Yes. I met Clyde Shively this afternoon when I went to get Acrasia behind Judge Shively's cottage. The two men had been watching her, and when I came Judge Shively brought his son over and introduced him to me."

"What time was this?" Adam asked.

"I think that it was nearly four o'clock. The storm was entirely cleared. Jeff might know. I met him at the gate a few minutes after that."

"It was close to four," Adam said, remembering that he had looked at his watch in the kitchen soon after I'd come in. "Very well. Now, Rosemary, the situation is this. You have confessed to killing your brother. You have admitted that you threatened to kill him before you fired. Is that right?"

"I said that I'd shoot, but I didn't mean it. I didn't mean to shoot."

"And why did you say that you would shoot him?"

"Twill couldn't understand my loving anyone but him. He was saying unkind things about Kent. He didn't mean them. But he kept repeating them over and over. We were both frightfully angry."

"I see," Adam said. "According to your story, then, you killed your brother shortly after half-past seven this evening. We have searched this place for hours and we have been unable to find him either alive or dead. We have found another murdered man, Clyde Shively. We have not found Judge Shively, aged and infirm.

"I've been patient. Now I insist that you tell everything that you know concerning the murder of Clyde Shively and the disappearance of his father. I am insisting, I am demanding that you tell the entire truth here and now."

Kent spoke up, mad as fury, "Rosemary doesn't know any more than you do about any of this. Probably she doesn't know half as much. Now—"

Adam interrupted. "Suave" is a word I hate. That's what he was. "It may interest you to hear," he said, "that I know twice as much as you and Rosemary think that I know. The revolver with which she admits killing her brother had been fired twice."

"No," Kent was the exact opposite of suave. "That doesn't interest me a damn. That revolver might have been fired any time during the year. Come, Rosemary—"

I'll never know where he wanted her to come because Adam interrupted again, speaking to the boys in the doorway. "You've heard her confess to one murder tonight," he said. "And you've found a murdered man, shot in the back. There's a horse here she can ride. Take her along. A few days in jail have been known to improve the memory."

Kent put one hand down on Rosemary's shoulder and remarked, carelessly and real friendly, "I wouldn't try it, boys, if I were you."

The boys weren't afraid of Kent. They had their six guns with them and he was unarmed; so they must have stood still more out of politeness than anything else, though they hardly looked it.

O'Dell says that my hearing is "phenomenal." I guess he's right. I don't think anybody else heard Mac, kind of whistling under his breath, though more breathing than whistling, "Looky, looky, looky, Here comes Cooky"; so maybe the others were more unprepared than I was for what happened then. If so, I'm sorry for them yet.

Brigid, who had been fooling around by the bureau, stepped over square in front of Rosemary and Kent, and I'll work for nothing and steal for a living if she wasn't holding a revolver in her hands. The pearl-handled one that I'd found earlier in the evening. To make it worse she was holding it the way a gun should be held to look like business and the way she circled it around was doggone near professional. She was a great one for threats; so that was what I expected and that was what I heard.

"If one of you dares touch Rosemary," she said, separating each word very distinctly, "I'll pop you right off. I'll pop you into little, spattering, tiny pieces."

For a second things were quiet. Not that anybody could have been scared—much. Just that everybody was shocked at seeing a nice girl like Brigid O'Dell acting up so horrid.

Kent reached out and took the revolver away from her, easy. "Not for little girls, Brigid," he said.

She turned around and kind of bored the top of her head into the front of his shirt and began crying, softly, in a ladylike way.

9

But our relief was short. Not that Kent started circling the gun at us. He held it in one hand, like he would have held his pipe, while he kept his other hand on Rosemary's shoulder and tried murmuring soothingly to Brigid. With two girls and a gun, I'd say the boy had his hands full.

"Don't you dare let them, Kent Oakman," Brigid was saying. "All that beauty. All that intelligence. Humiliated. Hurt. Taken to that horrible jail. St. Dennis would never forgive me.

"If you let them," she said, raising her head and turning on Adam and looking kind of cute, the way her little freckled nose stuck up, "I'll get a teakettle, and I'll run around, and I'll boil every ant in Oakman County."

Kent said, "That's all right, Brigid. No one is going to touch Rosemary," and looked across at the boys in the doorway. "Beat it, you fellows," he said, not rough but firm. "Sorry, but that's the way of it now. Ride over again some other time."

Adam began asking the boys questions such as, what was the matter with them, and couldn't they hear him, and why were they standing there, when to my utmost astonishment young Mac spoke up. I hadn't thought the kid was capable of such a burst of heroic action, no matter how pretty the girl was.

"Pardon me," he said, "but things are too irregular. You was trying to intimidate the lady and extort a confession. That ain't legal. We got no proof that she killed the guy on the bed. We can't go running ladies in like that."

"Proof?" Adam said. "You heard her confess to one murder."

"An accident ain't murder," Mac said.

"You heard her say that she threatened to kill him before she shot."

"Ugh-ugh," Mac said. "I heard her say she never meant to."

Joe Laud, being coroner and undertaker and his interests kind of running in those lines, put in: "If she killed her brother, where's the body?"

Brigid answered. "She didn't kill him. She wounded him a trifle, and he—went away. But the revolver's going off frightened her so that she's been—well, not exactly sane ever since."

"Temporary insanity," Mac said. I don't know where he picked the expression up, but he sounded as if he'd learned it long ago and admired it.

"We aren't sure of that," Adam admitted. "But we know that Kent isn't insane. Leave her out of it for the present. Take him. He knows all that she knows. Obstructing justice. Threatening officers. Are you boys going to make the arrest, or shall I get hold of some state men?"

Joe Laud, arresting being clear out of his line, stepped backward several yards. Mac had a good job as janitor in Adam's bank. Ernie was a prospector; so Ernie's wife, Ellie, had made both ends meet for years by working as chambermaid in Adam's hotel.

I'd liked staying out of it, in the breakfast nook, just fine. But I knew if this was going on I'd better get into it, fast. I reached Kent long before the boys did and spoke to him confidentially.

"Kent," I said, "I've never tried disputing with a mule's hind leg, because I always had an idea that if it didn't win the argument, I wouldn't know it."

"You're right," he said to me; and to Adam, not in a mean way, exactly, but not very pleasant: "O. K., Dad, if that's the way you feel about it."

He walked to the bureau and got shed of the revolver and came back to me, though not holding out his hands for the bracelets, which was just as well since I had none by me.

Adam didn't answer. I thought maybe the old codger was changing his mind about cutting off his own nose and I think yet he might have repented, if Reggie hadn't blown his nose right then and if Mrs. Duefife, instead of remonstrating with Reggie as usual hadn't begun remonstrating with Adam.

"Don't, Adam," she said, instead of "Don't Reggie," and went on. "Don't do this thing. Don't yield to your baser nature, your primitive lust for vengeance. Don't drag this splendid type of America's young manhood at the chariot wheels of your malevolent egotism. Don't—"

Nobody, not even I, could blame Adam for interrupting with a couple of cuss words though he spoke them to me instead of to her, wanting to know what I was waiting for.

"I'm not waiting," I said.

"You are waiting," he said.

Kent dropped one of his arms across my shoulders and said, "All right, Jeff. Let's go."

Brigid had been quiet for a few seconds so now she spoke up strong. "Don't you go, Kent Oakman. Don't you dare go. If you do, I'll—I'll find myself a pole and I'll sit on it, I swear I will, until you come out again. You can't leave Rosemary here with no one to take care of her."

Kent was never a hand for boasting, but there was a tinge of it in the way he said "Rosemary doesn't need anyone to take care of her, Brigid. She isn't like that. But, at any rate, you'll be here, won't you?"

"I'll be right here," Brigid answered, and though not a threat it sounded like a terrible one.

"You're a swell kid." Kent grinned at her. My only excuse for him is that I guess he found he had a grin and thought he might as well use it. But it slipped off his face while he was saying to Rosemary, "We've a date for tomorrow to be married. You'll not forget?"

She shook her head. I don't know to this day whether she meant she wouldn't be married or she wouldn't forget. Kent tightened his grip on my shoulder and the next thing I knew he was leading me across the room. The silence made by the folks holding their breath was something miserable. I shot a glance at Adam and, though he was the most unsightly view I ever saw, I wasn't ready for his next words.

"I've decided to change my charges against the prisoner, Sheriff. I charge him with murder. Premeditated. Do you understand?"

I understood. He was doing this so that Kent couldn't get out on bail for his wedding the next day. Kent didn't stop. He walked right on out-of-doors. I followed him, thinking that we could talk it over.

10

I never found a person in a less talkative mood than Kent was that night, or in a bigger hurry. If I hadn't made him pack his valise, he'd have gone right off without taking a thing with him. It seemed to me that there were better places for him to go than to jail. I explained to him how I, a merely helpless officer of the law, unarmed, couldn't stop him if he escaped; but he wouldn't listen to reason. I might as well have let the boys arrest him.

All the way to Ferras, jogging along in the starlight, every topic I'd open he'd close; so, finally, I gave up trying to talk to him at all.

We were in town, passing the depot, when he said, "Have you any idea how long it was, after we heard that shot this evening, before Dad came around from the back of the community house and joined us?"

"No, I haven't," I said. I judged it was a couple of minutes more or less, but if Kent wanted it more or less, much or little, it was all right with me.

"Dad," he said, "is the only one on the place who'd have the nerve to get Twill's body away in order to help Rosemary, or sense enough to do it effectively. But Rosemary thinks that she was with Twill when he died, and that she left him on that pillow when she ran out to us. Dad was with us then, wasn't he? You were behind us."

67

"He was right with me," I said. "But suppose he'd had all the time there was? After we began hunting for the old Judge we didn't leave a spot as big as a two-bit piece unsearched on the place. So if your dad swiped the body, which he never would, where in thunder could he have put it? Adam has his faults, or had when I last saw him, but he's shrewd and he'd know that the lake wouldn't be any better than a show window by the first streak of dawn tomorrow morning.

"You're right," Kent said. "Here we are."

We'd had to go by the hotel for me to get the keys to the jail. I begged Kent to come in there and spend the night with me, but he wouldn't. When we got to the jail he wouldn't even let me leave the key with him, so that he could step out of that dirty hole and get a breath of fresh air when he needed it. He had some notion, crazy as hades, that because he'd said he'd come to the jail he had to do it all in order.

That Ferras jail isn't fit to describe. It stood out like a blister on the burning desert, so that its red brick walls held the heat like a furnace and stored it up, getting staler and stinkinger day in and out, year in and out. When I left the boy there I felt as if I'd locked him in an oven knowing that a hotter fire would be kindled at sunup.

Back in the hotel I was surprised to see Joe Laud sitting there in the lobby alone, looking as if he was thinking about dead bodies and sure enough he was, as it came out later.

"Hello, Joe," I said. "How'd you happen to come home?"

He said, "Rimrock," but it sounded worse; added, "I'm supposed to get a boat out from Nameless and take it across the lake early in the morning;" added, "It ain't that I hate boats, but I do," and said nothing more.

After a while I said, "What is it then?"

He answered ugly, wrinkling his nose, "What is what?"

"Nothing," I said, knowing he'd lost track, and went on to ask if there was any more news from Memaloose.

"None," he said, "when I left. Just one dead man found and three bodies missing, either dead or alive."

"Three?" I asked, horrified.

"There's the good-looking girl's brother, Twill. There's that Judge Shively. There's whoever it was that killed that guy, Clyde Shively. I make it three. What does 'calk' mean?"

"They put them on horseshoes," I told him.

"I know it," he said. "But why on a boat? They say it is seaworthy. It'll leak like a sieve and sink like a bullet. Calks!"

"At that," I said, "you could walk out of almost any spot in that lake."

"Sure," he said. "I could walk out if I wanted to walk out," which didn't make sense then and never would and I knew it; so I turned the subject by asking him where he was getting the boat.

"Where'd you suppose?" he answered. "Sig Hansen. Only one in the county, I'll bet and hope. He calls it a canoe. He built that boathouse. His kids had the boat up to Tahoe all summer. Just brought it back and put some more calks on it. It's in Sig's woodshed now."

"How are you going to get it to the boathouse?" I asked.

"I suppose I'll have to take it out of the woodshed," he answered. "But you'd better hunt yourself a sailor. I'm sick of talking boats. Nothing but boats. I hate boats. But that ain't it."

"What ain't it?" I asked him.

"The boat ain't it," he said, as if he'd told me six or eight times and was all worn out with explaining.

I gave up, thinking that I might just as well worry some more in silence.

"Oakman got shed of all the boys," Joe burst out, after while, "because anybody would want to get shed of that bunch from any place. But he got shed of me because he feared me. I know he feared me. He can't fool me. I know it. But that ain't it."

I wasn't going to start whatever it was all over again, so I just kept on worrying.

Pretty soon Joe burst out, worse than before: "How does it look?" he said. "He's got Mac and Ernie and Taylor out riding wild all over the deserts hunting for dead bodies, live bodies, escaped criminals and so forth. No sense in any of it, but it looks all right. Why should I be counted out until time to go rowing myself across the lake in a boat by sunrise. I'll make a picture. Bringing Rimrock home is defaming enough. Insult to injury. Me, a licensed mortician and coroner out at dawn, posse of one, hunting criminals in a boat!"

"So that's it, is it?" I said, but he wouldn't answer.

I tried explaining. "Adam wouldn't think of asking you to hunt criminals in a boat," I said. "He wants you to look for the bodies."

"This is it," Joe said, and I kind of held my breath. "I'd of helped him and been glad to. I told him so. I'm obligated to him. But if I wasn't, even as cussed mean as he is, I'd have helped him because the dog-ratted son-of-a-gun's my friend. Oakman's this," Joe said, but naming it. "He's that," he said, naming it. "But he is my friend. I told him so. Took him to one side to tell him. 'Mayor Oakman,' I said, 'I'm your friend. You're my friend.' But he up and insulted me."

"He never meant to," I said.

"Telling me to get Rimrock home safe and sound. There's an errand. After I'd offered, point-blank, to help him."

"Help who do what?" I asked.

Joe leaned away over in his chair and spoke through his nose into my ear. "Aren't you on?" he asked.

"I can't say that I am, entirely," I said.

"Do you mean to say you don't know why Oakman got all the men off the place tonight?"

"Did he get Reggie off?" I asked, having one of those strange spurts of idle curiosity that comes even during tragedy.

"Him? The fat one?" Joe said, kind of taken aback. "What's he got to do with it?"

"Nothing," I said.

"What are you bringing him into it for then?"

"I wasn't," I said. "I just wondered what became of him."

"Nothing became of him," Joe said. "What were we talking about?"

"Dead bodies, I suppose," I said.

"In the lake," Joe took it up. "And Oakman's clearing the place so he could get them all out of the lake before morning."

I told Joe how crazy he was. He denied it, so I had to explain.

"Can you tell me," I asked, "what Adam would do with three dead bodies, or two, or even one if he did get them or it out of the lake? He'd have them or it on his hands, just the same, wouldn't he?"

Joe shrugged his shoulders, trying to let on that if I was so dumb I didn't know what Adam would do with dead bodies he wasn't going to bother himself to tell me. I kept on worrying in silence.

After quite a while Joe asked, "This fat guy? Can he swim?"

"I don't think so," I said. "But he floats fine with an inner tube," and went on worrying about Rosemary killing her brother by mistake and loving him. And about Kent, smothering in that damn jail, a good boy like him. And about little Betty-Jean, with her pretty face all spoiled from crying and suffering. And even about Adam, the old dizzard. Sure he bossed Oakman County, but there were plenty who thanked their stars that he did. Nobody went hungry in our county and the kids all had candy for Christmas. The pockets in every pair of pants Adam ever had wore out first from his digging down into them.

The more I thought about the folks over there, all deep in the mires of mystery and sorrow, the better I liked them. I thought of Betty-Jean lending a hand and fixing coffee for the folks when she was so heartsick and scared. I remembered how Mrs. Duefife had stood up for Kent, when smarter ladies than she was might have kept still on account of being beholden to Adam. Even Brigid covering us with the gun didn't seem so horrid now. While as for Reggie—well, as I'd just said he did float good, he floated fine on the lake with an inner tube wrapped around him.

Thinking about floating must have made me a little drowsy, because pretty soon when I heard Joe asking if I wouldn't even answer a civil question, the best I could do was to tell him that I didn't know the answer.

"Sure you don't," he said, very haughty, "because you don't think. Take me, I think. And pretty near always I think of something. When you asked me what Oakman would do with the dead bodies he fished out of the lake, I went right to work thinking about that. Listen here. I'm not accusing, see? But I'm hinting pretty strong that he could give them to the boys to drop off of Dead Man's Hook on their way home tonight."

After I got over being too disgusted to speak I spoke. "So that's all the better you know Adam Oakman, is it?"

Joe tried defending himself. "I'm not saying that under ordinary, every-day circumstances Oakman would ask anybody to drop dead bodies off of any place. But I'm saying that under desperate circumstances Oakman might act desperate."

I explained, seeing that as usual Joe had things all wrong. "You just told me that Adam cleared the men off the place so that he could fish the bodies out of the lake. Would he do that if he was going to give the bodies to the boys afterward? No," I said, answering my own question kind of like Mrs. Duefife. "He would not. Not wet work like that. He'd keep the boys right there and direct them how to get the bodies out while he himself stood high and dry on the shore."

Joe knew I was right so he was very vexed. "All you ever do," he said, "is pick flaws. Besides that," he added, "all you ever do do is sit and pick flaws. No matter what a man thinks up, all you ever do do is sit and pick flaws."

I didn't bother answering. I went on up to bed. I was worrying. I'd left Acrasia over in Slim's barn with Dollar. Adam's car, the only one belonging at Memaloose, was parked in front of the hotel right then. Short of borrowing one of the boys' horses, which couldn't be done without a lot of explaining which couldn't be done, I knew there wasn't any way that either Brigid or Adam could take anything that either of them, by any chance, might want to take that night up Tumboldt Mountain to Dead Man's Hook.

11

I'd meant to be up and stirring early the next morning; but, when I came down the steps into the lobby, Bert Thalen, the day clerk who comes on at seven o'clock, was just getting his coat off ready to assume his duties.

He looked surprised at seeing me and wanted to know what was going on to get me up at this hour.

"Nothing," I told him. "I just felt like taking a walk before breakfast."

"Walk!" he said, as if I'd said, "Poison," and came out from behind the desk and followed me to the door. So I just sauntered, loose-legged with my hands on my hips, until I'd rounded the corner. After that I made a bee line for Dollar and rode over to the Penroys'.

Eight or ten years ago Adam told Abe Penroy that unless the whole kit and caboodle of Penroys, including outside relatives and the dogs, would clean up he'd never do another thing for him. But Adam, being sometimes sentimental, couldn't let a large and increasing family starve. And so Abe still held his job of looking after the prisoners in the jail when there were any. It was handy, because the jail was close to the Penroys' and, as Adam said, since Abe got paid only when there were prisoners, it saved the taxpayers' money.

Abe was in bed in the kitchen when I got there, but Mrs. Penroy was up fixing breakfast.

"Yeah?" she said, being more talky than Abe, "I heard you say that President Roosevelt and his wife was over in the jail, but I didn't catch the third name."

"You heard me right," I said. "Kent Oakman is there. But get this. Kent has been traveling in high diplomatic circles with his ear to the ground, and—"

"What?" Abe said.

"Never mind," I told him. "Foreigners, crooks, are probably after Kent to get international secret information. Mayor Oakman coaxed the boy to come over here to the jail where he'd be safe for a few days. If a word of this leaks out you'll have to answer for the consequences. Life or death. Also, the Mayor says that you're to see to it that Kent gets the best that money can buy in every way."

"Whose money?" Mrs. Penroy wanted to know.

As luck would have it, I could take care of that for the present. I did; and then I rode on over to see what I could do for the boy.

I found him able to lie and say that he was fine. He had a note written that he wanted me to take to Rosemary and be sure that she got it, and he wanted me to lead Acrasia back to Memaloose so that Rosemary would have her to ride if she wanted to.

When I asked him if he had a message for his dad he said, "Not as yet," and added nothing. I've always considered "Not as yet," a kind of sinister combination of words.

Acrasia was no hand to be led. I had to go at a walk all the way and, of course, I did a lot of thinking. Some of it seemed sensible, so I was anxious to tell it to somebody and talk it over.

But, when I finally got to Memaloose, I found Adam and the boys (Mac, Ernie and Taylor) waiting for me at the gate, and at first glance I knew it was no use trying to tell those birds anything. The worst of it was they wouldn't tell me anything either.

Before I was in earshot they began heaping reproaches on me for being late. Come to find out it wasn't me that they wanted, but my nag, Dollar, for Adam to ride. While I was dismounting, Mac admitted that things were the same as they had been last night, that Twill and Judge Shively were both still missing. "And Clyde Shively is still murdered," he added, and then off the four of them rode without answering my questions about where in the nation they were going or what in thunder they were planning to do with the coils of rope they were toting. If we had been living in some other state—of grace, I mean—I might have thought of a lynching. But we don't do that way in Nevada, so such an idea never entered my mind.

It was early enough in the morning for the cozy smell of something frying topped off with whiffs of coffee to be mighty tempting to a man. So instead of passing by Mrs. Duefife's cottage I stopped in for a minute.

Mrs. Duefife, Betty-Jean and Reggie were sitting at the breakfast table. The ladies looked the way I suppose nice ladies should look after murders, but I wished I hadn't come in. Reggie was bearing up better, eating his breakfast as if somebody had coaxed him to, just to keep his strength up.

"Well?" Mrs. Duefife said to me when I'd sat down and put my hat under the chair.

If there's a harder word in our language to answer than, "Well?" I never heard it.

Reggie folded his napkin—come to find out, all the frying had been done for him and he'd finished his plate off smooth as satin—and moaned out, "Oh, my! Oh, my! Oh, my!"

Betty-Jean asked me if I'd had breakfast. And, though I said I wouldn't wish to be any trouble for anything, she got a cup and saucer and brought the percolator from the kitchen. She had to shake it three or four times before she could dribble the cup half full.

"There isn't any cream," she said. "I spilled the cream."

The way she said it made it sound like another terrible tragedy, of itself, and she went right along as if she hadn't changed the subject.

"When people say, 'Twill's dead,' I can stand that. But when I think, 'Twill isn't alive, anywhere,' I can't stand that. I do, but I can't. No. That wasn't what I began to say. I wanted to ask you, Jeff, you believe that Twill is alive somewhere, don't you?

Mrs. Duefife needn't have bothered kicking me under the table. "Of course he's alive," I said. Sure he is. Don't you go doubting that for one minute."

"I can't doubt it," she said. "I don't dare. But Jeff, where is he? The men have searched the deserts for miles. Twill couldn't walk far. I mean—if he hadn't been wounded at all. That cruel, heavy brace thing on his leg and foot."

I had to say something, so I said, "I expect he must have caught a ride with some tourists."

Mrs. Duefife gave me a queer look. I couldn't tell whether she meant it for pity or disgust. Of course I knew as well as she did that tourists couldn't have come or gone around Tumboldt that night on account of the cloudburst, and that the road beyond camp went into dry washes and was a dead-ender within half a mile. I think I knew better than she did that trying to drive an automobile, or even a buggy off the roads across our deserts with their soft sand, gullies, rocks and brush would be about as successful as getting off the streets and trying to take shortcuts in a town.

Nobody answered what I'd said about the tourists, so I said, "Or, maybe, he swam the lake."

Mrs. Duefife got me such a clip on the ankle then that I jumped.

Betty-Jean, who had been sitting holding her forehead with her hands, kind of shivered and one of her hands clenched up into a little, trembling fist. "No, no, no!" she said. "He couldn't swim with that heavy brace on and he couldn't walk six steps without it. I think, I suppose everyone thinks, that whoever killed Clyde did swim the lake and run away. But they can't accuse Twill of that because—because he was a cripple. I never thought I'd be glad of that. He hated it so dreadfully. But I am glad. Because he can't be accused. He can't be—"

Mrs. Duefife broke in very soothingly. "Of course he can't, dear. No one who ever knew Twill at all could or would accuse him of any wrongdoing."

"He was so good," Betty-Jean said. "Wasn't he? I mean isn't he? And think of me trying to make him better—taking his little pleasures away from him. He was so gentle and kind. His big brown eyes—"

She had been fumbling with the breakfast things, trying to be controlled and brave, but it was a relief when she stopped biting her lips and folded her arms on the back of her chair and put her head down on them.

It seemed to me the best thing I could do was leave. I got my hat from under the chair and tiptoed away.

12

Rosemary's cottage was next door to Mrs. Duefife's, so I was hesitating in front of it wondering if Rosemary had stayed the night there or at Twill's when Brigid spied me from the window and came out. Being younger and wearing her swimming suit she didn't look as terrible as the other ladies, but her hair was going all the wrong way in front and stood up behind like a turkey's tail.

She said that Rosemary was in her own cottage—that Adam had made her move in the middle of the night so that he could lock Twill's place—but that she had gone to sleep about half an hour ago and should not be wakened on any account, not even the note I'd brought her from Kent.

"How is Kent?" Brigid wanted to know, next. "And where?"

"In jail, but fine," I told her, sitting down on the stoop, and adding when she looked accusingly at me, "or so he says. I couldn't help it, Brigid. Honest. I tried every way to keep him from going there."

"Sorry, Jeff," she said, "I'm sure you did. Isn't Mayor Oakman revolting? Kent thinks he'd put Rosemary in jail if he didn't go in her place. What I'm wondering is, could Mayor Oakman have had any reason for killing that Clyde Shively?

"Skipping that," she went on, answering my remonstrances, "whoever killed Clyde Shively must have had a reason for doing so."

"Motive," I told her. "I thought about that. But then I thought I wouldn't."

"Yes, but you'll have to," she said. "Now here's something. When St. Dennis looked for Judge Shively's name in *Who's Who* and found the son, Clyde C., we wondered whether he could be the C. C. Shively who was editing a blackmailing paper in New York three years ago. We thought it possible, because Pasadena is close to Hollywood and this blackmailing Shively began his paper in Hollywood before he came to New York. I saw the paper myself. It was named *Stars and Asterisks*. Wholly rotten. St. Dennis and I were in New York three years ago, you remember?"

"You saw Kent off for Europe. I remember."

"Yes. Well, Mrs. Duefife, Reggie, Twill and Rosemary all came out here from New York. So any one of them might have known Clyde Shively, if he is the blackmailing one, back there. But it seems to me that Mayor Oakman is the only one here who is important enough to blackmail, or who'd have money to pay.

"Now I was with Betty-Jean for an hour alone last night. She is what St. Dennis and I thought, but she has something besides. Something decent, that can forgive. She's sorry for Rosemary instead of hating her. Something even decenter, that can spell courage backward and forward. I suppose I should admit that I can't really believe that Mayor Oakman killed that man. But, all the same, it isn't fair for anyone to go around thinking, as you are, that because Betty-Jean is the only one who knew Clyde Shively before he came here, she is the only one who had a motive for killing him."

"I never thought any such thing," I said.

"If you should," she said, "remember that Betty-Jean is Mayor Oakman's daughter. If that Clyde Shively came here with some idea of blackmailing her, and presented the scheme to her father— I heard what he said last night about times when he'd been glad he hadn't a gun in his hands. So did you hear him."

"He was talking through his hat," I said. "Coming over here this morning, I was thinking about the facts we had to date. At half-past seven last night Rosemary shot Twill. Within six to ten minutes after we heard the shot his body disappeared. Close to two hours later we found Clyde Shively shot in the back, a quarter of a mile away from Twill's place. Right after that we missed old Judge Shively and he can't be found high nor low. The footprints by the gate show that nobody left the camp after four o'clock, or came in after Kent did, around seven. Leaving the lake out of it—"

"Why leave it out?" she interrupted. "I swam over it at sunrise this morning. Later, when Joe Laud brought the canoe, I paddled it all over the lake with Mayor Oakman in it. Silly. From the center of the lake we could have seen any dark object bigger than my foot."

She went on then telling what I've told before and what I was told many times afterward, all about the close examination of the fence, inside and out; and about the lake shores being tracked up but no tracks being found by the fence ends, and all searchings and examinations revealing no way for any person to have got in or out of the camp. Except, of course, by swimming the lake.

I was kind of interested in how Joe had made out with the boat so after while I asked her if he came across all right.

"I swam over and pushed him across," she said.

"Did he get away all right?" I asked.

"He escaped with his life, if that's what you mean. But when I think how tyrannical and cruel Mayor Oakman can be, when he is angry with anyone, I shiver for Joe. It is just as Mrs. Duefife said this morning. Adam Oakman has every man, woman and child in his darned old county, except St. Dennis and me, utterly cowed. And when one of them dares revolt—"

"What did poor old Joe do?" I interrupted.

"As for that," she said, "your poor old Joe acted abominably. He arrived in some sort of high fury. And when Mayor Oakman asked him to take Clyde Shively's body across the lake in the canoe and on to Ferras, through Nameless, Joe exploded. It was a necessary, reasonable request, because the Tumboldt Road is still impassable for cars. The small truck they'd brought the canoe in from Nameless was at the boathouse over there waiting. I don't know what was the matter with Joe. He began, of a sudden, accusing Mayor Oakman of throwing dead bodies in the lake last night and 'fishing' them out and carrying them up to Dead Man's Hook and throwing them down there. I shall never dare tell St. Dennis. He'd think it amusing. It wasn't, I'm sure. Was it, Jeff?"

"No, child. It was sad. Very sad. Terrible."

"It was not," she said. "But everything else is. Don't call me 'child.' I wish Betty-Jean wouldn't call me 'Briggy.' Isn't it odd that I should notice, or care now?"

"What became of Joe?" I asked.

"I took the body across in the canoe. Joe would not. The Killaky boys from Nameless were there with their truck. They were grand. Don't bother saying that they are Indians. You've no idea how civilized they seemed after the white men on this side of the lake."

"Adam shouldn't have let you do an errand like that. Your papa wouldn't like it. Where did Joe go?"

"Mayor Oakman wasn't to blame. Someone who could manage a canoe had to take it. I didn't mind. It was all covered up. I haven't the slightest horror of death. That is"—she shuddered all over—"not much horror."

"But what about Joe?" I asked. I hate admitting, even now, that I was chump enough, for a spell, to be worried some about those ropes the boys had been toting. Nervous as I was, I didn't think for a minute that Joe's life was in danger. But I did think that if Adam had chosen a time like that to try scaring Joe to death it was very unseemly and would make a lot of talk.

"I finally got him across in the canoe," she said, "and he went with the Killaky boys in the truck. I waited over there and brought the rope back. Mayor Oakman had telephoned to Sig Hansen's for it."

"When?" I asked.

"What is it?" she said. "You're frightened, aren't you?"

I denied it up and down.

"I know better," she said, so pale that her freckles stuck out like stars. "You're afraid of what they are going to find when they climb down those ropes into the crevice below Dead Man's Hook."

"It is a pretty dangerous undertaking," I said, "even with ropes, getting down into that place."

"Jeff," she said, "tell me. I'll know soon. Are they going to find anything down there? I mean, what are they going to find?"

"Nothing that I know of," I said.

"If you've heard Mayor Oakman talking about refuting certain sorts of insinuations—"

"Stop hissing like that, Brigid," I said; she was getting me nervous.

"Shut up!" she said. "Whatever he may have been up to in all this he doesn't believe that anything is going to be found in that crevice. If anything is found he is going to be utterly pitiless."

"I can't help it," I said.

"You're mistaken," she said. "You can. You are going to. We have time to get Rosemary away right now. I'll telephone to the Killaky boys. They'll be back from Ferras. They always loaf around Sig Hansen's poolroom. They'll meet us with a car across the lake. They're grand. They won't tell. Have you any money? I've twenty dollars— enough for them. I can get more for Rosemary. Stop sitting there looking comfortable. If you don't tell me what you know, I'll swear that I killed Clyde Shively myself. I'll stick to it—"

She had stood up and was pounding me with her fists, so I was forced to hold them. "Listen to me," I begged. "I don't know what may be found down there. Honest, Brigid, I don't. How would I know?"

"Let go of me!" she said. "How would you know? You rode with Kent around there last night. Why were you frightened a minute ago, when you heard that the men were going there? Will you tell me that? Will you let go of me!"

After quite a while I got her calmed and convinced that no matter what might be found in the crevice below Dead Man's Hook, neither Kent nor I had put it there nor knew the first thing about it.

She sighed and sat on the stoop beside me and said she was sorry she had kicked my shins. "If you and Kent didn't," she went on, "then no one did and nothing is there. The boys wouldn't, unless Mayor Oakman had told them to. He didn't. He doesn't expect to find anything in that crevice."

Long before this I'd been sick of the whole subject, so I took my chance to change it. "Brigid," I said, "supposing old Judge Shively did shoot his son—"

"Idiot! The old man was sweet, gentle, diffident—"

"Never mind," I said. "I'm saying only supposing he did. And supposing that he escaped, afterward. What would his shooting his son have to do with the disappearance of Twill's dead body?"

"Nothing at all," she said.

"Why not?" I asked, wondering if she really knew. She did.

"Because no murderer would burden himself with an extra dead body. We're getting ludicrous. Judge Shively was a decrepit old darling."

"Supposing, then," I said, "that he didn't kill his son, but was killed himself by the same person who killed his son—"

"That is what has happened, of course," she said.

"I think you're right," I agreed. "But what would these two murders have to do with the disappearance of Twill's body?"

"Nothing at all," she said again, and sighed again.

"I don't know," I said, "but I was thinking that if Clyde Shively and his father were both killed by the same person, then this person might have had some good way of disposing of bodies, and might have disposed of Twill's and the Judge's at the same time."

"And left Clyde Shively's body there, for us to find? You're being tiresome, Jeff. The one thing we do know is that whoever killed Clyde Shively did not kill Twill. So why on earth should he bother stealing Twill's body in order to dispose of it?"

"Maybe to help Rosemary," I said. "Or maybe he wanted Twill's clothes, or something that Twill had on him. I don't know, but there might be any number of answers to that."

"Who killed Clyde Shively, and why?" she snapped.

I was taken aback. "I don't know. You know I don't know, Brigid."

"All the answers you have," she said, "are for the wrong questions. I thought I'd see if you could find a right answer for the right question."

"Suppose you try answering that right question."

"Yes. If you and Mayor Oakman are telling the truth about those footprints outside the gate, then either Mayor Oakman, or Betty-Jean, or Mrs. Duefife, or—"

"Shame on you," I interrupted. "Rats! Some outsider could have come in before the rain."

"Clyde Shively did so himself; but we found him here afterward."

"The murderer could have got away by swimming the lake."

"Taking two dead bodies with him?"

I heard someone stirring around in the cottage, and was glad to say so. Brigid knocked on the door and in a minute or two Rosemary opened it.

I guess she looked terrible, but it was becoming to her and the way she thanked me for Kent's note made me feel that unless I could do something more for her, right then, I'd burst out bawling as bad as Jeremiah. So I told her that I'd brought Acrasia home for her to ride, and blessed if she didn't start thanking me, again, for that, until I had to tell her it was Kent's idea.

"He knew riding would be the best thing in the world for you, Rosemary, dear," Brigid said. "Why don't you go for a ride right now?"

"I wish I could. But Uncle Adam would object."

"He's gone," Brigid said. "He and the boys have ridden over to see what damage the cloudburst did on the Tumboldt Road. He is going to direct the repair work over there. He won't be home for hours."

Brigid rattled this off so fast, not giving it the dignity due a good lie, that I believed her myself while she was talking.

Speaking of lies, though, and out of fairness to the kid, I think I ought to mention that she was not the only one on the place who could carry her lies like a gentleman, making one part fit into another snug as a lid, or coming along in such good order like Monday, Tuesday, Wednesday, that no decent person could ever think of doubting them.

I reproved her, though, as soon as Rosemary had gone into the house and left us alone together. "Your papa wouldn't like it at all," I said, "if he had heard you telling stories about road repairing like that."

"Like what?" she asked, vexed, and added: "Don't, don't sit down again. Come along with me. We're going places and look at things while Mayor Oakman is away."

I wanted to explain to her that I'd had a bad night and no breakfast, but I didn't. I tagged along with her to the back door of Twill's cottage, where she stopped and said, "Look."

I looked, but saw nothing except us and the landscape.

"Here," she said.

Nothing was there but a swimming suit spread out on a clump of sagebrush to dry.

"Twill's," she explained.

It made me feel sad. I'd liked the boy. He was a good clean boy, nice-appearing and full of fun—fine company.

"Don't grieve," she said, taking a key out of the little pocket on her belt. "Think. Remember it when Reggie begins telling you that he saw Twill in swimming yesterday afternoon. Come in, why don't you?"

I followed her into the kitchen, but I was bothered. "I thought you said Adam locked this cottage up."

"He did. And Kent's cottage, and Judge Shively's. But all our keys fit all the cottages, and Mayor Oakman, I've been told, is a brilliant man." She picked up a three-legged stool and carried it into the parlor.

When I got in there she had put the stool close to the wall between the bedroom and the parlor and beside the panel of that doggone wall bed. "Stand up on this," she said, "and you can see better."

I looked around the room, which was even tidier than it had been the night before because Mrs. Duefife and Reggie weren't in it, and told her I could see all right from where I was.

"Please, Jeff," she said, and so for the sake of peace I stood up on it. I had to stoop to keep from bumping my head on the ceiling and I couldn't see any better from there than I had seen on the floor, if as well. I'd known I couldn't, and I said so.

She made a sound that for a horse would have been a very mournful whinnying as she came back in from the breakfast nook where she'd just gone. "Turn around and look," she said.

I felt I had to draw the line somewhere at satisfying her whims and I drew it. I sat down on the stool.

"Here's a cartridge," she said, handing me one, so I hardly know why I asked, "What's this?"

"I hid it in the sugar bowl last night," she said. "I'm glad I did, because it was the only one I could find and now Mayor Oakman has taken the revolver. I'm sure that the bullet would fit that hole. What do you think? You'll have to stand on the stool to see."

Come to find out, the thing she had called a "spot" the night before was a bullet hole and if she had said so in the first place none of the misunderstanding would have occurred. The minute I got on the stool and looked at it I could see it was a bullet hole, and I could tell that the bullet in the cartridge she gave me would fit into it.

I was dumbfounded. "By golly, Brigid," I said, "but this accounts for that other shot that was fired from Rosemary's revolver."

"The revolver was Twill's, not Rosemary's," she said. "The bullet has hit a studding in there. It didn't go through to the other side."

"There's your second shot," I said.

"I didn't want a second shot," she said. "But in books this would have been Rosemary's shot, gone wild. Someone else would have fired the shot that killed Twill. Both shots would have been fired at the same instant, so they'd sound like only one."

"Tomfoolishness," I said.

"I know it," she said. "Of course."

13

I got out my jackknife. Brigid began trying to pull the stool out from under me, telling me not to dare touch that plastering, so I gave up and sat down on the stool again.

"I'd hate like thunder to think that her first shot went wild," I said, "and that she up and took a second nip at him."

"It would have been a long time between nips. Kent and I had been on the community house porch for at least five minutes. You were with us for several minutes. We all heard only the one shot."

"The door was wide open," I said. "I'd have heard it in the house. And another thing, if Rosemary had been threatening Twill and had shot once, he wouldn't have waited around in there for her to shoot again. He'd have left right off. Gone some place else."

"That gives me an idea," she said. "Let's us go some place else, right now, Jeff."

"What's the idea?" I asked her, while she was locking Twill's door again.

"Nothing. Just going somewhere else."

"Where?"

"Judge Shively's cottage?"

"Not me. We've no business there, prying around." The next thing I knew here she was saying, "Look!" again, but this time she said, "Look, oh, look!"

It was nothing but a mirage of the ocean, rolling and tossing out yonder above the fence. I never cared for the ocean—too noisy—and I always hated mirages—too eerie. But Brigid, having lived here only off and on for the past fifteen years, went crazy over any fool mirage the same as all outsiders go.

I had to sit down and wait for her until the entire disturbing display had melted out leaving the nice, dry blue sky again. She gave me a hand to help me up—she's nice that way—and, "Jeff," she said, quite solemn, "we just now saw the ocean, didn't we?"

"Mirage," I said.

She nodded. "But we didn't feel the wind, or the lovely coolness, or hear the old growling surf."

"Meaning that seeing isn't always believing?"

"Maybe so. It seemed to have some meaning. But I can't fall into pointing morals. St. Dennis would be stricken. And if here we aren't, after all."

"Brigid," I remonstrated, standing still on the stoop of the Judge's cottage. "What's the sense of this? What's it going to get us, prying and snooping around like this? What good can it do us?"

"What harm? You know that Mayor Oakman is keeping Kent in that horrible jail because he hopes that torture will force Rosemary into telling what he calls 'the truth.' Rosemary's told all the truth she knows. But, if by some forlorn hope we could find the truth, or even a part of it, and tell it for her—"

"Hold on a minute," I interrupted. "Suppose we could find out this 'truth.' Are you dead sure you want it, or would want to tell it if you had it?"

"I can use my own discretion about telling it, if I get it. Kent can't stay in that jail. Even a Mexican died there last summer."

"He killed himself," I said.

"Comforting," she said, and went on into the kitchen leaving me no choice but to follow her.

As I was crossing the room I heard something back of the cottage. I glanced out of the kitchen window and saw Rosemary leading Acrasia to the gate, unsaddled the way she always rode her in hot weather. I was glad she was braving it out for her ride, but I was bothered because she was carrying quite a sizable parcel and I knew it meant that she was going to visit Kent in the jail and take him some dainties. I didn't want her to see that jail, with or without Kent in it. But it was too late then to stop her, so I gave up and went on into the bedroom from where Brigid had been calling me.

Sure enough, there she was going over that laundry again. Gruesome sight, and she made it worse by insisting that I look close at the pillowslip she claimed was twisted on the pillow and wrong side out besides.

"Why," she asked, "should a murderer take a pillowslip off one of the pillows—only one, the other slip is blood-stained too—and then put it on again wrong side out?"

"He shouldn't," I said, "so he wouldn't. He'd have to hustle. No murderer on earth has time on his hands to change pillowslips backward and forward. It must have been on wrong in the first place."

"Except," she said, sounding pretty nervous, "that it couldn't have been. You won't look. If you would look, you'd see what I've told you. The blood soaked through the slip into the pillow and made this stain on the ticking. But the way the slip is on now, the stain on the slip doesn't correspond with the stain on the pillow. See here? After the murder someone found time to take the slip off this pillow and put it on again, twisted and wrong side out. Why? A thing of the sort wouldn't be done for no reason. What is the reason?"

She was all wrought up. I was weak from lack of rest and food. I believe that if either of us had been up to par we'd have seen the reason for a simple thing like that right off. Though, as O'Dell said, later, when there is but one possible thing to think it takes rare intelligence to think it. I guess that my intelligence never was very rare, but the one thing I was thinking that morning was that I wanted to get out of that direful place and take Brigid with me.

"Just a minute," she said, which is always deceiving, I've noted, and kind of pushed me into the clothes closet, insisting that I look.

Two suits of clothes, which must have been the Judge's, on account of appearing elderly, gray and wrinkled, were hanging on the rod, along with a very snappy light tan suit that certainly must have belonged to Clyde Shively. The old gentleman's broad brimmed hat was on the shelf beside a soft, stylish-looking one that matched the tan suit. On the floor were three valises, or grips, as we used to call them but Brigid called them by different names, and several empty liquor bottles.

"This Gladstone," she said, dragging out the large valise, "and this small bag were the Judge's. I know because I went with Kent and Betty-Jean to meet him at the station."

She opened them both up, but nothing was in them. The old Judge, of course, had unpacked and his tooth-brush, hairbrushes, razor and so on were around the house in the places where they should be.

Clyde Shively, planning on leaving that night, had not unpacked to any extent. His brushes and things were all banded up neat on one lid of his little grip, and the other lid had an envelope thing holding very fancy shirts and neckties. In between were socks, underwear and so on; but instead of being tossed in loose they were folded and fixed the fussiest I ever saw. Even his shoes were tied up separately in silk sacks with drawstrings. Unthinkingly, I remarked that the whole lay-out looked very sissy to me.

"I'd say 'fastidious,'" Brigid answered, "except that he didn't bring an extra suit of clothes with him. There's only the one he wore, hanging there in the closet."

"He wouldn't want to squidge a good suit down into that little space in his valise," I told her.

"No, he couldn't in this bag," she said. "But I should think that a man of his sort would have brought an extra bag—"

"Oh, well," I interrupted firmly, taking the bag and closing it and setting it back in the closet, "with all there is on hand we can't waste time worrying about his having only one suit of clothes. Or, wait a minute," I said, having a thought. "The boys must have put his other suit on him this morning when they were getting him ready."

"No," she said. "A lounging robe. What is there on hand?"

I had a mean, nagging feeling that there was lots; but I couldn't name it just then so I turned that off. "He came up here to fetch his father home," I said "So why should he bother with a big wardrobe? I like it in him," I added, easing her toward the door by her elbow, "coming just as he was."

"I'm wondering whether taking his father home was the reason for his coming. I keep remembering that C. C. Shively who edited *Stars and Asterisks.*"

I'd got her to the kitchen door by this time and was more intent on getting her out of there than I was on the conversation; so I said, "Well, whatever he came for he didn't come to get killed," and shoved her gently out on the stoop.

"He didn't come to *get* killed," she said. "I'm wondering whether he did bring another piece of luggage with him?"

"What in thunder if he did?" I asked, getting some impatient.

"If he did," she said, "where is it?"

My only excuse is that I was so sick of these "where-is-its" that I wasn't myself. "Where is it?" I said. "It's out cantering across the deserts. It's leaping the lake and swimming the fence, for all I care. The one thing I know for certain is that it wasn't cooked for breakfast and that I didn't eat it."

"Jeff!" she said. "Haven't you had breakfast?"

"Nor supper last night, either," I said.

She said, "No wonder you're bearish." But, she's nice that way, she took the sting out of it by inviting me right down to her cottage for something to eat.

"About that bag," she said, as we walked along. "If Clyde Shively did bring another piece of luggage, and if it had something of value in it—"

"Listen to reason, Brigid," I begged. "If he brought another bag, it'll be something else missing. We don't need anything else missing. And we don't need a robbery, either—if that's what you're hinting at. We've plenty without."

"I think that we have a robbery whether we need it or not," she said. "If you hadn't been in such a hurry I meant to show you that the pockets of Clyde Shively's suit, there in the closet, had been searched and every single thing taken out of them."

"I'll bet you Adam cleaned them out this morning. Effects for the bereaved, or evidence, maybe."

"No. I looked through those pockets last night when we were hunting for clues, or whatever it was we thought we were doing there last night. The pockets were empty then. Since, I've searched everywhere for the things that must have been in those pockets. I can't find them."

"Maybe," I said, "that was his best suit that he did bring extra. Likely his other suit, with the pockets full, is the one that is missing. Or, maybe, one of those suits that we took to be the Judge's was Clyde Shively's other suit, after all."

"Rosemary said that Clyde Shively was wearing a light tan suit when she met him. I asked her, particularly. No youngish man would own those old-fashioned gray Palm Beach things. And having the entire suit missing, instead of what was in the pockets, wouldn't help any, would it?"

"Say," I said, "I have an idea. What would any man, kind of dusty and travel-worn, do after meeting Rosemary and knowing that he was going to meet her again? He'd spruce up. Clyde Shively took off his suit and put on his pajamas, and pressed it up nice and hung it in the closet."

"But what did he do with the things that he'd take out of his pockets?"

I sighed, heavily on purpose.

"Pressing his suit does seem reasonable," she admitted. "Especially since he was wearing his pajamas when he was killed. Maybe the old Judge objected to nothing but shorts. I wonder whether the Judge was wearing pajamas, too? They'd be cooler. His watch was in one of his suit pockets—"

"Brigid," I remonstrated. "You didn't go through the old gentleman's pockets, too, did you?"

"Rifled them," she said, vexed, "while you and Mayor Oakman were searching the hardware in the kitchen. I found his watch, and his billfold with fifty dollars in it and a return ticket to Pasadena. A leather key-holder, too; and some of his cards, and some loose silver and a handkerchief."

"Would a robber pass up a watch and fifty dollars?"

She didn't answer. I guess she was thinking. I was. The old gentleman's hat on the shelf; his keys, his money and his watch in his pocket. His cane in the corner of the room—we'd noted the cane the night before—and his

glasses flipping out of Reggie's pocket. Wherever the old
Judge was it certainly didn't look as if he'd started out to
go there on purpose.

We had come to Rosemary's cottage by this time and
Brigid stopped. "You go on, Jeff," she said, "and fill the
kettle for some hot water. I'm running in to see Rosemary
for a second."

I was glad to be able to tell her that Rosemary had gone
for a ride. "The only thing is," I added, "that I hate like
thunder having her see Kent in that jail."

"She won't," Brigid answered. "That's one reason I told
her that Mayor Oakman and the boys were on the mountain. I knew she wouldn't want to pass them."

"I'll bet you she goes the other way," I said. "She could
by rounding the lake and picking her way through the low
hills. I know that she's going to see Kent, because she was
carrying a large package of dainties to him—almost as big
as a pillow."

"A—what?" Brigid asked, kind of startled. I thought
that she was remembering the pillow we'd been examining,
so I hurried to set her mind at ease.

"Not a bed pillow," I told her. "It was just a fair-sized
box. It might hold a ham, or a watermelon, but I doubt
it. I'd judge it would hold maybe half a dozen oranges,
a couple of grapefruit, a small thermos of that nice iced
coffee you folks make over here, with maybe some sandwiches tucked in around the edges."

"Come on, Jeff," Brigid said. "We'll eat."

14

Barely in the nick of time to ruin my breakfast for me, Reggie came prowling in, sat down at the table and began looking around for napkin, knife and fork.

"Don't bother about Reggie, Brigid," I said. "He's had his breakfast. He's not hungry."

He gave me a queer look before he began reciting, "'Thou wast not born for death, immortal Bird! No hungry generations tread thee down; The—'"

"Reggie," Brigid stopped him, she's nice that way, "won't you have some toast and marmalade and coffee?"

Seemed that he would, if that was all there was, though he peered pointedly at the bacon and eggs I was finishing as fast as I could.

"I think that we should all consider all alibis," he said, while waiting for his first slice of toast to pop up; but, after that, he didn't say much of anything until the butter gave out, when he asked, "Do you know where Rosemary is?"

Brigid said, "She went for a short ride on Acrasia."

"Dear me," Reggie said. "I hope she comes back."

"What do you mean, if you mean anything, by that?" Brigid asked very slowly.

"Of course," Reggie kind of apologized. "In some ways I'd really rather she didn't come back. You understand?"

"No," Brigid said. "I don't understand—at all." It was the "at all" that took care of the kick back.

Reggie blew his nose before answering. "I meant that if she did— Or, well, say that she merely knew about Clyde Shively's being killed yesterday afternoon. And—well, if she brought the bloodstained pillow down to Twill's cottage, and—"

"It is rather soon after breakfast," Brigid interrupted, coldly furious, "to go into details. But"—she dipped a corner of her napkin into a glass of water—"how long do you think it would take this"—she spread the wet corner out flat—"to dry in this heat and altitude?"

"Goodness!" Reggie said, vexed. "I don't know."

"Of course you do," Brigid said. "You know that it would take a very short time. But in plain language, for you, the bloodstains on the pillow in Twill's cottage last night and on Rosemary's frock were bright red, wet and fresh. The stains in the Judge's cottage were brown and completely dry. Sorry, Jeff. Repugnant, isn't it? Shall we talk of something else?"

Reggie was willing and glad too. He unscrewed his face and began: "Mummy says that no matter how much Uncle Adam may want to hush this up, and for no matter what reasons, he won't be able to do so for very long. We think he should engage a criminologist. Betty-Jean knows of some perfectly marvelous chap in Los Angeles."

"Nobody," I remarked, "in Oakman County, much less Adam Oakman, would import anything, much less a marvelous chap from L. A."

"Well, of course," Reggie said, very reprovingly, "we all thought of Uncle Adam's unreasonable prejudices against California. But Betty-Jean thinks that she can persuade Kent to engage him. Kent, you know, has a perfectly wonderful alibi. He left camp shortly after one o'clock, was in the poolroom most of the afternoon, and walked home getting here a few minutes before seven. So we think that Kent will be only too glad to engage him. Dear me," Reggie began snapping his fingers, "the name was just on the tip of my tongue. It began with a *G*. Gangrene—Gemini—Gooseberry—"

Thinking my own thoughts, I decided that Kent wouldn't be apt to warm up, much, on the subject of detectives. My idea was that since Twill's body was hidden, and well hidden, Kent would be willing to leave it wherever it was.

When I began listening again Reggie had either fought his way out of his *G*'s or had given up. He was talking, now, about this Miss Lynn MacDonald who, afterward, was engaged on the case.

"Betty-Jean mentioned her," he was saying. "But we think that Uncle Adam's prejudice against women is so strong that even if Kent engaged her, Uncle Adam wouldn't allow her to work on the case. Place? Case?"

"Never mind," I said. "But the guy who told you Adam was prejudiced against ladies is a zoophite. He's famed, noted, for liking the ladies."

"What is a zoophite?" Brigid asked. It was just like her.

"You ought to know," I said. "Your papa told me. An animal of the lowest origin bearing some resemblance to a plant."

"Mayor Oakman," she said, "adores 'the ladies.' He despises women with brains. No, he distrusts them, dislikes them—"

"Oh, my!" Reggie broke in. "I came here to talk about alibis. And all you'll do is bandy words. Just bandy and bandy and bandy words."

"Grand word, 'bandy,'" Brigid said. "It bears repetition. Bandy, bandy. But, Reggie, if you came to discuss alibis, as you call them—"

"That's the right word for them," Reggie said. "It means where were you, or—"

"If you came to discuss alibis," Brigid interrupted, "why don't you? Rosemary talked with Judge Shively and his son just before four o'clock; so, beginning with after that time—"

"No," Reggie said, and got solemn and said, "No."

"Why?" Brigid asked.

Reggie said, "We've only her word for it that she talked to them at that time," and added poutingly, "I don't care, that's all we have for it. I like Rosemary. I liked Twill, too. But any girl who could indulge in a mad moment of passion and kill her own brother— Well, for goodness' sakes, any girl who could indulge in one mad moment of passion could indulge in two or three, couldn't she? Besides, such things run in families. You can't rely on the words of such persons. And," he finished, out of a clear sky, "I am not forgetting that it was before four o'clock when I saw Twill in swimming."

"Listen to me, Reggie," Brigid said. "You and I talked last night, while I was making you sandwiches, about your seeing Twill in swimming. You declared then that Twill was wearing his own bright yellow and white swimming suit. That he saw you and waved to you. That he was swimming toward this shore, wearing his own swimming suit. You agreed that there is no other suit like it on the place."

"I said it," Reggie answered, quite noble. "I told the truth."

"I know you did," she nodded. "I knew it last night when I found Twill's swimming suit spread on the sage-brush outside his cottage to dry."

"Change the subject, if you want to," Reggie said.

"I am not changing the subject," she said. "I am saying that Twill's suit drying outside his cottage proves that he returned to camp after you saw him in swimming."

Reggie said, "Well, for goodness' sakes, of course he returned. He wouldn't have been here at half-past seven for Rosemary to shoot if he hadn't returned," and finished off by tutting his tongue against his front teeth for a long time, until Brigid said:

"Stop that, you Reggie Duefife. Stop that silly ticking at me, or I'll shake you till your glasses fall off, and I'll grind them up, and I'll put the pieces into—"

"Brigid," I warned hurriedly, "Brigid. Now, now."

Reggie arose and kind of staggered over to the window. "'O, the barren, barren shore,'" he stated.

Brigid rubbed her head with her hands, making her hair look very much worse. "Sorry," she said to me, after a minute or two, and, "You-hoo, Reggie. I'm sorry."

Reggie wouldn't answer. From a rear view he looked like he was telling himself he wouldn't deign to answer.

"Jeff," she said, lifting her voice a little, "do you suppose that Reggie was making some connection between Twill's being in swimming yesterday afternoon and Clyde Shively's murder?"

"I can't see it," I said. "Not since Twill came back. Of course if he'd swum off. But he couldn't swim with that heavy brace on, and anywhere he'd landed he couldn't have walked without it."

"Still," Brigid argued. "I think Reggie must have meant to imply some connection between Twill's swimming and Clyde Shively's being killed."

Reggie kind of quivered all over. "I expected that," he said.

There wasn't a lick of sense to that remark and I knew it. Brigid should have known it too. But one of the big troubles with her and her papa is that they always think everything everybody says ought to make sense. She shouldn't have asked him what he meant. He couldn't answer, and it was so humiliating for all of us that I was actually relieved when Brigid opened the door to admit Mrs. Duefife who had just tapped on it.

Just inside the room she stopped and said, looking at me, "What is done is done. But do not ask me to believe that any dear good soul here in this forsaken place has been driven into crime."

Brigid spoke up. I never knew her to do such a thing before in her life. "'What I did, I did,'" she said. "'Not with a random inconsiderate blow but from old Hate, and with maturing Time.'"

Everybody gasped, even Brigid, before she slapped her own mouth with one hand and held it there. I hope I didn't look as shocked as Mrs. Duefife looked, but I felt it. Reggie's features being too fat to display the stronger emotions just gave an impression of gradually melting down.

"I'm sorry," Brigid apologized. "The rhythm, you know. It sounded the same. And Reggie's habit of quoting— One falls into it, sort of—"

Reggie spoke up, directly to his mamma. "See there? They blame everything on me," he said.

"No, we don't," Brigid said. "But, Mrs. Duefife, I think you shouldn't allow Reggie to go roaming around saying that Rosemary lied about the time Judge Shively introduced his son to her."

Reggie said, "I did not," and blew his nose.

"Don't, dearest," Mrs. Duefife said, and added, "Mummy knows you didn't, dearest."

"Yes, but he did," Brigid said. "Didn't he, Jeff?"

"He just wondered—" I began.

"As we all are bound to wonder," Mrs. Duefife caught me off base, and went on talking straight along.

Reggie dozed a little. Brigid swatted the flies. I soon gave up swallowing my yawns and yawned them, but I listened for quite a while.

Seemed that, about a quarter past one o'clock the day before, Mrs. Duefife and Reggie had gone to the community house and found Betty-Jean, Adam and Kent there.

Kent was on a ladder in the storeroom—the ladder that collapsed, later, under Reggie—handing down things from the shelves to Adam for restocking the kitchen supplies.

Adam immediately resigned his job in Reggie's favor. Mrs. Duefife helped Betty-Jean pack the big electric refrigerator with fancy fruits and vegetables that the folks got every few days by express from Phoenix. Timmy Monk, the grocer at Ferras, had delivered them about one o'clock, as usual, along with the things ordered from his store. Betty-Jean was sick with disappointment, she said, because the candles sent from Phoenix were red instead of light green; and when on top of that she found that Timmy had forgotten the sherry wine she was so upset that Adam suggested that she and Kent drive over to Ferras and fetch it.

Kent was agreeable. He said that they'd get Rosemary and Twill and all go. Adam put a stopper in that by saying that Rosemary had agreed to make the fourth at bridge with Mrs. Duefife, Reggie and himself that afternoon, and proved it by telephoning right then to Rosemary and telling her that they were waiting for her.

By the time the ladies had finished packing the refrigerator Rosemary had come, so the four bridge players went to it in the big living room and Kent and Betty-Jean struck out to go to Ferras.

"Kent went by himself, though," I said.

Brigid said, "Betty-Jean told me that Twill was in one of his 'temperamental moods.' He refused to go, so Betty-Jean thought that she shouldn't either. Twill was jealous of Kent, you know. Besides, Betty-Jean had her place cards to write. She wanted Twill to help her with those, but he wouldn't. He was sweet, but he did sulk, and—"

"My dear!" Mrs. Duefife interrupted. "Those place cards! She should have asked Reggie to help her. 'Rosemary, our good fairy.' 'Mrs. Duefife's chair, she's always fair.' And—"

I found myself losing track, after that, catching only some of her easier sentences, now and then.

"No person but Adam Oakman," she said, "had opportunity to conceal with deliberate malice and crafty cunning those glasses in my son's pocket."

Brigid astonished me by answering, "Mayor Oakman wouldn't, I'm sure, Mrs. Duefife. And whoever did it wasn't so very wicked, because we all know that no one could think of Reggie in connection with a thing like murder. He couldn't be considered."

"Thank you, my dear," Mrs. Duefife said, and went on all about how no intelligent adult could consider either, or for one moment, that a woman of breeding who had left a bridge game to procure a tube of nasal jelly for her son had been gone less than ten minutes before returning not only to play but also to win, could have been a party to any conspiracy while absent.

It is a queer thing about these good talkers. They put in all the effort and yet I never saw one who didn't tire everybody else out long before she got tired herself. But, in time, even Mrs. Duefife admitted that she was overly fatigued and asked me to put down the wall bed for her. The doggone thing dropped pretty heavily. It was a big relief to me when I gave it a quick glance and found nothing in it but the bedcovers.

Is talking contagious? I've thought so. Brigid never was much of a hand for it in long attacks, but that day Mrs. Duefife hadn't much more than closed her eyes after throwing herself on the bed, than Brigid began. When the wind started tearing the world up by the roots, she said, she had run to the community house because, like everybody in this country, she adored thunderstorms but she liked sharing them.

Not getting such a very cordial welcome from the bridge players, she had gone into the kitchen where she

caught Reggie, who was dummy then, slicing and eating
nice rounds of fresh pineapple.

Sure enough, as soon as she had read Betty-Jean's dinner menu, tacked on the wall, she found that Betty-Jean
was planning to have Pineapple Supreme for dessert that
evening and that Reggie had already made away with most
of the fruit.

Trouble ensued. They hunted for canned pineapple
and, finding none, Reggie agreed that he'd go to his cottage and get some cans he had there, just as soon as the
rain eased up a little. Also, a bargain was struck that if
Brigid wouldn't let on that Reggie had known about the
pineapple being for the pudding, and the pudding being
for the dessert, Brigid could take his hand at the bridge
table for one hour.

"Pardon me, Brigid," I said, when she'd got this far,
"but considering all there is to do, I guess I should be doing something."

"What are you going to do?" she asked, and had me
there.

Reggie had gone into the kitchen. Mrs. Duefife was
snoring light, lady-like snores. Brigid glanced at her and
came closer to me.

"Jeff," she said, lowering her voice, "bloodstained pillowslips wrong side out, bullets in the wall, empty pockets, missing luggage, don't kill men or steal dead bodies.

"I mean," she explained, answering my protests, "that
people do. So it seems to me that studying the people who
might, at least possibly, be involved is more intelligent
than running about searching for other 'clues' as you say."

"I never did," I denied. "But I suppose what you mean
is that you are agreeing with Reggie, wanting to look into
alibis."

"No," she said. "Or, well—call it opportunity. But I
was thinking more, I believe, of reasons, provocations.

What happened yesterday afternoon might be important it seems to me. Don't you think so?"

I didn't. I'd have been smarter if I had. But then, being an ordinary man myself, I naturally wouldn't think that ordinary happenings could have anything to do with murders and disappearing bodies.

15

"When Reggie said I might play for an hour," she began again, "I looked at my watch. 'Until fifteen minutes to four,' I warned him, and went into the living room and explained that I was going to play in Reggie's place for a while.

"Mrs. Duefife didn't like it. She said that we'd pivot, if I played. Rosemary and Mayor Oakman seemed willing to have me; but, before the hand was dealt, Betty-Jean came in wrapped up in a blanket and out of breath from running.

"'Isn't this storm terrible?' she asked, while she was pushing the door shut.

"'It is, indeed,' Mayor Oakman answered, 'if it necessitates the sort of garment—or garb—that you are wearing. You should have a papoose strapped on your back to complete the effect.'

"Betty-Jean's lips quivered and she pulled the blanket off. 'I didn't bring any things for rain,' she said. 'I haven't even an umbrella here.'

"'Noah had no umbrella,' Mayor Oakman said. 'But he throve.'

"By this time the poor kid was just about limp from insults and surprise. 'Well, but what's the matter?' she said.

"I thought that Mayor Oakman was being so rude because she had dared criticize anything, even a howling thunderstorm, in his beloved county. But Rosemary explained.

"'We are worried about Kent, Betty-Jean,' she said. 'He's gone to Ferras. And while we are sure he wouldn't start to come home around a dangerous mountain road with a storm threatening, still I suppose whenever anyone comes in we all hope it will be Kent.'

"Betty-Jean questioned in that polite little way of hers, 'Why doesn't someone telephone to Ferras and inquire at the hotel, or at the garage, or somewhere, whether Kent has left town?'

"'A brilliant idea,' Mayor Oakman said. 'The telephone wires blew down with the first gust of wind on the mountain.'

"'But the lights are all on,' Betty-Jean observed.

"I think she believed that the lights came over the telephone wires. But Mayor Oakman couldn't conceive of such stupidity, so he explained that our power line came from several miles south of Tumboldt.

"'I beg your pardon,' she apologized, when he gave her a chance to speak again. 'I should have said that the telephone wires aren't all down, either. I telephoned to Judge Shively when the storm began. I was frightened, and thought that he might be, and—'

"'Frightened!' Mayor Oakman scoffed. 'I never thought that a daughter of mine would be afraid of a little lightning.'

"'I'm not, Father,' she said. 'It is the wind I'm afraid of, and the thunder. Shall I try getting Ferras now?'

"'If you like.' Mayor Oakman answered. 'But try hard.'

"He was my host, so I simply got up from the table and went over to Betty-Jean, who was trying to ring Ferras, and explained to her that the cottage to cottage telephones weren't connected with the outside wires.

"Mayor Oakman said, 'We are waiting for you, Brigid, if you please.'

"I longed to say, 'Wait hard.' But, after all, there is something about the man that prevents one from piping insults at him, so I said, 'Sorry. I'll get Reggie. Do you mind?' and went into the kitchen before the thunder gave him an opportunity to answer.

"Reggie had opened a can of ham and a bottle of pickled onions and was making sandwiches. Arguing with him was useless.

"When I returned to the living room I was glad to see that Betty-Jean had taken my place. I couldn't have stuck it, playing with Mayor Oakman the way he was snapping his cards down on the table and gloating and quarreling.

"I picked up some magazines and read a story or two; then I noticed Rosemary, who was dummy then, standing at the window.

"The air was still gray with rain, but clouds were drifting away from bright blue patches of sky. Rosemary was surprised at the storm's clearing so soon. I looked at my watch. It was twenty-five minutes past three. That made more than an hour since the wind had begun and rather a long storm for this country.

"'I believe,' she said, speaking to all of us, 'that I'll get Acrasia and ride over now to see what has happened on Tumboldt.'

"Mayor Oakman jumped right up. 'An excellent idea. Splendid!' he agreed. 'I've a rubber slicker you can wear. Just a moment.'

"He went into the storeroom and returned with that big black coat of his and held it for Rosemary. 'Don't take any undue risks,' he was saying, when Twill opened the front door and came in.

"'Where are you going, Rosemary?' he asked. 'Why are you putting on that thing?'

"Mayor Oakman explained. Twill went into one of his worst rages.

"'You can't do it,' he said. 'You can't send my sister out in a storm to hunt for a big lummox who hasn't sense enough to keep out of danger.'

"'I'm not sending her,' Mayor Oakman declared. 'She is going of her own accord.'

"'The hell she is,' Twill said.

"'Don't "hell" me, young fellow,' Mayor Oakman warned him.

"'I'll "hell" you or any man who'd send my sister out in this weather to satisfy his own old-womanish fears.'

"'If you weren't a cripple,' Mayor Oakman answered, 'I'd slap you over,' and turned and walked to the bridge table where Mrs. Duefife and Betty-Jean were sitting.

"'If I weren't a cripple'—Twill was white and trembling—'I shouldn't be a coward. I'd walk a few miles to look after my child, if necessary, rather than send a girl—'

"Mayor Oakman interrupted, 'If you can't behave yourself, get out of here.'

"'I'm leaving,' Twill said. 'I'll return to Betty-Jean's friend. Stout fellow. Affectionately minded, too—at least when he's blotto. Ugh, Betty? "Sweet little Betty-Jean," he said, though thickly. Fancies himself as a temptation to women, doesn't he, Betty?'

"Betty-Jean looked at Twill and then around at all of us with an utterly stupefied expression on her face.

"Mayor Oakman asked, 'Who is he talking about, and what? Do you know, Betty-Jean?'

"'No, I don't, Father,' she answered, sort of breathlessly. 'Unless this is a joke of some sort—'

"'A joke,' Twill said. 'But not funny. I went to Judge Shively's cottage just now, looking for you, Betty, and found instead this—well, this son of a judge."

"'What is all this?' Mayor Oakman demanded.

"'I'm uncertain, myself,' Twill answered. 'But Judge Shively said it was his son when he introduced it. Clyde Shively. Arrived around noon today. Caught a ride out from Ferras with some tourists—'

"'Who couldn't read?' Mayor Oakman interposed. You know how tourists' disregarding all those 'Private Road, Keep Out' signs of his always throws the Mayor off any subject.

"Betty-Jean stood up. 'If Clyde is here,' she said, 'I must run right over to see him. I don't understand why Judge Shively didn't tell me—'

"Twill stepped in front of her and spoke straight to her as if he'd forgotten all the rest of us. 'Betty-Jean, honor now, didn't you know that fellow was in camp?'

"'No. I had no idea that he was,' she answered. 'I haven't seen him for ages. I must run right over—'

"'Wait a minute,' Twill said. 'I've pulled a boner. Sorry. Judge Shively told me that he was saving his son to crown your feast this evening, as it were. A grand surprise for you. I didn't believe him. I thought that you must know the son was here. I also thought— Well, you'll admit there were numerous things I might have thought. But, since you honestly didn't know he was here, I suppose the surprise story was true. I'd no notion that the old gentleman was so childish.'

"'I don't know that that's so childish,' Mayor Oakman disagreed. 'I know of nothing that cheers up a party like a pleasant surprise.'

"'I've often suspected that I am unfortunately adult,' Twill answered and, after glancing at his wrist watch, he made an ugly twisting gesture with his shoulder and walked fast to the front door.

"Betty-Jean ran after him and caught him as he put his hand on the doorknob. I'd looked at my watch when he looked at his, so I know that it was twenty minutes until four right then.

"Mayor Oakman said in a low voice, 'That boy gets crazier by the day. Does anyone know what is the matter with him now?'

"We knew. He was the only one too dull to know that Twill was insanely jealous of Betty-Jean, and that the idea of anyone's thinking that another man could be a grand surprise for her was destroying him, and making him fancy all sorts of impossible things. None of us explained.

"Twill banged the door shut. Betty-Jean came back to the bridge table. I'd seen Twill give her an angry shove and she was holding her hand over the place on her shoulder.

"'Sit down, daughter,' Mayor Oakman said. 'We'll try a few hands together since Rosemary has gone. Brigid, will you make the fourth?'

"'If you'll excuse me, please, Father,' Betty-Jean said, 'I think I must go to see Clyde. I mean, in case Twill wasn't joking or mistaken or something. I mean, Judge Shively would think it was rude of me not to come.'

"'Use some sense, Betty-Jean,' Mayor Oakman scolded. 'Twill had no business to tattle and spoil the old Judge's little plans. We must consider that Twill behaved like a gentleman and not like a lunatic. We'll do nothing and say nothing and this evening when the son—Clyde, is it?—appears, we'll all be enormously surprised.'

"And," Brigid finished, very grimly for a nice girl, "we were. Remember, Jeff? We were all enormously surprised."

16

As I said, Mrs. Duefife, being such a good talker herself, had gone to sleep as soon as Brigid began talking. But she woke with a start, during the pause after Brigid's grim remark and asked, "Where is Reggie?"

"In the kitchen," I answered absentmindedly, my mind still being on Brigid's story, and forgetting that I'd seen him walking toward the community house quite a while ago.

"I was telling Jeff," Brigid said, "about Twill's leaving the community house after the quarrel yesterday afternoon. Rosemary left a moment later. Before I went to the bridge table I looked out of the window and saw her running to catch him. She linked arms with him and they went on together toward his cottage.

"A few minutes after that Reggie came in from the kitchen. But, in the meantime, he'd been to his cottage for the canned pineapple. It was on his way back that he saw Twill in swimming."

"So odd of him," Mrs. Duefife murmured.

"If you mean Twill," Brigid snapped, "it wasn't odd at all. The storm had cleared and it was hot. Swimming was the one exercise Twill had and the relaxation was splendid for him.

"At any rate, as soon as Reggie came in, Mayor Oakman decided that we were all tired of playing bridge and should stop. But, since he couldn't command us to do so, we were going on with Reggie and Mrs. Duefife playing together, when Mayor Oakman called Mrs. Duefife into the kitchen."

Brigid stopped talking on a questioning note and looked straight at Mrs. Duefife who didn't seem to notice for a couple of minutes. Finally, though, she spoke up a little less collectedly than usual.

"He did interrupt right then, didn't he? It seems to me we hadn't bid the first hand, or had we?"

"No, we hadn't," Brigid said, and stopped, still questioning.

"He didn't want anything really important," Mrs. Duefife said. "He had noticed that Reggie's sinus trouble seemed a bit worse—the dampness, you know—so he suggested that I should get his nasal jelly for him. He knew Reggie would not trouble for himself."

I never was more embarrassed in my life. Brigid blushed until her freckles didn't show. We both knew that whatever Adam had told Mrs. Duefife in the kitchen, it hadn't come within shouting distance of Reggie's nasal jelly.

Mrs. Duefife swung off the bed and began taking hairpins out of her hair to stick them in again. "The whole thing is entirely trivial, of course," she said, stopping at the screen door and holding it open for more flies to come in, "but, do you know, I think I shall ask you not to mention to Adam this matter of the nasal jelly. He is—could one say a bit overly sensitive?"

She had been feeling her way through each word, but she tripped on that "sensitive" and knew it, and took it right back.

"No. Sensitive is not the word. One avoids 'vain.' One rejects 'fussy' for a personality so richly vivid. But Twill's calling Adam an 'old woman' cut very, very deeply. It was this, I firmly believe, that caused Adam, after suggesting the nasal jelly, to request particularly that the suggestion should not seem to come from him. Dear man. How he does brood over his little fuss. I mean, how he does fuss over his little brood. We should all help him, I think; smooth his path—"

"We won't say a word about the nasal jelly," Brigid interrupted, sounding tired.

"Well," I said to Brigid who just sat there looking glum after Mrs. Duefife had finally gone, "come to think of it, who thought up the plot of fetching Reggie's nasal jelly can't make a lot of difference; can it?"

"Liars make a difference," she said.

"Any lady," I told her, "who can't do better by a lie than that, is more than likely the most truthful person on the place. How long was she hobnobbing with Adam in the kitchen?"

"Only two or three minutes; long enough for Reggie to turn on the radio. You came in just after she did. You must have noticed how nervous she was and how eager to have you play her hand?"

"She went to get the nasal jelly," I said.

"She had it with her when she came back, yes. She was gone rather long. And it was after four o'clock."

"If 'rather long' is just about time enough to go to her cottage and get the nasal jelly, you're right," I said.

"Do you think that Mayor Oakman sent her for the jelly?"

"No," I said. "I think what you think. That Adam was planning to bump off Clyde Shively, so he called Mrs. Duefife into the kitchen and told her all about it—just to be on the safe side."

Brigid got up and began swatting the flies.

"Or," I asked, "did he send her to do the killing? In some ways that would be more like him. Saving himself steps, I mean."

"If you don't stop trying to be funny," she said, landing about one fly for every two words, "I'll— I'll—"

"Own up that it was you who slipped Judge Shively's glasses into Reggie's pocket last night?" I interrupted.

"That's nice, too," she said, very offhandedly.

"You went through the Judge's pockets last night in the clothes closet. You've some crazy idea that because Reggie is fat he couldn't be guilty of crime, or even accused. I don't know why. And I don't know why you thought it would be a nice complicating plan to move the glasses from the Judge's pocket to Reggie's. But I'll bet you know."

"I didn't take one thing out of those pockets last night," she said. "The glasses weren't in them. I suppose you don't believe me, and I don't care. Why should you? Some of us must be lying. I'd probably be more deft with it than any of the others, except you and your precious Adam, of course."

"Look here now, Brigid," I said. "Adam is no liar. He may be kind of diplomatic at times—"

"Diplomatic! Throwing Betty-Jean at Kent's head all summer. And it wasn't until last evening, when Kent finally said straight out that he was going to marry Rosemary, that any of these horrors began happening."

"Kent told us well after seven o'clock yesterday evening. Clyde Shively was killed, the best we've figured yet, close after four in the afternoon. And, come to think of it, Kent wasn't going to marry Clyde Shively."

"No. He was going to marry Rosemary. Mayor Oakman knew that no girl in her senses could be in love with a Twill if a Kent wanted her to love him, so all the Mayor had to do was to change Kent's plans, not Betty-Jean's. For that matter, I don't see how any girl could be in love with any man but Kent. I've adored him madly for years. Didn't you know? I thought I'd told everyone. That's the reason I adore Rosemary—or one of them. What was I saying?"

"I don't know," I said.

"Oh, yes. About Mayor Oakman's thinking that if Twill and Rosemary were out of the way all his troubles would be over. I asked Rosemary yesterday evening what he'd said to her by the gate when she came home from her ride. She told me that he'd said only that she and Twill must leave on account of Twill's behavior. That was his plan—just to kick them out. But when Kent took a hand and spoiled that plan, Mayor Oakman might have decided that he'd have to find another one. Suppose that he could make it appear, even temporarily, that Rosemary had done some wicked thing?"

"I'd be ashamed!" I said.

"I'm not. When St. Dennis first met Mayor Oakman in New York he told Mother that he'd met an up-from-the-soil product of the Far West who looked like Ramsay MacDonald and thought he was the Lord Almighty. He is proud of the Ramsay resemblance, so he doesn't tell that his father left him tons of that funny stuff he found in California in '49. He is a poseur; and he still thinks that he's the Lord Almighty and meddles with people's lives. He meant to stick a finger in this and he fell in up to his eyebrows, but—"

It was a big relief to have Betty-Jean come in just then. She had tried to fix up a little; but she wasn't pretty, yet, and she'd forgotten to rub any of the powder off her neck.

"Father and the men are home," she said. "They didn't find anything at all in the crevice below Dead Man's Hook."

Brigid gave me a look that meant "I told you so" several times, but all she said was, "Take this chair, Betty-Jean, honey. Lean back, and rest."

"I don't want to rest," Betty-Jean said, but she sat down and slumped a little. "I was going to tell you something. Oh, yes. Joe Laud telephoned a few minutes ago. He says the bullet that killed Clyde Shively was much larger than the bullets in Twill's revolver. I mean, Twill's in his pearl-handled revolver were smaller. Did I say larger? What I mean is that the bullet that killed Clyde was too large to fit into Twill's little revolver. Clyde used to bring me chocolate marshmallows all the time when I was little. I choked on one once, but Clyde didn't laugh. Another time he gave me a boy doll in a red velvet suit. It had big brown eyes, like Twill's. If the bullet wouldn't fit into Twill's revolver, no one can blame Twill now, can they?"

"Of course not." Brigid went over to her and began petting her up. "But no one blamed Twill, anyway. Truly. Brigid wouldn't fib to you, darling."

"I love you, Briggy," Betty-Jean sighed. "But Reggie just talks and talks about Twill's being in swimming and then people look funny. I forgot. Jeff, Father told me to ask you to come to the community house. Reggie told him that you were here. Father is very angry. I loved Judge Shively. Mother loved him, too. He used to call us his two best Bettys. It was a joke. Oh, dear, isn't it hot?"

Brigid came out on the stoop with me. "Betty-Jean is half out of her mind," she whispered. "I wish I knew what to do. But, anyway, you tell Reggie that if he mentions Twill's swimming again, ever, I'll tell Mayor Oakman that he's in love with Betty-Jean. I will, too."

"Reggie you mean? Is he?"

"Desperately. He fell in love with the first meal she ever cooked when a tick bit Jeremiah months ago at Hay Patch."

"There's something to be thankful for," I said. "That Jeremiah isn't here now."

She didn't pay any attention. She was peering out at the lake.

"Can you imagine," I said, "what we'd have on our hands, and how sickening it would be if Jeremiah was here now bawling all over the camp?"

"Who, Jeremiah?" she said, so I turned around to see what in the nation she was staring at with that creepy look on her face.

I saw. Old Memaloose, sprawling; and sitting on it, empty, motionless, reminding a person of nothing on earth but a waiting coffin, that doggone canoe.

"I'll swim to it, presently," she said, as if we'd been talking about it all the time, "and push it across to the boathouse landing."

Her own papa who, if not a smarter man than the average, certainly thinks that he is, said himself that if he had been in my place right then he wouldn't have seen a mite of harm in letting the kid move the canoe since it was an eyesore to her. Yes, leaving the canoe alone might, possibly, have saved two lives. But how could I know that? I couldn't. Nobody could have known it, then. So I stepped off the cement, in order to walk in peace and quiet on the ground, and started out to meet Adam at the community house.

17

Walking on the ground made going slower—our rocky deserts resemble in no way the seashore sand— so I had time for thinking, some, as I went along.

The first thing I did, was to give all that alibi business up as a bad job. According to Brigid's and Mrs. Duefife's stories, there had been too much gadding around. It did kind of look as if Kent and I had pretty fair alibis; but, come to think of it, ours weren't so hot, either.

Take my own. I met Rosemary at the gate, after the storm had cleared, and got into the kitchen with Adam at about four o'clock. But I could have had a leeway in there of ten minutes or so—long enough to hurry off and kill one or two men, easy, before I started my alibi, first with Adam and then with the other folks playing bridge. (If anyone should think that my playing contract bridge needs an alibi, or something, maybe I should explain that I learned when a couple of big bugs from Denver came to spend the winter with Adam in 1927. I like it fine. Next to poker it's the best card game I know except solo.)

Kent's alibi went up in smoke if, instead of walking home from Ferras and making good time in under three hours, he'd jumped a horse and ridden home. His footprints showed for walking through the gate, but he could have dismounted and walked into camp.

What became of the horse? I'm well acquainted around here and I don't know a single horse that wouldn't light out for home if it had half a chance.

Of course I knew that Kent had walked home as he said he had. And I was pretty certain that I hadn't just finished up a few killings when I went into the living room and took Mrs. Duefife's place at the bridge table that afternoon.

As soon as she came back with the nasal jelly, Reggie said that he was tired of playing and went into the kitchen; so the four of us, Mrs. Duefife and Brigid, Betty-Jean and I, settled down for a session.

We didn't play for big money, but enough to be interesting to lose and interesting to win. Betty-Jean was a terrible player, but as usual she held the cards to even things up. After Reggie stopped fussing around, turned off the radio and went sound asleep on the sofa we had a mighty good game and time got clear away from us.

The first thing we knew, here Adam came in all dressed up in spanking clean white and whewing about the air being stuffy as folks always do who feel superior on account of having been outdoors when others have been indoors. He whewed so much and so loud that Reggie woke up, and Reggie wanted his dinner right off.

"You'll have almost an hour to wait," Adam told him. "It is only ten minutes past seven—"

"Ten minutes past seven!" Betty-Jean said, and went on saying she had never done such a thing before in her life, and that there wouldn't be any dinner, and what in the world, and why hadn't somebody told her.

Adam tried soothing her by suggesting that she turn us out to graze, and by saying that give him a frying pan and he could fix a meal fit for a king in under twenty minutes.

He didn't soothe her. Everything he'd say she'd say something that didn't answer. "I saw some fine roasted fowls, in the ice-box," he said. "Instead of fixing them fancy, as you told me you were going to, why not slice them cold? Nothing better."

"Hot consommé would be horrid," she said.

"We're all homefolks here," Adam said, "and there is plenty of food on hand. A little later, or not so elaborate, what's the difference?"

"And that makes my salad too simple. Perhaps if I used a Roquefort dressing, and curled some cucumbers. No. And I did want everything to be so nice."

Brigid said, "Don't worry, Betty-Jean. We'll all help and everything will be grand. I'm running down to my cottage to get into something decent. I'll bring Rosemary back with me, and she's marvelous with salads, and—"

"Don't bother Rosemary just now, Brigid," Adam interrupted. "Leave her alone. She'll join us, perhaps, later when she feels better."

"But what is the matter with Rosemary? Brigid asked.

"Nothing more serious than a pouting spell after tears. She and Twill will be leaving here tomorrow—"

Kent came in just then, and I knew at first glance that the boy was mad all over. "Skip it, Dad," he said. "Rosemary, Twill and I are all leaving here tomorrow, as soon as the road is opened. Rosemary and I are going to be married in Ferras."

Adam never was a hand for slang phrases, but I guess he forgot himself. "What are you going to use for money?" he asked.

"Money," Kent said.

"Your poker winnings today, I suppose?"

"I came home with more money than I had when I left here. You seemed to hope I'd be broke, so I haven't bothered mentioning it to you."

"Or to Rosemary, either, before this evening?"

"She knew, of course. I've been begging her to marry me and leave here since the first week I came home. She hoped, not knowing you, that you might come to dislike her less and be willing for us to marry."

"Let me tell you something," Adam said. "If that girl knew you had money, the only reason she didn't marry you the minute you asked her was that she wanted to give that damn crippled brother of hers a chance to marry my daughter and the money they thought she'd have."

Kent didn't answer. He walked over toward the back hall door. Adam stepped in front of him and gave him a clap on the ear. I caught Adam's arm and he slammed one at me, but missed it a mile.

Kent walked to the front door and out of it. The trouble was he took his time, lazy as whittling. He should have hurried. If he had, Adam wouldn't have had a chance to say so much while the boy was crossing that big room.

Betty-Jean, Mrs. Duefife and Reggie had skipped out into the kitchen. Brigid followed Kent. Adam shook the door open, kicked it shut, and left me standing there alone.

Mrs. Duefife, hearing the door bang I suppose, peeked in from the kitchen and then came tiptoeing toward me, hunching her shoulders and biting her lower lip as folks do when acting stealthy.

"Shall we go on with the dinner?" she asked.

"You bet you," I told her. "Food will be the best thing for everybody around here."

"Reggie is trembling all over," she kept on whispering. "Such brutal language. And Betty-Jean is crying. The shock of it. Her own father, threatening to kill, threatening—"

"Hold on," I said. "You all misunderstood Adam. He didn't mean a thing—"

"That is all very well," she interrupted; but I, always being doubtful of sentences beginning with those particular words, made five or six excuses and got out to the front porch where Brigid and Kent were.

He said, "Sorry about all that in there, Jeff. Is Dad cooling down?"

"Like everything," I said. "He's gone outdoors. He'll be fine."

"I hope not," Brigid said. "Is the dinner party off, do you know, Jeff?"

I said it was on, and the three of us chatted for several minutes after that, chiefly about Brigid's not wearing briefs to a dinner party, before we started to walk down to her cottage.

It was then that we heard the gunshot. It couldn't have been more than two or three minutes later when Adam showed up from around the community house and met us as we turned to walk east.

And then, as I've told, Rosemary came running out of Twill's cottage, making those pitiful outcries and telling us that she had killed her brother. We went into the house, and saw the blood on the dented pillow, and on her arms and pretty white dress and heard her grieving; but we couldn't find Twill anywhere.

A quarter of a mile away, and almost two hours later, we found Clyde Shively murdered, shot in the back. Soon, as I've also told, we realized that the old Judge couldn't be found; and it was then that terror came creeping like a storm cloud's shadow over us all. It was bigger than we were. We couldn't get away from it any more than we could get away from the dark night itself with its evil hours that turned our very hopes against us, changing them into blind dreads and dull bewildering fears.

18

If I'd stopped to think about it that Wednesday night, though I didn't, I'd have said that I'd never be at myself again. But Thursday, with the sun shining as usual, and finding myself alive and with my health in another day made me feel a lot better.

I don't mean that I was cheerful or very sensible when, after Betty-Jean had given me Adam's message, I started out from Brigid's cottage to meet him at the community house. I was worried about Kent in that boiling hot jail, and about everything else in the world. But I had my two feet on the ground—desert ground, where they belonged—and, speaking symbolically like O'Dell, I thought that I was going to be able to keep them there.

So, seeing Adam coming toward me too fast with that curly white hair of his standing out every which way and with twiggish things in it besides like a maniac's was very discouraging. I felt myself slipping. I waved and hollered the one cheering thought I'd had that morning.

"It's lucky Jeremiah isn't here—"

"What?" he hollered back, slowing down and looking over his shoulder.

"I just said—"

"Who?"

"Jeremiah," I said, and gave up, sick of the whole thing.

He stopped and waited for me to come to him. The twiggish things in his hair were bits of sage and greasewood; his clothes were torn, showing scratches that he'd got climbing down into the crevice, but the worst of it was he looked old. I'd never so much as thought, before, of Adam's being old; so I began feeling sorry for him, and to what lengths I might have gone with my sympathy I don't know, if he hadn't said, right then:

"Get on the sidewalk and walk, can't you? What are you minching along like that over the rocks for?"

"I am not minching along," I said.

"You are minching along," he said. "What were you yelling at me? It sounded as if you were saying that Jeremiah wasn't here."

"I was—" I tried telling him.

"By the Eternal! What next? Why did he come over here? How did he get here? Who saw him last?"

"He never started for here, even," I said, trying to explain in a hurry while I had a chance. "He never came. He hasn't been here—"

"Well, well, what about it?"—I'd known he wouldn't let me finish.—"Who said he was here?"

"Nobody. I just said he wasn't."

By this time I wished like everything that I'd never brought the subject up. I thought maybe if I'd change it, he'd let the whole thing drop.

"Hot, isn't it?" I said.

"Not particularly," he said; sweat was dripping off his bushy white eyebrows into his eyes and trickling down the creases around his mouth. "But, before we leave this news concerning Jeremiah, I'd like to clear up one point. I've gathered that he is safe at Hay Patch. I've gathered that he isn't here. Am I right?"

"I was trying to tell you—"

"You told me. Now I have news for you, Sheriff. Unsensational. Less exciting. Not the sort that must be shouted from far distances with warning gestures. Rosemary isn't here."

"I know it, Mayor," I said, disgusted to the point of turning around and starting to walk off.

"Wait a minute, Jeff," he said, more politely. "Let's go in here and get out of the heat."

I humored him and went with him into Reggie's cottage. We'd been standing in front of it.

The parlor, very untidy and dusty-looking, smelled of stale oranges and peppermint. A lot of the pictures of things to eat were curled up like pinwheels on the walls, but some of the extra delicious ones were fastened at all four corners and fly-specked.

Adam walked around a minute or two squinting at them as if they didn't agree with him and then an idea struck him and it was a dandy.

"Jeff," he said, "I'm a damn fool."

"Yes?" I said, making it a question but insinuating that I'd take his word for it.

He went on, not quite so pleasantly and this goes to show how Adam sticks to things, never leaving go until he's finished them—"You were telling me that Jeremiah wasn't here," he said, "because, being in one of your lighter, more whimsical moods, you thought that I would appreciate the jest—the absence of his tears, so on. The good taste might be questioned, at the moment, but I'd rather question a man's taste than his sanity. I thought you'd gone insane. Have you as good a reason, humorous or otherwise, for allowing that girl to escape?"

"Meaning Rosemary?" I asked. "If you do, 'escape' your foot!"

That shouldn't have made him mad, but it did. Seemed that he'd left me in charge of the camp. Seemed that he'd trusted me and expected me to be on the go every minute getting evidence from hither and yon all over the place. Seemed that he hadn't expected me to spend a minute off my feet, to say nothing of talking to the ladies. Seemed that he'd have overlooked my doing or not doing anything if I'd just managed to prevent Rosemary's going for a ride.

"You never said a word about keeping her on the place," I stood up for myself.

"I must have forgotten, momentarily," he said, "that you were County Sheriff."

"What do you want her here for, anyway?" I asked.

He was looking in the wastebasket where the orange peelings were, but he put it down before answering. "It isn't," he said, "that I blame a man for being crazy. What I blame him for is enjoying it, taking pride in it."

"Just because Rosemary killed her brother, by accident, and admitted it right away, is no reason," I told him, "for thinking that she had a hand in everything that happened here last night, or in anything else at all."

Adam, who had been lowering that doggone wall bed, now sat on the side of it to rest for half a second, and say, "I'm by no means convinced that Rosemary did kill Twill yesterday evening."

"Be that as it may," I said, and when he said, "What?" I repeated it, "Be that as it may, somebody was killed by somebody in that cottage last night at about half-past seven. Remember hearing the shot? Remember the pillow? Remember Rosemary's white dress and her arms? Remember that some of it rubbed off, red, on Kent's white shirt?"

"Distinctly," he said, "and you may omit particulars. Reggie has been giving a demonstration. He isn't as dull as I thought. It is true that things do dry rapidly in this heat and at this altitude. You are right. Someone was killed in Twill's cottage last evening. But suppose that 'someone'

was Judge Shively and not Twill? Suppose that Twill killed
the Judge and took the body away while Rosemary ran out
in front to stop us."

"Stop us from what?" I asked. "She never made a move
to stop us. If she hadn't come running out, we'd have
walked right along without going in there at all."

"Exactly," he said. "You have answered your own question."

"No, I didn't," I said.

"You have answered your own question," he said, as
I'd said nothing. "When we heard the shot," he went on,
"the four of us, Kent, Brigid, you and I walked toward
Twill's cottage. If he had left there a minute or two after
the shot was fired, he could have been getting away with
the body behind the cottages—using them for screens—
while we were walking in front of them. After the boys
rode through the gate the footprints were effaced. Anyone
could have ridden out, after that, without leaving traces.
The boys' horses were here, too, you know. And there was
a short time when we were all together in Twill's cottage,
before you arrested Kent."

"I didn't arrest Kent," I said. "But have it your own way.
Twill shot the old Judge and skipped out in daylight with
the body. Six people hunting at fever heat couldn't find
him. But he waited, somewhere and nearly three hours, for
his chance and rode away. He couldn't ride far, because the
horses were here when Kent and I struck out, and later, I
guess, when the boys were ready for them. No, Twill just
rode a little piece, got off and sent the horse back. Would
the horse come over to Memaloose, or would it light out
for Ferras where it eats its oats?

"Never mind that, though. Since we're going crazy, we
might as well, as you said, be proud of it. So Twill dis-
mounts on the desert, a cripple hampered with a dead

body. The boys spent the night and until long after sunup
this morning scouring the deserts. Where is Twill? Where
is the body? You take the story and go on from there."

"Shut up," Adam said, "you talk so much you make me
nervous," and went walking to the front door in order to
turn around and come back in a careless manner except for
shooting quick glances across the floor.

"What are you doing now?" I asked, knowing—I don't
know how—that he was doing something.

"I am looking under the bed," he answered, being dignified very slowly, something like Mrs. Duefife.

"A couple of minutes ago," I told him, "you were walking where under the bed is now. Did you drop something?"

"When we went into Twill's cottage yesterday evening,"
he said, "the wall bed was down. I am trying to discover
whether, if someone had been under that bed, then, we
should have noticed him."

"Who would it be under the bed?" I asked. "Twill, or
the Judge, or both?"

"If you please!" he said, mad again about something,
and went off into a long rigmarole about how Kent had
stayed alone with Rosemary until after Clyde Shively's
body had been found, and finished by stating that Kent
was the only person in camp who would have sense enough
to get Twill's body (seemed that Adam had gone back to
Twill's being shot) away and hidden where it couldn't be
found.

I didn't answer. I was thinking.

"Well? Well?" he burst out. "What now, Sunbeam? Astounding," he added, "this propensity of yours for thinking up jokes and grinning over them in times of deep tragedy. Astounding and repellent."

"You'd know better than I would about the joke," I
said. "I was just remembering that Kent mentioned to me
last night that you'd be the only one on the place with

nerve enough to steal the body or sense enough to hide it where it couldn't be found."

There was never any telling about Adam. I hadn't aimed to make him mad before and he got mad. I had aimed to vex him a little, then, and he was pleased as Punch though he tried to hide it by chucking some of the covers under the bed and walking off, to see whether they'd be notice-able or not. The upshot of this was that, trying our best, neither of us could see anything in that room, from any point in it, except those covers under the bed.

While he was picking them up and shaking the dust off them I happened to remember that I'd looked under the bed in Twill's cottage while Kent was sitting on it beside Rosemary and not so very long before we'd found Clyde Shively's body.

"That doesn't change matters, so much," Adam said, after thinking it over. "We had all been searching at the back of the place for almost two hours. Kent, or anyone, could have taken the body out the front way—"

"Where?" I interrupted. "Could have taken it where?"

"Stop that everlasting 'whereing'!" he said. "Is there no word in the language that anyone on this place can use except where, where, where?"

"Why," I asked, as much to change the subject as any-thing else, "did you want to search Reggie's cottage, in par-ticular?" It had dawned on me, by this time, that he hadn't stopped there wanting to get out of the heat by accident.

"The Judge's glasses in Reggie's pocket," Adam admit-ted. "Even during the excitement, Reggie couldn't have picked them up without noticing what he was doing. Some-one here on the place slipped them into Reggie's pocket deliberately."

"Reggie might have slipped them in there, more or less deliberately," I said. "Or some stranger—" I saw my mis-take there, and stopped but not soon enough.

"You think that Reggie wouldn't have noticed a stranger, coming close enough to him to put something into his pocket? But, as I was saying, before you interrupted, I've wondered whether the person who disposed of the glasses might have put other clues here in Reggie's cottage, in order to mislead us? You know as well as I do that Reggie wouldn't commit murder—"

"Why not? Too fat?"

I had him there, and he knew it, so he didn't answer.

I happened to look out the front window just then. "I don't know what there is about the way she walks, I said, "but there is something that makes it the handsomest walking I ever saw walked."

He bit excitedly, giving himself dead away on one count, anyhow. "Rosemary?" he asked.

"Home from her ride and on her way to her cottage right now," I said.

19

I'd rather have gone with Adam when he went to talk with Rosemary, then; but he said he wanted to talk with her alone. I understood, in a way, what Kent had said about Rosemary's not needing anyone to take care of her. I remembered O'Dell's saying, months before, that if she and Adam ever came to a conflict she'd win. So I found myself a patch of shade between two empty cottages; but, as far as peace and quiet went, I might as well have been lying under the hose cart at a fire on Main Street.

Brigid was in swimming, splashing and slapping the water; moving the canoe at first and, later, just splashing and slapping. The two horses were tramping around in the back. Every once in a while somebody had to get out and walk a piece, just so there'd be footsteps making big clatters on the cement. Naturally in a tumult like that I couldn't rest. I had to think; and, like Joe, I thought of things.

It's queer that knowing something and knowing that you know it should be two entirely different matters. I guess I'd known the night before as well as I knew afterward, when it was proved for certain, that old Judge Shively was dead, murdered. But just then, in between the houses that Thursday afternoon, was the first time I knew for sure that I knew it.

That sudden, positive knowing led me, against my will, into a whole parcel of questions. Who? When? How? Why? And— No, I wasn't going to tangle up with those "wheres" again, so I stopped at the "whys."

Suppose that somebody had feared or hated Clyde Shively bad enough to shoot him in the back. If his father hadn't seen the killing, he'd more than likely know about the hard feelings. So it was sensible to think that whoever had killed the son had killed the father to keep him quiet. But what was the use of hiding one body and not the other? Had the killer been pressed for time? Was there room for only one body in this hiding-place? And there I was spang-bang into the "wheres" again. I wouldn't have it. I went back to the "whys."

If Brigid was right about Clyde Shively being the blackmailer, then everybody in camp who had ever been in New York or in southern California might have had a reason for killing him. As nearly as I could figure that took in everyone on the place, including myself. I had never been back East, but I'd been down in California now and then when I couldn't help it.

I wasn't sure, but it seemed to me a person would have to be pretty well acquainted with another person before he'd hate him enough to kill him. I kept trying to stick to that "he," but finally I gave it up and faced facts. Betty-Jean was the only one in camp who had known the Shivelys all her life. Suppose she was afraid that Clyde would tell something on her, and get her in bad with Twill or Adam?

Nobody could imagine Betty-Jean's doing anything very wrong, but I'd heard that the quietest ones were the deepest. Adam wasn't quiet, but he was deep. Or—this came to me like a flash—suppose that Betty-Jean wasn't Adam's daughter, after all, and that Clyde knew it? That was exactly the way it would have been in a book, and all books weren't all crazy, either.

She didn't look a bit like Adam, except for a few little mannerisms, such as starting her smiles with one side of her mouth first, which looked cute for her though queer for him. But Joe and I, and some of the other boys who had seen Adam's wife, thought that Betty-Jean favored her considerably—small and dainty, with curly yellow hair and pretty blue eyes. Elizabeth's dimple had been in her cheek, but Betty-Jean had one in her chin besides.

I hadn't known Judge Shively myself, but from what I'd heard of him I didn't think that he'd be part or parcel of any plan to palm off a daughter on Adam. The folks who had known him had liked and respected him, and I'd been led to believe that *Who's Who* didn't make a point of being an index to the Rogue's Gallery. Still, I couldn't get away from the fact that persons who had known each other all their lives—especially relatives or close friends—were very much more likely to murder one another than strangers were.

Before very long I was going to feel meaner and more miserable; but I felt mean and miserable enough right then—a big husky man taking his ease and considering, accusingly, a little thing like Betty-Jean—when here Brigid came, asking me at the top of her voice, almost, if I was asleep.

"Why?" I wanted to know.

"Because if you aren't," she said, "I've something to tell you. Clyde Shively was that C. C. Shively. I asked Betty-Jean. She tried to defend him. Said he'd begun with a little weekly of dramatic criticism, but that temptations had been too strong for him. She didn't say so, but I sort of gathered that she hadn't liked Clyde too well. You know—she keeps remembering the few sweet things he ever did for her. All the same, she is much more disturbed over the Judge than she is over Clyde. And, of course, she is grieving, sickeningly, over Twill—it's terrible not being able to do anything for her. I wish St. Dennis were here."

"What could he do?" I asked.

"Nothing," she said, and went tangenting off. "Jeff, do you know that if St. Dennis were writing this as a story he'd have either Clyde Shively or the old Judge be the culprit?"

"I didn't even know your papa wrote that kind of stories," I said.

"Small discriminating publics are luxuriously grand until dividends stop. We talked it over and decided not to give up eating."

"Clyde Shively couldn't be the culprit," I reminded her, "because he was the victim. He was shot in the back, and—"

"Mechanical devices," she murmured, kind of half-heartedly.

"Abound only in books," I said. "But even in books—"

"Men can't strap themselves in beds, after death, and dispose of the weapon—always 'weapon' to authors—I know. But what about the Judge? He's gone. With the gun, maybe?"

"Nice old gentleman like he was! His own boy."

"St. Dennis would have him do it for some perfectly sweet, nice old gentlemanly reason."

"That wasn't the way it was done, though," I said, remembering and shuddering in spite of myself.

"I didn't say 'way.' I said 'reason.' Method doesn't matter as long as the motive is pure. Beautiful, virtuous, sacrifice stuff. For the good of everyone. So many people like justifiable murders—satisfying, or excusing their own urges, you know. Besides making them feel superior for not killing their own uncles and aunts when such charming and wealthy people have killed theirs."

None of that seemed to call for an answer, so I didn't answer.

"You've done nothing but yawn all day long," was the next thing she had to say.

"If your papa was writing this in a story," I said, kind of goaded into it, "how would he explain all these disappearing or invisible bodies?"

"He'd say that, since they couldn't disappear, they hadn't disappeared."

"But they have," I said.

"He might possibly manage it in some way with a garbage incinerator."

"There isn't one," I said.

"I know it."

(The folks emptied their small cans into the big covered can by the gate. Timmy Monk took it away for his pigs every afternoon, when he had delivered the groceries, leaving a clean can in its place.)

"The big can couldn't possibly hold a man's body," I said.

"I know it. It is three feet high and eighteen inches across. I measured it."

"I hope then," I said, "that we can forget the garbage."

"You started it," she said.

"No, you started it."

"Well, at any rate, here comes Mayor Oakman, so I'm leaving. I think he knows how we got into the garbage, but that he can't find a way for us to get out. Ask him, just to see what he says."

20

"So here you are," Adam said, before I'd had a chance to open my mouth. "Good old Sheriff. I knew if we'd give you time you'd take it."

I stood up and brushed myself off.

"I'm hurrying to my cottage for a bath and clean clothes," he stated, and I never heard words less invitational in spirit.

I said, "What I want to know is were you sitting out at that anthill by the gate from four o'clock yesterday afternoon until around seven in the evening?" and went walking along with him.

"In other words:" he said, "where were you from four o'clock until nine-fifteen on Wednesday afternoon, September the tenth?"

"In still other words," I said, "where were you?"

"The devil of it is," he said, as if he thought he was giving me a straightforward answer, "that I am forced to believe that girl. I'd have believed her sooner if I'd found time to talk with her alone. She shot and killed her brother—there's no doubt of that. She shouldn't have had the revolver in her hands. She shouldn't have threatened. But I am now thoroughly satisfied that the thing went off by accident and that she didn't intend to shoot him."

"All the rest of us," I said, "were thoroughly satisfied of that by eight o'clock yesterday evening. Shall I get over to Ferras now and let Kent out of that damn jail?"

"Remember St. Augustine's prayer?" he answered. "'Lord, make me pure and chaste but not quite yet.' Not quite yet, Jeff. By the way, your question just now. Are you trying to convict me or protect me?"

He was walking fast and furious so I plunged right in, not pausing to bandy words, as Reggie might have said. "I met Rosemary going out of the gate at about five minutes to four o'clock. Between that time and when I got into the kitchen where you were, if a gun had been fired I'd have heard it. I'd have heard it several miles off, on my way here—but never mind that. After you left the kitchen and all the time you were sitting out there, just inside the gate, you'd certainly have heard a gunshot even with your hearing."

"My hearing is as good as any man's, young or old, except your own."

"Well, you'd have heard a gunshot out there then, wouldn't you? That's just what I said. But when you and I were talking in the kitchen the doors and windows were all shut tight—they hadn't been opened after the storm— and the radio was going like blue blazes in the front room. During that short time in there maybe none of us would have heard a gun fired. So it seems to me that sets the time of the murder pretty exactly. It must have been during those few minutes while we were in the kitchen. You looked at your watch then and said it was four o'clock. That's why I want to know if you were outside from then on."

"I beg your pardon, Jeff," he said. "I should have known you were talking sense. That is sense. I was outside by the gate until half-past six. Of course I'd have heard a gun fired anywhere on the place. Now, let me think—"

"Think first about getting that boy out of jail," I said. "And then you can take your time thinking of other things."

He didn't answer, so I went at it again hammer and tongs. "I saw Rosemary leaving camp just before four—say five minutes to four. You sat out by the gate from then until she came in. When?"

"I should say about twenty minutes past six. We talked not more than ten minutes, I think, before she went along to her cottage and I went to mine."

"There you are. The prints at the gate show that she left once and came in once. We know that the murder must have been after she left and before she came back. What can she know that she isn't telling? Nothing. What could Kent know? Nothing. He got home at a quarter to seven. He talked to Rosemary for a while, and then he came on to the community house. You know what happened then. The folks all like you fine, of course, and I don't know whether or not they'd say much if it came to a showdown. Just the same, it didn't sound so pretty, Adam; your saying that you'd kill both the young ones and mentioning how before you'd let them marry."

"Fortunately, then, for me and perhaps for them," he said, "neither Rosemary nor Kent has been killed by any method. Fortunately, also, for me though perhaps not for them, I haven't been killed. I should have been, you know—according to all precedent. I made a new will a few weeks ago and, being in one of my less malignant moods, I left rather a neat little amount to everyone here in camp— some of it conditionally, but wisely so."

"Have you told anybody about it?" I asked.

"Iverson fixed it up for me. His wife is Joe Laud's sister. But you miss my point. I have not been killed."

"Not as yet," I said, and wished I hadn't, because it sounded too sinister. "But never mind about that—"

"No, no," he said. "I insist upon minding about that. I have a peculiar personal interest in it. What do you mean 'not as yet' I haven't been killed?"

The worst of it was I hadn't meant much of anything, so I had to think fast. "In books," I told him, "quite a lot of times the killer gets the wrong man by mistake."

"Sheriff," Adam said, "you're getting crazier and crazier, rapidly. You're as crazy as O'Dell."

"At that, Mayor," I said, "O'Dell isn't crazy enough to keep a good boy in jail smothering him to death and breaking down his health for life, just to show off."

In the nick of time to ruin any good I might have done, Reggie came rounding the corner of one of the cottages, right then, like he was riding a bicycle—a very silly, swaying way he had of rounding corners, almost worse than the way he had of jumping around on the cement walks to keep from stepping on cracks. He was whistling, too, and carrying the most gnawed and disgusting-looking large bone I ever saw.

"Don't dance," Adam said. "Don't whistle. Don't carry bones," and went into his cottage.

"Oh, my, what rot!" Reggie said, as soon as the door was shut tight.

"If I were you," I said, "I'd give up on that bone. You've got all the good you'll get out of it."

"I'm looking for *De Profundis,*" he explained. "I think that sounds better than 'Funny' at a time like this, don't you?"

"I expect," I said, and tried walking off and leaving him and the bone, but he came right along talking nothing but "wheres" and "where is its."

It seemed to me I'd walked a mile before I got to the shelter, with Reggie chatting all the time. "I mean, Funny wouldn't follow anyone but Twill off the place. And he couldn't have followed Twill off because Twill was killed.

Twill—kill. I never noticed that before. But if he didn't follow Twill away, where is he? Not Twill. The dog, I mean."

Adam, the old dizzard, hadn't unsaddled Dollar. He knew better than that, in the heat; but I was glad to be able to swing right up on her, then, and ride away. I had some things in mind to attend to, and going about my business seemed harmless enough—just as Brigid's moving the canoe seemed harmless. But neither of them was, entirely so, I guess.

On Tumboldt I found the road gang boys repairing the road, getting it "passable but dangerous" as the signs all say in California. Just to show what Adam's influence amounted to, none of the boys stopped me asking for news. Meaning that the fact of there being news hadn't leaked out much as yet.

When I went into the drugstore at Ferras, though, Shinny Lang asked me what about that accident over at Memaloose. By saying that was what I was wondering, I got him to tell me that Oakman was claiming that a shooting accident had taken place over there; but that some were saying things about suicide. Joe Laud, Shinny told me, had the body at his place and said that it was a shooting accident, but Joe owed Oakman money.

I turned that off by saying that I'd come to buy an electric fan. Shinny got so excited over my getting one, after refusing to have truck with them all these years—I can't bear the noise they make—that he forgot all about shooting accidents and suicides.

Over in the jail Kent was barely able to claim that he was fine. The fan didn't do much good stirring that stale blasting hot air around, but the ice I'd brought in a gunny sack helped some for the minute or two it lasted.

Almost right away I got next to the fact that he thought nobody knew Rosemary had visited him that morning; so

I never let on, and kept not looking at the oranges and grapefruit there on the bench until, pretty soon, he said:

"Have one, won't you, Jeff? The Penroys are treating me fine, thanks to you, and lots of thanks."

I thought that I'd better be going.

He asked me to wait while he wrote another note to Rosemary. I wondered whether two notes in one day were love or blinds to make me think he hadn't seen her. He didn't take long, but before he'd finished writing the heat almost got me. I was beginning to feel those chilly trickles crawling over my skin. So, when I was leaving, I read him the riot act.

"Kent," I said, "I'm sick of this foolishness. Few pass this way. You'll not be seen if you step out once in a while for a breath of fresh air. It's hot, but it's clean outside. When dark shuts down you get out there and stay out until morning. Here's the key." I threw it on the floor, and went on the run.

I'd had to get my car out to tote the ice, so I jumped into it and headed for Joe Laud's place. I had a question to ask him.

21

Joe was sitting outside in the shade when I got there, growling like sixty about curiosity seekers.

"Where are they?" I asked, seeing he was all alone.

"That's what I want to know," he said.

I was afraid, maybe, we were talking about different things, so I came out hurriedly with my question. "Can you tell from the bullet," I asked, "what kind of gun Clyde Shively was shot with?"

"Thirty-six Colt's," he said. "Same as yours. Why?"

"Same as everybody's around here," I said. "I just wondered."

"That pearl-handler was a twenty-two," Joe said, and went on, knocking me right off the Christmas tree, "but they are both revolvers and you can't put a silencer on a revolver."

"How did you happen to think of that?" I managed to ask him.

"I never happened to," he said. "I thought of it on purpose. I always think of things on purpose. Would you like to view the body again?"

I had what I'd come for; so I refused, thanking him just the same, and got into my car to hit out for Nameless. Differing from Joe, I'd happened to think, when Brigid had mentioned how obliging the Killaky boys were up to twenty dollars' worth, that a visit to Nameless might be a good plan.

The fact that the outside telephone wires had been down from after two o'clock when the wind began until well past eight the night of the murder was something. But the other fact was something, too. Any strong, sturdy person could have swum the lake, walked to Nameless, found the Killaky boys and their truck that could go to Mesquite Forks to catch a train, or back to Ferras, or elsewhere.

One thing opposing this idea was that any stranger dripping wet or entirely dry would attract considerable attention in Nameless, a town of fifty-four population and one block of Main Street. Another thing opposing it was the notion of anyone's swimming back and forth, unseen and unheard, towing dead bodies.

If the murderer had planned ahead of time, he might have had his own car and left it across the lake behind the boathouse. But he'd have to come and go through Nameless, turning square in front of Sig Hansen's (Sig runs the general store, butcher shop and poolroom all in one) for the lake road, going and coming. A stranger's car that leaves the highway stands every chance of being noticed in Nameless.

So when I got there I circulated myself around, careless, but freely inquisitive, and found that nobody had seen a stranger, wet, dry, afoot or horseback, in a car or out of one, any time yesterday.

I had a bite to eat at Ma Whal's, the alertest old lady for news that I ever met. She knew to the minute what time all the ladies in town had got their washings out on the line on Monday. She knew that a man and woman and three children, driving a blue Buick sedan with an Oregon license—number 23112—had come littering into her place on Tuesday, on their way to the Grand Canyon, and used the paper napkins so rough she couldn't iron them out again. She knew all about the shooting accident across at Memaloose on Wednesday—or so she thought, the poor old soul—but she was positive that the men I was hunting, helping out the Reno police, hadn't come near Nameless and wouldn't dare if they knew what was good for them.

At Sig Hansen's I'd already learned that the Killaky boys had been shooting pool there all afternoon and evening and that practically the whole town had seen them doing so at one time or another. Like all Indians, they never bothered much about eating, so they'd missed their suppers and had fine alibis the same as everybody else had—that is, everybody except one of the victims.

Coming back from Nameless some little thing went haywire with my car again. When I got to Ferras I drove into Goldfield Red's garage to have him look her over. Doc Sprague was outside there with his old Ford getting gas. I had an idea that maybe the folks had called him to come to Memaloose and, sure enough, they had. Instead of taking Dollar out again I asked the old Doc if he'd give me a lift. He said he'd be glad to and I got in with him.

It was nearly eight o'clock and the mountain road was worse than it had looked from horseback. We agreed that another slide was likely at the place I pointed out. We agreed that we'd wait until daylight to come back over the road, spending the night at Memaloose. Fine agreeable man, the old Doc. Quiet, too. He answered my question about why he had been called by saying that the heat had affected some of the ladies pretty bad. I asked him nothing more. He asked me nothing at all. So neither of us, as the saying goes, had to tell lies.

Not speaking of Adam, in particular, he met us at the gate and told the old Doc that one of the girls had shot her brother by accident and that the young man, more scared than hurt, had left camp. Another young man, he said, had been examining the revolver the girl had used and he'd be damned if it hadn't gone off again by accident and killed the second young man dead.

Doc said, "Joe called me in this afternoon. He had to by law to protect himself. I couldn't give a certificate of self-inflicted gunshot wound resulting in death for the man I saw. He was shot in the back. But I suppose Joe had things wrong as usual. He told me that a lot of tenderfeet over here—dude ranchers—had been fooling with revolvers, target practice or something of the kind, and not knowing the first thing about handling firearms a lamentable series of accidents had resulted."

This sounded to me twice as much like the old Doc as it did like Joe, so I remarked in a good clear undertone, "The Mayor has been so upset over all this that he hardly knows just what has happened, except, to use his very words, that hell has burst loose all over the place."

"Um-hum," said the old Doc. "And Joe told me that while you weren't issuing extras over here, Oakman, or broadcasting for a while, you had Jeff, Ernie and Mac on the job, working hard. I assume that Joe is right about that, at least?"

"Did Joe also tell you," Adam asked, "that we have one man in the Ferras jail right now?"

"No. If he had, I'd have visited him. If he's a white man, I'd advise you not to keep him there in this weather. A Mex or an Indian might stand it. A white man can't, for long. If he has to be in jail, send him down to Sackawash."

There is an unfriendly rivalry between Ferras and Sackawash, so Adam made a few preliminary remarks and wound up by declaring that a little heat never killed anybody.

"Let's hope not," Doc said, "if you're responsible for keeping him there."

"I have good reasons for keeping him there," Adam said.

Doc said, "Shooting scrapes aren't in my line. Trying to keep folks alive is what I work at. I'm advising you, and not forgetting that you assisted me in sending my Julia and Charles through the university, that there aren't any reasons good enough for keeping a white man in the Ferras jail in this heat. I'm warning you, though still remembering your favors to me, that if a man dies over in that damn jail I'll make it as hard for you as I can. Where are the sick ladies?"

Seemed that Mrs. Duefife was the worst off of anybody. She had fainted dead away while helping get supper for the boys in the community house. She was in bed in her bedroom. Reggie, Betty-Jean and Brigid were milling around in her parlor. Rosemary was there, too, but not milling. She was sitting by the window with her quiet hands folded in her lap. I slipped Kent's note to her and then I went outside again and sat down on the stoop waiting for Adam. I knew he'd leave the old Doc with Mrs. Duefife and come out pretty soon.

He did, in a tearing hurry. I told him that the old Doc and I were planning on spending the night in camp.

"All right," he said. "But what do you want me to do about it?"

That wasn't such a good opening, but I grabbed my chance of putting in some words for Kent, using the old Doc to back me up.

"Everybody in this county," he said, "is crazy about good, healthful heat doing harm. Do you want the boys here any longer? The three of them are making a lot of extra work for the ladies."

"I never did want them here, especially," I told him. "Why not send them with word to the Penroys to let Kent out and tell him to come home. He'd be more useful than six of them."

"The boys have been exceedingly useful," he said. "But they are worn out now—no sleep for twenty-four hours. I'll stop here at the community house and send them home. See you later, Jeff," he finished, adding, "maybe."

I sat down and waited. I knew he was going to warn the boys about keeping mum and liked issuing his orders in private. When he came out again he greeted me like something he had been trying all his life to forget and asked me what I was waiting for.

"You," I said.

"Why?"

"To tell you that, while it is real nice of you wishing to keep everything pleasant for everybody, just the same right is right. And, notwithstanding—"

"What's that?" he asked, like he was deaf.

"Notwithstanding all the trouble over here, you'll be letting yourself in for worse and more of it if you don't get in touch with the Shively's kinfolk pronto. The immediate family, the bereaved—you've got to inform them, Adam. There's no two ways about that."

"I am a patient man," he answered, very solemn, "and I am long-suffering. I never tell anyone to mind his own business. I always explain all things, including my most private affairs, to everyone who asks, because I am patient and long-suffering.

"The Judge and his son had no immediate family. I telephoned this morning to the old gentleman's lawyer. I began guardedly—to spare him any shock you understand. He told me that Judge Shively had gone, a few days ago, to join his foster daughter, Betty-Jean, at some summer camp in Nevada. The post office address was Ferras—apparently where I was telephoning from. Clyde Shively, in so far as the lawyer knew, was in New York.

"Fortunately, despite Ivy Duefife's objections, I had had both Rosemary and Betty-Jean identify the body. This brings an interesting question. Were they, actually, the only persons on the place who could have done so? At least, they are the only ones who admit ever seeing the man before."

"Yes," I said, "but did you tell the lawyer that Clyde Shively had been killed here?"

"Most assuredly. I also told him that the old gentleman had left the camp and that we didn't know where to get in touch with him."

"What did he say?"

"Well, he wasn't overly agreeable at first. He insisted upon knowing whether we were certain that the shooting had been accidental. But when I assured him that the verdict at the inquest—"

"What inquest?"

"The inquest. The coroner's inquest, of course."

"This is the first I've heard of it," I said.

"You should have attended it, instead of sitting over here all morning."

"Have you held the funeral yet?" I wanted to know.

"I spoke to the lawyer about that. He hadn't our geographical limitations clearly in mind. He was sure that Judge Shively had stepped out and boarded a train for his home. And so he suggested that we wait to consult the old gentleman's wishes as to 'the disposition of the remains.' A California lawyer wouldn't be any better than a Nevada mining man if he talked about 'funerals' and 'burying.' In the end, though, he was very decent. He seemed sincerely grieved over Clyde Shively's accident—said the boy had been a fine, faithful son to his father. Also, he had some very pleasant things to say about my little daughter."

He stopped talking. I sighed. I thought that he'd ask me, "What's the matter?" But he didn't, so I told him.

"You didn't do right, misleading the lawyer. There comes a time when there has to be an end to hushing things up—"

"By the Eternal!" he burst out. "What should I do? What do you want me to do? Cite me a single instance where publicity has helped in finding criminals. Doctor

Sprague knows that I am doing everything possible—except inform the universe. I'll not do that. These people are my guests. I'm responsible for their being here. I feel particularly responsible for Brigid O'Dell. I'm the one who will have to face her father when he returns. Could I face him, if I'd allowed his young daughter's name to be blazoned in headlines all over the country in connection with an affair of this sort? O'Dell has a small fame of his own. 'Author's Daughter Involved in Murder Mystery. O'Dell Girl Guest at Millionaire's Murder Camp.' Is that what you want? Or do you want me to arrest that girl who accidentally killed her brother? She's fairly young to stand a criminal trial. Or is it that you think I have no right to keep my own daughter's name clean?"

I didn't have an answer for so much as all that, so I just sighed.

Seemed that my sighing got on his nerves. He burst forth again, worse than ever, saying so and finishing, "As for that, what is the use of our keeping up this infernal pretense with each other? You know as well as I know what has happened here, and that no hue and cry is going to do any good now."

"How do you mean 'know what has happened'?" I asked.

He didn't answer. A spry breeze had sprung up and kept on springing, whistling between its teeth and lapping the lake into nice little sounds that blended fine with the silence.

"Cooler tomorrow," Adam said.

"Speaking of the weather," I said, "what did you mean by saying that I know what's happened here and that hues and cries won't do any good now?"

"Don't you?" he asked. "Don't you know that Clyde Shively was killed? That his father undoubtedly has been killed? That Twill was killed?"

"Sure," I said, mad all over and hoping to get him the same way. "I know that. And, also, that 'I or you can or may be killed.'"

"But not eaten," he said. "Oh, I beg your pardon, Jeff. My mind was wandering. I was thinking of ants. Scamp ants, you know. Most unpleasant customs. Carnivorous. Good night. I'll see you in the morning," and off he went into his cottage, leaving me alone and glad of it.

22

If there is anything that makes a man who is behind on his sleep feel more resentful than waking up bright and early when there is nothing to wake up for, I don't know what it is. That is what I did the next morning, Friday, and the pink ruffled bedroom curtains were the last touch. Not that pink ruffles aren't pretty and romantic; just that no man on earth wants to wake up to them in the early morning.

Reggie, agog, was the first person I met when I stepped outside. After saying that he'd just had a splendid shower—he being the type of man who never takes a bath without talking about it—he sprang the other good news.

"Uncle Adam is going to take us all back to Hay Patch today. I'm so glad. Mummy's so glad. Aren't you glad? We are motoring over. We are all glad."

I walked down to the lake where Brigid was swimming around, kind of half-heartedly. When she saw me she hollered for me to wait. I sat down and waited.

"Jeff," she asked, while she was shaking the water out of her ears, "do you know what or how much Mayor Oakman knows?"

"You mean about all the goings-on over here?" I asked.

She just slumped her shoulders, pressed her lips together and looked at me.

"He was hinting around last night that he knew some-thing," I said. "But I doubt it like sixty."

"What did he say?" she demanded. "Word for word?"

I told her how he'd said that I knew as well as he did what had happened and that no hue and cry would do any good now.

"Fine! Grand!" she said, leaning back and shaking her bright hair like it was a flag.

A man is hard to suit. I hadn't liked it yesterday morn-ing when all the folks had been so sad. I liked it less this morning when they seemed happy. I said so. I said I saw no reason for Reggie's jumping up and down and clapping his hands, or for her celebrating something—I didn't know what.

"I'm not either," she said. "Here comes Mayor Oak-man, the poor, sweet, precious old darling."

Adam came up to us just then asking hurriedly, "What is it? What's the matter now, Jeff?"

"Nothing," I said. "Why?"

"I don't know. You looked stunned."

"It was the language Brigid was using," I said.

"These modern girls," he said, smiling a very little, and turning to her. "Run and get dressed, child. You're going with the first load to Hay Patch."

"Jeff hasn't had his breakfast," she objected, being nice that way sometimes. "I was going to get it for him."

"Betty-Jean is getting breakfast for the Doctor in her cottage," Adam said. "I told her to count Jeff and me in the pot. Run along, child. Come, Jeff, to breakfast. We haven't much time, the Doctor is in a hurry as usual. You and I, Brigid and Mrs. Duefife are going with him in his car to Ferras. I'll pick up my car there and take Brigid and Mrs. Duefife on to Hay Patch. You can bring your Ford back for the girls and Reggie."

"Do you think it's all right?" I asked. "Leaving Betty-Jean and Rosemary here alone?"

"Reggie will be here," he said.

"I meant to say alone with Reggie," I said.

"Still joking and jesting, Sheriff?" he said, very sour.

"Have it your own way, Mayor," I said and looked at my watch. It was eight o'clock.

Anybody would think that five people could get fed, fixed up, loaded into a Ford car and started off, especially from Memaloose, in half an hour. It was twenty minutes past nine when we got under way with the old Doc driving.

Some of the reasons for our delaying were as follows: Brigid didn't want to go with the first load. Mrs. Duefife didn't want to go, either, if Reggie couldn't go. Adam got mad, of course, and said that Reggie could go in my place and bring my car back for the other folks. Reggie said he couldn't drive a car. Brigid said she could; so why couldn't Rosemary go in my place? Adam told Brigid that he was responsible to her father for her—meaning that he didn't want her driving a car over the road in the shape it as in. Mrs. Duefife began crying, then, and saying that Adam admitted there was danger for those left behind. This made no sense since Brigid was not going to be left behind. But Adam mentioned, anyway, that he was leaving his own daughter.

We'd likely be arguing there yet—and in some ways it might be better for all if we were—but the old Doc stepped on it and we were off with a jerk according to Adam's first plans, which at the time seemed good to me.

Mrs. Duefife was sick from heat and strain and had to get to the cool of Hay Patch. Brigid was a kid under his care. I had to bring my car back for the folks. Doc, of course, had to go. And Adam, besides wanting to take the ladies on to Hay Patch, wanted like everything to talk to Kent in the jail. Of course, though, besides all this sensible planning he did have an ornery plot on foot for the

arrangements he made. I didn't know it then; but I knew
then and know yet that he believed with all his heart that
those going and those staying were safe from harm.

The old Doc, cranky at starting so late, drove like fury
until we came to the place where we'd agreed the night before that another slide would be apt to come. It had come.
The road gang boys were clearing it off with hand shovels,
not daring to bring their outfit up to such a place.

Trying to turn around there would be sudden death.
Trying to back down, even in a Ford, would be slow suicide. So we stayed stopped. The old Doc—it was just like
him—had to have a shovel in the box on his running board.
He, Adam and I took turns with it helping the boys who,
also, found quite a bit more for us to do, such as shoving
boulders over the brink and so on. They were nice about
it; said we needn't turn a hand unless we were in a big
hurry. They'd have the road passable but dangerous in five
to six hours anyway.

Mrs. Duefife was chilling again and it looked serious
so early in the morning. Brigid and the Doctor fixed her
up as comfortably as they could in the back seat and the
Doc gave her a pellet with some water out of his canteen.
Pretty soon she went off to sleep, but kind of moaning and
fussing even then.

Brigid, though she meant the best in the world, didn't
do so very well. She insisted on helping roll rocks, and
half the time somebody was stopping work and yelling at
her to watch out where she was going. So, toward noon,
when she came crumbling through the rocks by the outer
edge of the car, leaving maybe three inches between her
and dropping to destruction, and told Adam she was hungry and was going to walk back to Memaloose, he was all
for the idea. The only stipulation he made was that she
pass the car on the inside of the road as she went.

Right then and there, while she was climbing around the car, I had another foreboding of evil and I stated it again in advance.

"Adam," I said, "I don't like it. I don't like letting the kid put out alone that way. If I thought I could make the four miles in this heat, I'd go with her."

"What heat? You're better off where you are. Can't a girl of her age take a walk on the deserts in broad daylight without your getting nervous? She is certainly much safer walking to camp than she was dangling over the sides of this mountain."

The old Doc came up just then insisting that it was his turn at the shovel, so I went and sat down on the running board of the car and stuck my fingers in my ears. The grinding, gritting noises were getting me ready to fly into pieces.

Before long, of course, Adam had come and sit beside me, bent on talking, and I had to listen to him and to the noises both.

He was worried about Mrs. Duefife's being ill, he said, and he went on, getting sentimental, saying how essentially she was a good woman, a very good woman if only she didn't happen to make a man's nerves raw at times. But, after all, she had supported herself and her son for years and it was easily enough for a person who had never known the gnawing fear of poverty or the curse of charity to carp at those who had.

"Damn it all," he said. "What if she and Reggie did have a few signals for bridge? I edit Betty-Jean's check book and I could have fixed it up with Brigid later. I've known it for months and liked the extra handicap when I played with Rosemary against them. Rosemary played like an idiot Wednesday afternoon and we lost. I'd hate to think that was the reason that I spoke as I did to that poor, frightened old lady. I could have gone about it decently. I needn't have humiliated her as I did. Besides that, I've ruined our bridge games from now on."

I thought it over for a minute and then I decided I might as well ask him if that was why he had called Mrs. Duefife out in the kitchen for a talk on Wednesday afternoon, just before I got there.

Never before in his life, he said, had he lived where his every word, move and gesture were not only noticed but also gossiped about. Hotbed of whispering. By the Eternal he'd stood all he was going to stand. From now on he'd have privacy or die, but he'd rather have privacy. He'd pension Mrs. Duefife and Reggie and send them packing tomorrow. Yes, yes, yes, that had been the subject of the kitchen conversation, since I insisted. Just as soon as Kent and Betty-Jean were married he'd send them away too.

Up to then I hadn't said a word, but I couldn't keep still any longer.

"Well!" I said. "Kent and Betty-Jean are going to get married, are they?"

"I'm inclined to think so," he said, lightly but very knowingly.

"Where?" I said. "In the Ferras jail?"

"At it again," he said.

"No. But the only thing is, I understood Kent to say that he was going to marry Rosemary."

"Nothing is coming of that nonsense," he said, moving his hands like he was bouncing soap-bubbles with them. "In fact, I am confident that the whole thing has fallen through, completely, since we left Memaloose this morning."

Any man hearing that kind of talk would think what I thought and nothing more—that Adam was talking through his hat. But, when I finally got into the hotel at a quarter till two, and Bert Thalen told me at Brigid O'Dell wanted me to call her at Memaloose as soon as I came in, I remembered Adam's words and thought that Brigid had got hold of some silly notion that had to do with love affairs.

I'd be the last person in the world to think that love affairs weren't important. I just thought that helping the Doc get Mrs. Duefife up to my room, and collecting fans from the other rooms so that she could be comfortable until Adam was ready to take her on to Hay Patch, was more important.

There happened to be a pint of real liquor on my bureau, and the old Doc thought a dose of it would be good for Mrs. Duefife and fine for us. Before we'd finished, Shinny Lang came up to tell me that Brigid O'Dell wanted me to call her at Memaloose. The Doc went on about his business. I waited just long enough for Shinny to have his drink.

Going down stairs I met Joe Laud coming up to tell me that Brigid O'Dell wanted me to call her and, before I'd got to where the phone was, Slim came in the back door telling me that Brigid O'Dell wanted me to phone her pronto at Memaloose.

She answered the first ring. "Jeff," she said, "get Kent out of jail and bring him over here as fast as you can in your car. Hurry. Don't let Mayor Oakman know—"

"Hold on, Brigid," I began, still confused about those love affairs and thinking, also, I'll admit, that good jobs like mine didn't grow on trees.

"Don't argue!" she said. "Something terrible has happened. It is a matter of life or death. Rosemary's. We must have Kent—"

"Doc Sprague, too?"

"No, no. Kent. Stop talking. Hurry. Run. Bring Kent and your car."

I went to the garage and got my car—Red had put a new spark plug in it—and from there fast to the jail. It was a big relief not to see Adam's car standing in front of it. I had feared, too, that the boy might give me trouble about leaving; so, before going to the garage, I'd skipped up to my room and got my six gun. I didn't need to show it to him. The minute I told him that Brigid had said it was a matter of Rosemary's life or death he beat me out of the jail on the run.

We jumped into my car. He wanted to drive and I let him. He drove fast. But at that Adam kept far enough ahead of us so that we didn't have to eat his dust.

Brigid should have known better. As soon as Adam had left me and started up the street all the boys began hailing him and telling him that Brigid O'Dell wanted me to phone her at Memaloose right away. She had called up only half a dozen or so, but they had passed the word around. I don't know yet why Adam was scared. Premonitions, it must have been. He just said that he knew there was trouble and so, without waiting for anything, he had headed straight back to camp. The only thing that had delayed him at all was stopping the first five or six times when hailed, thinking that maybe it was other news.

Anybody will tell you that a Ford is the only car for this country; and, if it happens to be a model T like mine, so much the better—fine clearance. But there is something about these sixteen-cylinder cars that goes. In spite of Adam's having to back before he could take any curve on the mountain, we wouldn't have known he was in front of us if we hadn't spied him on the hairpins, and when we got to the straightaway there wasn't even a speck of dust left in the air.

The Memaloose gate was open. Kent brought my car through it—I wouldn't know how fast, since the speedometer has been out of whack for years, but at a rate I didn't know the old bus had in her, and kept going a little faster until Adam, who had come dashing out of the back door of the community house yelling and waving one arm, headed straight for us. Kent had to choose between running him down or turning into the brush. He turned into the brush. We stopped at full speed.

23

Kent said, "Where's Rosemary?" and jumped out of the car.

I said, "What's happened?"

Adam yelled, "What's happened? Nothing. Everything. I don't know. Hell's broken loose again all over the place. What do you know? What did Brigid tell you? Answer, can't you?"

"Where is Brigid?" I said.

"Where is Rosemary?" Kent said.

"I don't know," Adam said. "I just got here. I've had my hands full. Why don't you answer me?"

Kent swung up on Acrasia who, horse-like, had come nosing over to see what it was all about, and gave her a slap that started her on a dead run down the road toward Rosemary's cottage.

By this time I was out of the car.

"Take your hands off me," Adam said. "What's the matter with you? Brigid's here. I just told you. She's in the kitchen there on the floor. I found her unconscious beside the open gate when I got here. I thought she was dead. She's not. But I can't revive her. Of course it's serious, you forsaken fool. I've telephoned for the boys and the Doctor."

I kept on running. But I spared breath to holler, "Sure somebody didn't get her, after she phoned?"

Come to find out Adam was right beside me. "Sure of nothing! She's not been shot. Dead faint. I can't revive her."

"Throw water on her."

"I have."

"Loosen her stays," I said, from out of the past as I went running up the back steps.

"She's in her swimming suit," he said.

He needn't have told me. I was several leaps ahead of him by that time and I could see for myself. She was lying there as flat as something spilled on the kitchen floor. But not as motionless. No, it took her, I'd judge, about one-sixteenth of a second to settle down into unconsciousness again. She'd done it fine, though, before Adam got in.

"She'll be all right," I said, sitting down on my heels beside her and mad all over for a minute. "What about the other folks? Are they all right?"

"Probably not," Adam said. "I don't know. I just got here and found this child by the gate. Reggie has been scared into imbecility. He told me that Betty-Jean was all right, but I doubt that he knew what he was talking about. He had locked himself in the storeroom there. He came out when I carried Brigid in here.

"He has some wild story about hearing shooting all over the place at five minutes till twelve. What did Brigid tell you when you telephoned?"

"Nothing," I said, remembering that she'd told me not to let Mayor Oakman know, and giving her the benefit of the doubt, "except to get Kent and come over. I tell you what, Adam, you get out and rustle around and see about the shooting—if any—and I'll sit here and tend to Brigid—"

"You'll sit nowhere!" he said. "I'm responsible for this child. She's been out too long now. There's some brandy around here somewhere. I can't find it. Get it and bring it here."

I got the cooking sherry instead and poured some in a cup so he wouldn't notice the bottle. Whatever had happened I knew that Brigid couldn't take a drop of anything stronger without getting cock-eyed and that having her that way wouldn't help a bit.

"By the Eternal!" Adam said. "I knew from the first instant that this wasn't a mere fainting spell. I knew there was something unnatural about it. Look here, Jeff. Her teeth are clenched. It can't be rigor. She's warm. Sweating. Her heart is beating. You listen. It is beating? Of course it is beating. Well then, why hasn't she relaxed. What can we do? What would you do?"

I could think of several things to do, such as tickling her since she was very ticklish. But if she wanted to stay swooning on the kitchen floor with her teeth clenched, I thought I'd better humor her for the present.

All I knew about Reggie's hearing shooting was that it had been Reggie who had heard it—so that was nothing to bother about, much. I remembered Brigid's phoning that the trouble was a matter of Rosemary's life or death; but I knew doggone well that the kid wouldn't be acting this way unless she was certain that it was smarter than acting any other way. My idea was that, now she had Kent on the job she wanted like fury to keep Adam off the job. I was just thinking how lucky it was that she was a girl instead of a boy, on account of Adam's susceptibility to being hoodwinked depending almost entirely on gender, when—

"She's been poisoned," he decided at the top of his voice. "Poisoned. That accounts for her clenched teeth. What shall we do? She may be dying. What can we do? She probably is dying. Get warm water. Hot. Tepid. Get mustard. Salt. Egg whites. Stop sitting there. What's the matter with you? We can pry her teeth open—"

"Listen, Adam," I interrupted. "Take things easy now. I've had a lot of experience with poison—"

"The devil you have! Where?"

"The Spanish-American War," I said, it being about the only place I'd ever been where he hadn't. "You'd be surprised—"

"I am," he said. "Go on. Go on. Go on."

"I am going on. This is the same thing as shellshock, but a little different. Brigid's had some shock and fainted, and instead of coming to, she's gone off into kind of a coma. Best thing in the world that could have happened. Forcing anything on them or waking them up is very dangerous. They come out raving. This way they sleep it off. Nothing to do for her that is as good as making her comfortable and keeping her very quiet."

"What's all this to do with poison?" he said.

"Nothing. That's what I'm trying to tell you. I don't know how many soldiers I've seen in this fix—exactly the same. Dozens upon dozens. Young fellows, mostly."

"I hope you're right," he said. "But I doubt it."

I went and picked her up and carried her to a sofa by the window in the living room. "Brigid, honey," I whispered, "this is going too far. Call a halt as soon as you can, won't you? Kent is here now, and—"

"What's that?" Adam said. "What are you muttering for, Jeff?"

"I was not muttering," I said.

"You were muttering. I saw you. Your lips were moving."

I tried looking reverent, hurt and bashful.

"I beg your pardon, Jeff," he said, and for almost half a second things were as quiet and solemn as Sunday without the church bells.

"Tell you what," I whispered to him, taking advantage of the calm, or trying to do so, "I'll sit right here with Brigid—"

"No, you will not," he said, speaking soft but very savage. "I want you to get outside and find Betty-Jean and see what's happened here. I'll stay with Brigid now, and I swear by the Everlasting that if the poor child does pull through this I'll keep her with me after this. You warned me. I'll never let her out of my sight again until I hand her over to her father. Here, wait a minute before you go. Isn't she relaxing, slightly? Give me something to fan her with. I've no excuse. My own criminal negligence. Why don't you go and get Betty-Jean? I sent Reggie for her. He may have locked himself in the storeroom again. Telephone and see what has happened to Doctor Sprague? This paper is not any good—find me a fan. A fan! The place is alive with fans. Find Betty-Jean. Find Reggie. Will you please do as I have repeatedly asked you to do and telephone to Doctor Sprague's home?"

I got the old Doc's house and Julia there said her father was on his way now, though he'd had to stop to see a patient after Adam had phoned—the little Potter boy who had been stung by a scorpion, but who was going to be all right in a day or two.

"That's good," I said to Julia.

"What's good?" Adam said. "Gossiping at a time like this!"

I chatted a decent half-second more with Julia and then hung up the receiver and told Adam that the old Doc would be here any minute.

"You've done it now," Adam said. "Yelling over the telephone like that. You've waked Brigid up too soon."

"I had to yell," I said. "Julia Sprague's deaf and you know it."

"You did too yell," he said. "You deny everything. See here, Brigid's eyelids are fluttering."

I thought that they'd better be fluttering with the old Doc due at any minute. But I was so kind of embarrassed for Adam, or something, that I thought I'd rather not face her when she made up her mind to be revived.

"Here!" Adam said. "Where are you going? Don't leave me for a few minutes. I may need some help."

I guess he was thinking about my soldiers who woke up raving.

Brigid opened her eyes—not bad-looking if you care for eyes large and freckle-colored—and said, faintly but politely, "How do you do?"

"Dear little girl," Adam said, fanning her like sixty now. "Dear little girl. Are you all right?"

"Thank you. Yes, of course," she said. "But I seem rather confused. I know that I'm in Italy, but this room is unfamiliar."

She and her papa had been in Italy several years ago. I began getting a little scared right then, being entirely unable to remember for sure whether or not I had really seen her settling down on the floor in the kitchen, and things went from bad to worse.

She didn't know me. She didn't know Adam. She was mannerly but not cordial, and she got pretty insistent about seeing her friends. Adam kept introducing us to her over and over and pleading with her that we were her friends. She was too nice to deny it up and down, but she showed pretty plainly that she doubted it like fury.

Adam got me to one side and asked me if those Spanish-American War soldiers ever came out of it with their memories gone. The only excuse I can make for myself is that by this time I was scared enough for two men twice my size. The minute Adam mentioned those soldiers I believed in them stronger than I believe in the Democratic Party, and I could remember hundreds, troops of them, who had come to with their minds complete blanks. Whether they were ever cured I couldn't remember for sure, but I thought not.

Adam had a bright idea. "We'll call your friends, dear," he said. "But you must tell us who they are, dear. What are your friends' names, dear?"

"Brigid O'Dell," she said. "And St. Dennis O'Dell, and another close friend named Kent."

Adam began tearing through his pockets like they were full of hornets. When he found his notebook he went to the telephone.

"I'll have to call her father," he said. "This can't go on. I've his hotel here somewhere. Could I telegraph? No. I must talk to him. Explain. What can I say? What would you say? What is the confounded name of that hotel?"

He was licking his thumb and flapping through the pages of his notebook fast, like they were red-hot. I was looking at Brigid. She looked straight at me, gave a long, slow wink with one eye, shook her head and shuddered.

If it had been a saucy wink, or even a cute wink I don't know what I'd have done. It was not. The only thing I can say about that wink is, that if the kid had raised her finger and poked her eye out instead of shutting it I couldn't have been much more horrified. It was a ghastly, awful, horrid, blood-freezing wink, I guess.

"Hold on, Adam," I said. "She named Kent. He's closer than New York. Most of these cases one person that they remember is as good as another. Phone down to Rosemary's for him."

Adam threw his notebook away like he was aiming it at something and picked up the telephone. I put myself between him and Brigid and stooped over her.

"Angel!" she whispered, warming my frozen blood a little. "Help me. I had to do this. Sorry, darling. I must see Kent alone."

"Yes, you bet. But—"

"Get Mayor Oakman away."

Before she'd had time to say another word Adam had finished delivering his orders to Kent and was demanding, "Why is she whispering? What did she whisper? What did she say?"

"I can't understand her," I said. "See if you can."

He leaned over her. She kept on whispering. She's nice that way.

"Something about Italy, I think," he said, sighed despairingly, took out his watch and dropped it into his pocket again without opening it. "I telephoned hours ago," he went on, "for the boys and the Doctor. Why aren't they here? Why? Why should they take this time to dawdle?"

"You couldn't possibly have telephoned hours ago," I said.

"I did telephone hours ago," he said. "I cannot understand this propensity of yours for contradicting or denying every statement on any subject that I chance to make. I telephoned hours ago."

I didn't answer. I was wondering whether I should go to meet Kent and tip him off about Brigid, or whether he'd do better as long as Adam stuck around, without the tip.

Just as I'd decided that ignorance never helped anybody, I heard him coming in the kitchen door; so I went to meet him. Adam came, too, nearly stepping on my heels.

"Where have you been all this time since I phoned you?" Adam said, stopping in the doorway so that he could keep an eye on Brigid.

"Walking up here," Kent said. "Acrasia had gone to the shelter, so I had to walk—"

"Get your mind off horses," Adam said.

"What is the matter with Brigid?" Kent asked.

"Don't talk so loud!" Adam said, and went on explaining in murmurs to Kent how she had had a bad shock and come out of it minus her memory, but that she had asked for him, so he must do the best he could; adding, in some detail, my experiences with similar cases during the Spanish-American War.

Kent cocked his ear and gave me kind of a funny look, but all he said was, "Yes; though what could have shocked or frightened Brigid to this extent? Rosemary says that nothing has happened here this morning. Except that she found this roll of bills on her table. I'll return them to you now, Dad. She didn't care to ride away on Acrasia, even with two thousand dollars. Sorry to disappoint you. Count them, please, if you don't mind."

Adam just stood there for a minute, looking sheepish and a little old and bent. Kent changed his tune.

"This isn't like you, Dad. You are usually fair. I wish you'd be fair with Rosemary and believe her—"

"Damn it all," Adam said, tossing the roll of bills on the table like it was turnips. "I do believe her. But if she'd had her share of common sense she'd have gone away when I gave her a chance to go. I couldn't have done her a bigger favor, or you either."

I tried changing the subject before Kent got sore again. "Brigid is looking out of the window now," I said. "I'll bet she'll be fine before long."

Somebody knocked kind of timidly on the back door. Kent opened it, and Doc Sprague came into the kitchen.

We all knew right away, I think, that something was all wrong. The Doc's knock had been queer. The way he came in was queer. And he looked all broken up as he went over to Adam and put a hand on his arm.

"Old friend," he said, in that nice grave voice of his, "I'm bringing you bad news. I wish I could soften the blow, but I don't know how. Your daughter. The boys found her about a quarter of a mile away from here on the desert."

"Dead?" Adam asked.

"Yes," the old Doc answered, very sad.

Adam waited a minute, and then he didn't sound like himself when he said, "Murdered?"

"Yes," the Doc said.

24

Kent went over and stood beside Adam. I guess he didn't
know anything else to do, or what to say. I didn't.

"She is in my car, now," Doc said. "I wanted to come
in first."

"Should we bring her in here?" Adam asked, very help-
less-sounding. "Or—what, Son? What do you think?"

"We'll bring her in, Dad," Kent said. "You wait here."

But Adam went along outside with Kent and the Doc. I
walked in to where Brigid was on the sofa, still sitting up
and looking out of the window. I knew she hadn't heard,
but that was all I did know.

"Brigid," I said, and I had no just call for being cross
to her, so I don't know why I was, "get off that sofa. It's
the nicest one. Help me get it straightened

"Is Betty-Jean ill?" she asked, but absentmindedly, as
she stood up. "Listen, Jeff, I must tell you—"

Set me down for a brute and a fool, both and worse, if
there is worse, which there isn't. "Wait," I said. "I want to
tell you something first. I guess you don't know it. I hope
to my soul you don't. Betty-Jean is dead. She has been
murdered."

I had never believed, much, that people did those queer,
jerking things with their hands and arms, or that their
faces could change in a second into looking like crazy

181

faces, until I saw Brigid right then. I had never heard
anything half as terrible as that long hurt sound she made
before she began, almost screaming, "Not Betty-Jean. No.
No. Not Betty-Jean. No. No. No—"

She brought me to my senses fast. I took hold of her
hands so she'd stop pounding them like that. "Brigid, honey," I begged. "I'm sorry. I'm awful sorry. Please listen to
me. They're bringing Betty-Jean in here now. Adam's all
broken up. Everybody is. You can't act like this. It will
make everything worse. For the love of Heaven— For the
love of your papa who is so awful proud of you, always,
quiet down before the folks come in."

She nodded. I got her into a chair. She folded her arms
over her face, crying but making hardly any noise.

I was glad that she kept her arms over her face when
Adam came carrying Betty-Jean in like he would have carried a baby, she was such a little thing. He put her down
on the sofa. The Doc had got a sheet from somewhere and
he covered her up the minute Adam put her down.

Ernie and Mac had come in, too, and were standing
hanging their heads and fiddling with their hats; but their
shoes made a noise even standing still.

Adam looked over at Brigid, "Poor child," he said. Kent
eased him down into a chair. The Doc went to Brigid and I
could hear him trying to soothe her in his nice grave way.

Maybe it wasn't long, but it seemed long before Adam
asked the boys, "Where did you find her?"

Ernie never was any hand for talking, so Mac had to
answer. "In a gully, about a quarter of a mile or less from
here. Riding down the mountain I saw something white
over there. We'd been searching the deserts, you know, or
I hardly think I'd have noticed it. I said to Ernie that we'd
better take a look. I was thinking of the other folks who
were missing from here."

"Did you find a revolver over there? Did you look for one?" Adam asked.

"We looked," Mac answered. "But we didn't find anything." He was so embarrassed that the old Doc helped him out.

"She wasn't shot, Mayor Oakman," he said.

"What killed her, then?" Adam asked. "I mean to say, how was she murdered?"

The Doc looked the other way for a minute and then back at Adam. "I think," he said, "that we might go into that a little later, after you've rested—"

"Rested?" Adam said very quietly, but like he couldn't believe his ears. "My daughter is dead. I want to know how she met her death, and when."

"When," the Doc said, still trying to put Adam off, "I don't know. I haven't any particular knowledge about that sort of thing. Within the past two or three hours, I should think. Perhaps Joe Laud could tell a little more definitely."

Adam said, "Some one telephone for Joe," and Kent went to the phone.

"Doctor Sprague," Adam said next, "was my daughter a suicide? Is that it?"

"Not the least possibility of such a thing," the Doc said, and gave up despairingly. "The cause of her death was primary cerebral hemorrhage, induced by a severe blow on the head. An instantaneous, merciful death, old friend."

"You'd tell me that, I know," Adam said, and went right on as if he was trying to reason things out. "But why was she there? What was she doing out on the desert a quarter of a mile away from camp?"

Nobody answered. After quite a while Mac spoke up, very nice and polite. "Pardon me, but I was wondering if somebody might have told her there was something out there for her to see, or get, or something, and lured her over there?"

"'Lured?'" Adam said, puzzled, like he'd never heard the word before in his life.

"The old Judge," I said, kind of thinking out loud and meaning that if someone had told Betty-Jean that the old Judge was out there, either living or dead, she'd have gone to see, as I knew she would.

"No," Adam said. I don't know what he thought I'd meant. "But this explains Brigid's fright and shock, the poor child—"

"Brigid," I begged, putting my very heart and soul into it, "can't you please remember what happened to give you a shock?"

She shook her head but didn't raise it from her arms. I didn't know what to think of her. I knew she aimed to be a good girl and usually was. I didn't think anything. I wouldn't let myself think. I listened to Adam.

"It is possible," he said, "that she was killed right here on the place and carried out there afterward."

Mac said, "We figured it that way. Her white shoes weren't scuffed up for walking that far over the rocks. She's as light as a feather."

"Yes," Adam answered. "And she wouldn't have been walking out on the desert. It must have been done here on the place. Brigid must have seen it. God send that the poor child may be able to help us later. In the meantime, Jeff, please find Rosemary and bring her here. Mac and Ernie, I want you to look around for Reggie Duefife and bring him here."

We all started for the door on our tiptoes. Kent came along with us. Adam said, "Son, I'd like to have you stay here with me."

I'd have thought better of the boy if he had minded at a time like that; but, "I'm sorry, Dad," he said. "I have to tell Rosemary. Jeff can stay with you. I'll hurry."

"Very well," Adam answered. "If you will, Doctor, you had better go with Kent. Another shock for the girl, you know."

They all went then, and Adam and Brigid and I were alone except for Betty-Jean there. Adam pulled himself up and went over and turned back the sheet that was covering her. I went to Brigid. She had stopped crying and was sitting there stooped over with her face still hidden in her arms, catching her breath once in a while.

After a minute Adam said, "Don't bother her, Jeff. Tears are good for women."

I hadn't been bothering her. I'd just been smoothing her hair down a little; but I didn't say anything. She took one of my hands—she's nice that way.

Doc Sprague and Kent must have used one of the cars, for they were back in faster than walking time. Brigid dropped my hand and waved me off a little when she heard them coming. I found myself a chair. Adam had put the sheet in place and was sitting down again. He didn't move when they came in.

Rosemary stepped away from Kent and walked straight to Adam. "I'm sorry," she said. "I am so sorry, Uncle Adam."

He pointed at a chair, meaning for her to sit down there and she did.

"Kent tells me," he said, "that you say nothing out of the ordinary happened here at camp after we left this morning."

"I didn't know that anything had happened," she answered.

Just then the boys came walking in with Reggie just walking, nothing official about it. Reggie was crying a little, taking the tears out of his eyes with one finger and one at a time like the girls do in the moving pictures.

"He was asleep out here between the houses," Mac said.

"Reggie," Adam began, before Reggie had had time to offer a word, "when I came in this afternoon you told me that Betty-Jean was all right. Now—"

"She was all right," Reggie broke in. "The last time I saw her she was all right."

"But when was that?" Adam asked.

"Oh, dear me," Reggie said. "I don't know exactly. It was quite a while after breakfast and long before lunch. I didn't look at my watch. I never even thought of looking. Maybe it was about eleven o'clock."

"Reggie," Adam said, sounding only very tired, "do you mean to admit that you reassured me about my daughter when you hadn't seen her after this shooting that you say you heard?"

"I did hear shooting," Reggie said. "I heard shooting. But when you came in carrying Brigid and yelling at me about Betty-Jean I just naturally wanted to calm you down. I thought she was all right. Oh, my, of course I thought she was all right. Who in the world could think of anyone's shooting Betty-Jean? She was so pretty, and good, and—"

"If you please, Reggie," Adam stopped him. "About this shooting that you say you heard here before twelve—"

"All over the place," Reggie said. "Exactly five minutes before twelve noon."

"And you, Rosemary, didn't hear anything of the sort?" Adam asked.

"I wasn't here at noon," Rosemary answered. "I went for a ride on Acrasia. I left shortly after ten o'clock. I didn't return until one."

Right then Kent made a big mistake by speaking without thinking. "But, Rosemary," he said, sounding surprised, "you didn't tell me that you'd been away from camp almost all morning. You said that nothing had happened here."

I knew he didn't mean to make trouble, or contradict or bother her, but it hadn't sounded just right. I was so embarrassed I didn't know where to look. I happened to look at Brigid. I wished I hadn't.

She had her nose stuck up so high that the crown of her head was in line with the back of her chair, and the expression on her face, I thought, boded evil. It was far from a wholesome expression. It was very superior, as if she wouldn't turn the whole kit and caboodle of us over with the toe of her shoe. Also, there was something do-or-die about it, with quite a pinch of malice.

25

"I'm sorry," Rosemary answered, "but you didn't ask me, Kent. When you came in you were frightened because Brigid had said that I was in danger. I told you that she must be mistaken, because nothing had happened at all. You didn't tell me that Reggie had heard shooting here at noon."

"I didn't know it," Kent said.

"Neither did I," she answered. "And so I didn't think of mentioning, when you first came, that I had been riding. It seemed unimportant. We were talking of other things, you know. And then Uncle Adam telephoned for you."

"Just a minute," Adam said. "Your story, as we have it now, is that you went for a ride at ten o'clock and didn't return until one. And yet you knew that Jeff was coming to take you all to Hay Patch."

"I left word with Reggie," she said, "to tell Jeff that my bag was in my cottage. I was going to ride to Hay Patch on Acrasia. She hates being led."

"I see. And where did you go on this three-hour ride of yours?"

"Out across the deserts, where I always go."

Reggie took his face out of his handkerchief and said, "The last I saw of her she was riding, hard, bare-back, too, straight out toward the White Cracker Mountains."

Adam's next question to Rosemary was a little nicer-sounding. "You rode out across the deserts and returned at one o'clock. Then what did you do?"

"I went straight to my cottage. The camp seemed deserted, so I supposed that Jeff had come for the others. My bag was in my sitting room, but I thought that Reggie had forgotten to mention it to Jeff."

"That would be probable, wouldn't it?" Reggie piped out.

"Very probable," Adam said, and went on talking to Rosemary. "Did you close the gate, after you came in?"

"Yes, I did. But it was so warm that I remounted Acrasia and rode to my back door."

"The gate was wide open when I drove in," Adam said, and thought a second. "Brigid may have left it open. She couldn't have walked that four miles from the mountain and got into camp until after one o'clock."

Leaving gates open wasn't like Brigid. I hoped she'd say she hadn't, that she had opened it again when she heard the car coming; but she didn't say a word. I kind of glanced at her and then I thought I'd as well not say anything either.

"Yes," Rosemary was answering Adam's question that I'd missed in part. "I was hot and dusty and rather tired, so I thought I'd rest an hour or so before riding on to Hay Patch. Acrasia needed a rest, too. I took a shower, ate some bread and milk and lay down on the bed in my bedroom."

"Have a good nap?" Adam asked, getting meaner again all of a sudden, I don't know why.

"I had been asleep only a few minutes, I believe, when Kent came."

"That must have been about half-past two," Adam said. "I suppose you couldn't get to sleep because you were thinking—worrying?"

I didn't blame her for not answering that, the way he'd asked it.

"I'd give a cool million," he said, "to know what you were thinking."

"I was thinking of Twill. And of Kent in that frightfully hot jail."

"How do you know that the jail is so 'frightfully hot'? Have you been there?"

"No, I haven't. Kent sent me a note yesterday morning asking me not to come. But I've been told that the jail is dangerously hot. You told me so yourself, Uncle Adam; remember?"

Up to that minute I had believed her word for word. But this about her not having been to the jail rang so true that it made me feel kind of sick. And right then, of course, Adam had to turn on me.

"What did Brigid say when she telephoned to you this afternoon?"

"I told you once, Adam," I said, trying to sound reproachful and forgetting in all this uproar exactly what I had told him.

He gave me a very sneering look and turned on Kent. "What did Jeff tell you that Brigid said when she telephoned to him?"

Before Kent had time to open his mouth, he was often a little slow spoken, Brigid asked, "What is all this about my telephoning? I did not. Who says that I did? And why do you all act as if I weren't here?"

"Bless my soul!" Adam said. "Brigid, my dear child, are you feeling better?"

"I don't know what you mean," Brigid answered. "But, thank you, I'm feeling well enough, if that matters. I am sure that I didn't telephone to anyone."

"You telephoned to everyone who had a telephone in Ferras," Adam said, getting a little beside himself and then remembering. "But I beg your pardon, my dear—you have forgotten."

"Forgotten?" Brigid asked, and though she didn't pull her chin back she sounded something like Mrs. Duefife.

Kent was the only person I ever knew who a man could nudge without getting into some kind of hot water for his trouble. I walked over beside him and nudged him a couple of times while Adam was explaining to Brigid what had happened to her and how he had found her unconscious by the gate and all about it. I gave him one or two more very meaning nudges, while Brigid was admitting, bewilderedly, that the time between when she had come into the gate at camp after leaving us on the mountain, until I told her the bad news about Betty-Jean, was a complete blank in her mind. After while, Kent moved a few steps off from me, but he never let on.

"You must have been in swimming," Reggie said, very interested, "because you are wearing your swimming suit. Don't you even remember being in swimming?"

Brigid shook her head and tried looking sweetly pitiful, but her voice was snaky poisonous as she asked, "Did you see me in swimming, Reggie?"

"I did not," he answered right up, like she had accused him of something terrible.

"That's odd," she said. "I mean, where were you all this time after twelve today? That is—after you say you heard shooting here?"

"I?" Reggie took time to straighten and look noble. "I was where any sensible man would have been considering the circumstances. I was in the storeroom."

Brigid repeated, more surprised than chiding, "The storeroom?"

"Certainly in the storeroom. I was in the kitchen here by the refrigerator. Suddenly shots to the right of me, shots to the left of me—and so on. I stepped into the storeroom and secured the door—"

"Didn't you look out of the window?" Brigid asked.

"There is only the one window facing east. After securing it, I pulled down the shade at once. I had myself well in hand. I consulted my watch. It was five minutes before twelve, noon."

Mac said, "Yeah, sure. But didn't you see a thing of these shooters, or what they'd shot, or shot at, or anything when you came out?"

"I didn't come out," Reggie said, very offended.

"But," Brigid reminded him, "you *are* out."

"He came out when I came home," Adam said. "Drop it. What I want to know now is what Brigid said when she telephoned."

Rosemary said, "Kent told me that Brigid had said that some terrible thing had happened here and that my life was in danger."

"Was this what she telephoned to you, Jeff," Adam asked.

"In effect," I said.

"And what Jeff told you, Kent?"

"Yes, Dad."

"Brigid," Adam turned to her, "my dear child, do you suppose that if you were to go quietly away by yourself, you'd be better able to make an effort to remember? Kent— anyone can go with you. We won't leave you alone again, of course."

I was so sure that Brigid was going to grab her chance to get alone with Kent, after all this time, that I saw her walking right off with him until I noticed that she wasn't doing anything of the kind. She sat tight as a tick and got some hysterical—I'll bet you that was easy for the poor kid right then—and said that she couldn't remember, and that her head ached, and that she wasn't to blame, and that she was certain she had not telephoned to anyone. Doc went over and began talking to her again in this nice soothing voice of his.

Ernie spoke. "This—" he said. "I mean to say, that—" He was blushing and very nervously twirling his forefinger at Reggie. "I didn't catch the name."

Reggie straightened his glasses and looked all the way down Ernie and all the way up again. "Reginald Duefife," he said.

"Pleased to meet you," Ernie said. "The only thing is, I was wondering if this Reginald Duefife would know if the shots were around here, or off some place, or were shots, or what."

"For goodness' sakes," Reggie said, getting fretful, "why do I have to keep telling this over and over and over? The shots I heard were shots. Loud shots. At hand. On the front porch, or close by. Discretion is the better part of valor. Oh, dear me."

I saw my chance and I took it. Whatever the old saw is about getting away from it all was how I felt. But I stopped when I came to Brigid and asked her quietly to come out on the front porch with me, please, and help me look for signs of the shooting. Please.

I hardly thought she'd come. She did, though her first words when we were alone were very discouraging.

"You're a nice one, aren't you?" she said.

"Listen, Brigid, honey," I pleaded, "I couldn't help it. Adam got the word before I did. I brought Kent and did the best I could."

"Sorry," she said. "I know you tried, Jeff. Why did you want me to come out here?"

"Why?" I repeated, all taken aback. "I want you to tell me about it, now we've a good chance. Talk fast, though. Somebody may butt in any minute."

"Talk about what?"

"Everything. What happened. Why you phoned me to bring Kent."

"I can't remember telephoning," she said, but the way she said it meant, "I'm lying and you know it. Try getting anything out of me."

"Brigid," I begged, putting my very heart and soul into it again, "you wanted to tell me a while ago, in there. I'm just the same now. I never went back on you, ever; did I? You need help now and I know it. Just give me the chance."

"I can't remember telephoning," she said.

I sat down on the steps. I never felt so useless in my life. A broom would have scared me worse than a gun right then. But I daren't give up.

"You liked little Betty-Jean, didn't you, Brigid?" I said.

She caught her breath in sharp. "Betty-Jean was a peach," she said, and sniffled quite a bit.

"Yes," I said. "And some brute has hit her over the head and killed her and thrown her out there in a desert gully and left her there. She was young and pretty and sweet— and her life's gone. You're the same, but you have your life yet. You can hear all the nice quiet on the deserts, and can see things, and laugh—"

"Torturing me won't do any good," she said.

"I wouldn't hurt you for the world and all," I told her. "The trouble is, I'm afraid you're on the wrong side. I don't know for sure. Maybe you aren't. What I do know for sure is that you're too thin and all to go it alone."

She began crying again and I hoped like everything that she was also relenting.

"Honey," I said, "when you and your papa came to these parts you were a couple of years old. You stayed at the ho- tel while you were getting your house built. You found out then, in short order, that there wasn't anything I wouldn't do for you from walking on all fours down Main Street to ringing the fire bell. You've known it ever since. We've both known it. Your own papa couldn't do more for you than I would, if you'd give me a chance."

"I know it," she said, crying hard now and using the backs of her hands. "I know it."

"Hell's bells!" I said, being clear beside myself. "Why don't you trust me then? Stop that crying. I'm practically crazy," I told her, "the way you act." And I was, and I didn't even have a handkerchief clean enough to offer her or anything.

"I'll never trust anybody again," she said, swallowing after every few words. "And anyway, now, I think I shouldn't. Only—if you do want to help me, if you really do, then please don't forget that I can't remember telephoning."

Before I'd begun recovering from that blow I had another one. The front door was open and ripping out through it came the loudest, hottest and most capable cussing that I'd ever heard in my life.

Brigid stopped crying. "That can't be Doctor Sprague," she said, awed, and kept her mouth open.

It sounded no more like the old Doc's nice grave voice than the cat on the fence sounds like itself purring under the stove, so how we both knew that it was the Doc, I'll never know. But we did.

"Why! Listen!" she said.

She shouldn't have wanted to listen. I didn't; but I couldn't help it. Doc Sprague was talking about his getting Rupert Potter, the bank cashier, to open the bank up for him last evening and give him two thousand dollars cash to bring to Adam. Doc was calling it bribe money and hush money and was going to put the fact in all papers west of the Mississippi with a sworn statement.

"Doc's wrong about that," I said to Brigid. "The money roll is on the kitchen table right now. I can prove it."

"Listen!" she said.

"I've warned you, Oakman," the Doc was saying, still cussing but that isn't necessary. "I mean it. I swear it.

I'll have you sent up for murder and in spite of your pull and your money I'll get a conviction if I have to carry it through every court in this country."

26

Mac and Ernie came slinking out on the porch. They looked as if they had been slinking for miles. Mac shut the door behind him and said, "They're having trouble in there," just above a whisper.

"But why is Doctor Sprague accusing Mayor Oakman of murder?" Brigid asked.

"He ain't," Mac said, shocked.

"I heard him," Brigid said, vexed.

"She means," I explained, "about the old Doc's saying he'd have the Mayor sent up for murder."

"Aw, that," Mac said, relieved. "No, you see the old Doc is saying that he'll send the Mayor up if he puts the pretty girl in the Ferras jail. The Doc claims that she'd die there and that it would be deliberate murder against Oakman."

"Adam's all upset," I said, "and no wonder. When it came right down to it, he'd never think of sending any lady, let alone Rosemary, to jail."

"I don't know about that," Mac said. "He was thinking of it Wednesday night. And now he has it in his head that his girl, Betty-Jean, was killed here on the place and carried out to that gully. He thinks you saw the killing, Brigid, and that that's what knocked you out cold. Seems that the only person on the place who could ride Kent's horse, which they say is the only horse on the place, is this pretty girl. I told Oakman and the Doc told him that it wouldn't take a horse to carry that little thing—"

Brigid interrupted, "I could carry her myself."

"You could not," I said. "But I don't see why the Doc is getting so excited. I'll bet you he could take her out of jail within an hour and put her over at Mrs. Enfield's." (Mrs. Enfield has her front rooms fixed up for a hospital.) "Nobody would dare stop him, if she was sick—and she would be, in under an hour."

"Yeah, sure," Mac said. "And I whispered that to the Doc, myself. He told me to shut my mouth. He said that keeping her out was a damn sight easier and more important than getting her out. He's on a rampage right, the old Doc is."

"What about Kent?" Brigid asked very coldly. "Is he whispering? Or has he lost interest? Or is he leaving it all up to Doctor Sprague?"

Kent was well liked in these parts. Neither of the boys said anything. I thought I knew something. I thought I'd heard something. I didn't have time to go around outside, so I went as fast as I could through the house to the back. Adam hollered at me, "Jeff! Here, Jeff," like he was calling a dog by that name, but I didn't have time to stop.

Sure enough, there was Kent in the big car, just finishing bringing it around for a quick getaway.

"Hold on, Kent," I said. "You can't go off the highways, boy, and Adam will have you stopped before you've started. Leaving always looks bad.

"Lend me your gun, Jeff," he said. "I'm taking Rosemary out of this."

I offered it to him, but he was sore and wouldn't have it. Come to find out, he had wanted it loaded to the hilt. I'd just turned around and shot it empty, due west.

I had acted on a sudden impulse. But nobody would believe me. They all came tearing out, jumping to the conclusion that just because I'd been shooting I'd been shooting at something. I was so blamed upset from the noise that I just sat down on the running-board of the car and told the truth—that I'd shot on a sudden impulse at nothing, and stuck to it. I must have stuck to it ten or twenty times.

Kent came in for his share of questioning, but he also told the simple truth and stuck to it. He said he didn't know what I had been shooting at. He hadn't seen a thing to shoot at. He positively did not know.

Adam decided in a nice way that I had gone stark raving insane and that he had feared as much when I'd torn through the house just now on a dead run.

"No, I am not," I said, hating the way the circle of folks widened out as if I was a pebble dropped in their midst. "I felt like shooting due west. And I shot."

Rosemary was suggesting that they get me in out of the sun when Reggie showed up from behind two or three of the folks and said, "I think he is fibbing like everything."

"Shut up, Reggie," Brigid said. "If you had seen what Jeff saw you'd have done something worse than firing a gun."

"What should I have done?" Reggie asked, all curiosity; but nearly everybody else asked what Jeff saw.

Brigid answered, shuddering, and making even me half believe her word for word. "I think Jeff saw what I saw before I fainted. I saw Clyde Shively. Alive. Riding one horse and leading another. He had a hammer in his hand. He was riding toward me."

In the midst of one of those fearful, petrified silences, Adam said, "You couldn't have seen Clyde Shively."

"I know it," Brigid said. "I knew it then. I suppose that is the reason I fainted. I did see him."

"Was this before or after you telephoned?" Adam asked.

"I don't remember telephoning," Brigid said. "All I remember is seeing Clyde Shively. Alive. Coming toward me on a horse. He was leading another horse. He had a hammer in his hand. He was coming from over there." She pointed, and the way she did it we were all afraid to look. "So I think that Jeff saw him, as I did, and shot. I fainted. Jeff is seriously shaken."

"Was the horse he was leading Acrasia?" Adam asked.

"No. She was in the shelter when I opened the gate and came in at twenty minutes past one. I looked at my watch to see how long it had taken me to walk to camp. I remember closing the gate. I think it must have been shortly after that when I saw Clyde Shively."

"Impossible," Adam said.

"Did you see him before you put on your swimming suit?" Reggie asked.

Mac said, "The Killaky boys are twins. Some folks can't tell them apart."

"Whoever she saw, Oakman," Doc Sprague said, "there is your extra horse—two horses, in fact."

"Two horses but only one weapon," Reggie said worriedly.

Adam came and stood over me, putting one hand on my shoulder. He'd had a thought, but he was ashamed of it, so, "Mirage?" he asked, kind of feebly. "Jeff, did you see someone who resembled Clyde Shively riding on the deserts over in the west there? Was that why you shot? It is nothing to be ashamed of, you know. We have all been fooled by the confounded things at one time or another."

I'd have liked to tell some more of the truth, with Adam being so nice thinking up excuses for me, but I couldn't see my way clear. It wouldn't have sounded right for me to say that I'd had the impulse to shoot because I wanted to keep Kent from attempting a dangerous getaway with his girl, his Dad's car and my gun. No, there was nothing for me to say except, "I felt like shooting so I shot. Due west."

Mac said, "I saw the Ferry Building in 'Frisco, once, with crowds of people rushing around between here and Injun Ridge."

Ernie looked like he had a good notion to speak, but before he'd made up his mind to it, Brigid said, "What I saw wasn't a mirage. I heard the horses' hoofs on the cement road."

Kent said, very solemn, "Joe is coming. If you'll get up, Jeff, I'll drive this car out of his way."

Sure enough, here Joe came bringing the hearse.

We haven't an ambulance in Ferras, so I suppose he thought he had to, and that it would seem disrespectful to drive any hearse in a hurry. The worst of it was, that the black thing crawling with its shadow up the white road in the blazing sun should have looked out of place and it didn't; not any more than it looked out of place in the graveyard.

Some of the folks went into the house with Joe and Adam and the Doc. Some of us just stood around watching the hearse. I had an eerie feeling about it; as if it liked Memaloose, meaning death, and felt right at home there. I found myself kind of thinking words to it, such as, "Make the most of this trip because you'll never be here again."

I was wrong about that, and I guess I halfway knew it then without knowing that I knew it. I went and sat down on the steps, wondering what kind of pass a man had come to when he started talking to hearses. In a minute Brigid came and petted the top of my head and whispered, "Angel," taking my mind off the hearse for a few seconds. She was nice that way.

27

When Joe had finally got off again with the hearse, Adam, Kent and Ernie rode out to the gully where Betty-Jean's body had been found. Mac and I stayed in camp trying hard to do some investigating concerning this shooting story of Reggie's, but we couldn't find a thing to investigate. The Doc told us that Joe thought the time when Betty-Jean had been killed was between one and two o'clock. He said guessing time was one thing Joe was usually pretty nearly right about—that is unless rigor was complete. In this case, the Doc said, though he was no judge of such things himself, he'd an idea that Joe wasn't far wrong. Rigor had begun, but the body heat hadn't entirely left the body when the boys found it a few minutes after three.

Adam with Kent and Ernie didn't stay long away from the place. As soon as they got back the old Doc went home, surprising and confusing me quite a bit by giving me a pat on the back and saying, "Good work, Jeff," just before he left.

He was no sooner gone than, trying my best to avoid it, I found myself rounded up alone with Adam in the community house kitchen.

"Here, wait a minute," he said, so I had to.

"It seems to me," he went on, "that all our lives I've been accusing you of being a fool only to discover that you weren't anything of the sort. It seems to me, too, that I've apologized to you more frequently than I have to all my other acquaintances and friends combined. I presume you are tired of it. I am. But now, besides apologizing, I want to thank you. I am deeply grateful—"

"Oh, shut up, Adam," I said, getting embarrassed and sick of it anyway.

"There'd have been the devil to pay, sure enough," he said, "if Kent, the young jackass, had tried running away with that girl."

I thought, maybe, it would be good for him to get just a little vexed; so I said, real gently, though, "I don't know what's got into you here lately, Adam. You are always accusing somebody of something. Kent had no idea on earth of running away."

It didn't work. He gave me a queer look, but all he said was, "Is it an accusation if I state, and I do, that Brigid O'Dell could not have seen Clyde Shively alive here this afternoon?"

"That's just exactly what she thought," I said. "It wasn't the two horses that scared the poor little kid out of her wits."

He sighed. I felt so sorry for him I didn't know which way to turn. And my conscience was bothering me like a bugle playing taps off key and keeping it up.

"Adam," I said, "why don't you get away from this blazing place and take the folks on over to Hay Patch like you planned? It'll be cool and dark and comforting over there. And I'll bet that Mrs. Duefife is getting awfully nervous by this time, waiting in the hotel."

Precisely what he was going to do, he said, as soon as he got his long-distance call from L. A. Up to that minute I'd had no idea how desperate Adam was. He was trying to engage that criminologist, named Jones, that Reggie had mentioned. And even at that I didn't know how desperate he was; because, when the word came that this Jones was in the hospital, what did Adam up and do but put in a call for Lynn MacDonald in 'Frisco. He excused himself for this by telling me that she had been on a case for a friend of his, Sam Stanley, up north at his Desert Moon Ranch, and that Sam spoke highly of her.

While we were waiting for the 'Frisco call Adam walked the floor. After a while I said, "Adam, you told me last night that you knew and that I ought to know what had happened here. I don't know—"

"Fortunately for you," he interrupted. "If I had known less, though that is impossible since I knew nothing, this might not have happened here today."

"And," I said, "if the L. A. wise guy hadn't built the camp here, it wouldn't have happened, either. There's never any stopping when you start going backward over the *ifs*'," I told him.

"Very true," he said. "But if you hadn't started talking to me about not hearing a shot here on Wednesday afternoon, and if you hadn't happened to have an unusual sense of hearing, and if— What the devil!" he broke off, just when he was beginning to get interesting. "Why should we go into all this again? Talk! I'm tired of it. I'm getting a professional on the job, or attempting to do so. Since she's a woman she'll probably talk enough for six of me. I'm through."

With that he went wandering back into the kitchen and I got up from my chair and followed him. No reason—just some place to go into and get out of. I noted the roll of bills on the table there and told him that he'd better put them in his pocket.

He paid no attention to me so I picked them up and just idly counted them. "There's only fifteen hundred dollars here," I said, after I'd run through them twice. "I'd understood that there were two thousand."

"Kent probably borrowed it when he was deciding to skip out with Rosemary," Adam said. "It will turn up all right."

"If it shouldn't, though," I said, "I wouldn't want you to accuse the boys, or—"

"By the Eternal!" he said, and went on declaring that he had never accused anybody of anything in his life, and went on some more cussing me out for accusing him of accusing. I didn't mind. It seemed to be doing him some good and me no harm. For that matter, he wasn't much more than well under way when the phone bell called him to the front room.

I heard him say, "Hello," a couple of times, and that he wanted to talk with Lynn MacDonald herself, and then Brigid came in through the back door all dressed—I mean, with a dress on and shoes and stockings and everything, looking as gaunt as a starved coyote, but kind of pretty though a little smug.

"Brigid," I said, speaking fast and earnestly, "Adam is in there right now phoning to that Lynn MacDonald detective woman in 'Frisco."

"I can't help it," she said.

"The thing is," I said, "maybe you need some help yourself?"

She stuck up her nose, but I noted that her lips and her voice kind of trembled when she asked, "You haven't made up your mind that I killed Betty-Jean, have you?"

I was plumb disgusted with her and I said so. "There are plenty of crimes besides killing," I added. "There is aiding and abetting; there's being an accomplice—"

"Yahweh!" she said. "Will you please let me alone and stop talking to me like that?"

"I don't know what in the world you are mad at me about now," I said. "You were calling me 'Angel' a while ago."

"A while ago," she said, "I liked the way you changed the subject with your six gun and kept Kent from sneaking off."

"That boy was not 'sneaking' off with Rosemary," I began.

"Did I mention Rosemary?" she said.

"And now you ought to be ashamed," I said. "The idea that a good boy like Kent—"

"Shut up!" she said. "I told you a minute ago that I wanted—"

"Quarreling?" Adam asked from the doorway. "I never saw anything like it. No two persons can meet anywhere on this place without instantly plunging into a quarrel. Tragedy, grief, nothing can prevent everyone's bickering with everyone else on sight. Petty bickering!

"I can't get that MacDonald woman on the telephone," he went right on before we'd had a chance to deny a word he'd said. "I am positive that she was in her office. I could tell from her secretary's manner. I explained to her that we had no time for fiddle-faddle and that money was no object. Useless. That's what I get for dealing with women. No method. No sense of responsibility. Any man on earth would call his office from time to time. I finally left this number and told the secretary to have her call me the instant she got in touch with her. She was sure that wouldn't be earlier than five o'clock. At that rate she can't get here by plane much before ten tonight. I told the secretary to call the airport there and have a plane and pilot in readiness. I doubt that she'll do so. All this serves me right for engaging her in the first place."

"But," Brigid tried telling him, "you haven't engaged her."

"I have decided to engage her," he said, stubborn as usual about sticking to anything he had started. "The thing now is to get you all on your way to Hay Patch."

I couldn't see a bit of sense in Adam's staying at Memaloose when he might as well and better have left the Hay Patch phone number for Lynn MacDonald to call. I couldn't see any more sense in Adam's sending Brigid, Rosemary, Kent, Reggie and Mac off in the big car and keeping Mac's horse and gun and Ernie with his horse and gun there in camp with him.

Naturally I waited around after the folks had gone to find out about all this, to explain to Adam that he wouldn't have any way to get to Hay Patch himself and to try persuading him to have the phone call transferred and come on with me.

"I'll ride Mac's horse to Ferras," he said, "and get a car out of Goldfield Red's to drive on to Hay Patch. I feel like being alone now. I may take Mac's horse and ride out on the desert to an ant nest that I haven't seen for months. Interesting but exceptionally ungrateful creatures—ants. I'm keeping Ernie here. I won't need anyone else. His gun's loaded. He's the best shot in the country and is practically inarticulate."

"You never needed any help before to look at an ant-hill," I said.

"But I have needed ant nests," he said, "to help deliver me from my friends—and other evils."

He came back, though, while I was trying to get the car door shut. "I beg your pardon, Jeff," he said, and got red and vexed all over again. "There I go!" he said. "Why in the name of the Everlasting are you always around making me apologize to you?"

"I never make you apologize," I said. "You always just up and do it. At the drop of a hat."

"Yes, it is becoming an obsession with me," he said, "as your flatly contradicting my most casual remark has long been an obsession of yours."

"No, I don't, Adam," I said. I was going on to apologize, some, myself, if he'd have let me. But the last thing I heard he was hollering after me, "You do. You contradict flatly every word I happen to utter."

At the first turn on the road I looked back. Sure enough, there was Adam on Mac's horse, riding lickety-split toward the White Cracker Mountains.

28

Driving back to Ferras I didn't even glimpse the big car on the hairpins, so I knew when I got to town that the folks had picked up Mrs. Duefife and were well on their way to Hay Patch; I was glad of it, for it gave me time to drive around the outskirts and come up to the back of the hotel where I could dive in through the kitchen entrance without being noticed.

I knew that with Joe taking the hearse through town to Memaloose and back, everybody would be on Main Street talking things over and waiting for me in front of the hotel to give them the latest news. Adam had told us all that there weren't any secrets to be kept any longer; but I hate being the center of any attraction and I didn't feel in the mood for talking anyway.

I parked my car on the circus lot a block away from the hotel and the only sign I saw of anybody after that was the carpet sweeper standing with its handle straight up in the hall where Ellie had left it when she had run downstairs to hear the latest news.

Feeling pretty good over giving everybody the slip, I decided to feel a little better and see what I'd missed. My own room is at the back of the place, so I had to go into one of the front rooms.

The rooms are always unlocked, of course, but the door
I picked out wouldn't open. I thought it was stuck and
raised it a little, giving it a shake.

Brigid said, "What is it?"

I had reason for being surprised. Why I was scared I
don't know, except that I had a fool notion that, maybe,
someone had locked her in there.

"It's me," I answered, sounding kind of silly.

She opened the door just wide enough to stick her nose
up in the crack, and asked, vexed, "What do you want?"

"What are you doing here?" I asked.

"Nothing," she said. "That is, I'm staying here until St.
Dennis comes home. I'd go home and stay, but I promised
him I wouldn't. I didn't say I wouldn't stay in the Ferras
Hotel. I'm going to stay here. I won't go to Hay Patch. I
will not. I won't talk about it. I won't talk about anything.
Mayor Oakman can't make me go to Hay Patch. Neither
can you. I won't go."

"You just bet you won't," I said, all admiration or trying hard to be. "You never did a smarter thing in your
life," I went on, "than finding yourself a good safe place
to stay and staying in it."

She shut the door and locked it.

Lucky for me nobody thought of looking for my car
anywhere but around the hotel or over at Goldfield Red's,
so I got some rest until, around seven o'clock, I woke up
and found myself thinking of Reggie and deciding that I'd
never had enough understanding sympathy for the lad. No
wonder; the last food I'd even seen had been at breakfast.

I wrote a note saying, "Dear Brigid, let's eat. Jeff," and
within a couple of minutes after I'd stuck it under her
door she came tapping on mine.

"I haven't eaten since yesterday," she said. "So if you'll
promise not to scold or ask me any questions at all, I'll go
with you to Slim's."

Feeding her, the way she looked, seemed a lot more necessary than putting her through the third degree. So I promised; but I complained a little until she began crying, leaning against the door-jamb, and I had to take it all back and promise over again.

"It's this way, Jeff," she said. "Something goes wrong with my tear ducts when I try to talk. But I'm not responsible for anything that has happened and nothing I could say or tell could help anybody or do any good. I haven't been wicked—but I'm hungry. I feel odd, very odd. And I'm hungry."

We took a table at Slim's, instead of sitting up to the counter, and we weren't bothered, much, except for a dozen or so of the boys sidling up and asking whether I'd be in the poolroom later or where would I be. The folks around here always stood quite aloof from the O'Dells. They liked them fine, but they kept a distance. I never knew whether this was out of respect to O'Dell's being an author, or whether it was that most everybody thought that the O'Dells were kind of crazy.

On our way back to the hotel we saw Mac and Ernie, riding east, but taking it easy as if they weren't bent for any place in particular. We didn't think about Hay Patch being to the east. I guess we didn't think anything except that Brigid, noting that Mac was riding his horse, remarked that she was glad Mayor Oakman had got a car and gone on to Hay Patch instead of stopping and finding her at the hotel and arguing with her.

"Brigid, child," I said, knowing she'd be a lot better off at Hay Patch than she would be in that hot hotel, "if you'd tell me which one of the folks you're afraid of, over there, I know I could prove to you that you had no cause for fearing any of them."

She didn't answer. All the way up the steps she didn't answer. She stopped at the door of her room. "Don't call me child," she said, and went in and locked the door behind her.

I went to my room. Shinny, Taylor, Quebec Red and several of the other boys were waiting for me. I decided it would be better to go down to the poolroom and shoot a few games in public than it would be to hold a big private reception. It wasn't a bad idea. As soon as the boys found out that I was sore on the whole subject of Memaloose, fighting sore, knew nothing anyway and would say less, they were very white about it. I didn't have to arrest a one of them for libel, defamation of character, interchanging opprobrious epithets, being private nuisances, or anything else that I'd mentioned.

Things were going all right until, around nine o'clock, Shorty, the night clerk, came in to tell me that a drummer in the lobby was acting very ugly, trying to make trouble just because Brigid O'Dell had borrowed his car and gone for a ride. She had told Shorty she wanted a breath of fresh air and would bring the car right back, so Shorty had said "O. K." because the drummer was upstreet. But it seemed that the drummer had noted her leaving town, and here he was back in the hotel and raising Ned.

Strolling to the door, I asked what direction she'd taken. Shorty said that the drummer claimed she had struck out to the west of town driving like hades. I told him to tell the drummer that he'd sent the sheriff to get his blistering old rattle-trap for him but that Ferras, Oakman County, or the State of Nevada would stand for no monkey business when it came to anybody's objecting to a lady borrowing a car for a few minutes, and sauntered on my way.

A Ford is a fine car for this country, but I guess the drummer's car was a good one for whatever country he came from. It went. I heard it and followed it, getting a

glimpse now and then of its headlights spotting the hairpin turns for a split second, and being so scared at Brigid's
spinning around that mountain road like a top that I forgot to be scared of anything else until I got to Memaloose.

The gate was wide open. The camp was as dark as down
the well except for the drummer's car with its lights on
standing where the hearse had stood that afternoon. The
back door was locked. I knocked hard and I heard someone
who I knew wasn't Brigid coming to answer.

Adam opened the door and said, "Is that you, Jeff?"
Sure enough, I found out in a minute that it was me.

Only one shaded light was burning in the living room
but I could see Brigid sitting by the telephone with her
mouth shut. To this day I never have seen anything half as
much shut as Brigid's mouth was then.

Before I'd even found myself a chair Adam was asking a
hundred questions, all of them about why had I come and
what for.

I was afraid I couldn't change his mind, so I thought
that I'd try changing his tactics. "I came to see why in
thunder you sent for Brigid to come over here alone at a
time like this," I said, adding, "Dangerous business for a
grown person, let alone a child."

"What are you talking about!" he said. "Send for her! I
didn't send for her."

"If not," I said, but hardly giving him the benefit of
the doubt, "why did she come? Tell me that."

"She didn't come," he said. "I mean to say I didn't.
That is—I tell you she didn't even know that I was here."

With that he went on, less confused but more bitter as
he described how he had been lying there in the dark, resting, when Brigid came creeping in through the front door
with a flashlight, making a bee-line for the telephone.
He should have kept quiet and listened to her telephone

message. But, being unaccustomed to criminal plots and methods, he had spoken to her. She had screamed. He had spoken again. As nearly as I could gather, he had been speaking ever since. She had not uttered a word and would not.

"I suppose," I said, "that instead of speaking to the poor kid you hollered at her and gave her another terrible shock. It's too bad. I'd think she had had enough for one day. This afternoon she lost her memory. Now I suppose she has lost her voice."

"No, you don't," he said. "Not this time. You know as well as I do that she didn't lose her memory this afternoon."

"Know what? Know what?" I said, twice on purpose.

"At any rate," he said, "you know it now. You've been told. I've told you. I'll tell you, further, that she has been making a fool of you. Oh, yes she has. Just as that girl has been making fools of us all for days."

Generally he meant Rosemary when he said "that girl," but I asked him, anyway. "Not Rosemary?"

"Rosemary," he said. "She didn't kill her brother there in his cottage on Wednesday evening."

"Where did she kill him, then?" I asked. "And when?"

29

"She didn't kill him," Adam said. "She helped him get away after he had killed Clyde Shively and the Judge. Every hour she could keep us searching for him, believing that he was dead, was an hour to his advantage."

A very disgusted utterance came from Brigid's direction. It sounded something as if she was saying "Fist!" with her mouth tight shut, but since she couldn't do that it didn't sound like that, either.

Adam pretended he didn't hear it and went right on talking to me. "I've known that Twill was the murderer ever since you spoke about our not hearing shots here on Wednesday afternoon," he said. "The shots must have been fired during the thunderstorm. With your hearing, you'd have heard a shot fired here in camp from at least half-past three o'clock on. You'd have heard it while you and I were in the kitchen, despite the radio. During the storm, Twill and his two victims were the only ones on the place who weren't in the living room, right here."

"I doubt it," I said.

He went on talking. "Why he did it, I don't know. Jealousy, perhaps. Or some past scores to settle. But I do know that he committed both murders. I've known that for some time. But I firmly believed that he was dead. I shouldn't have believed that girl's story for a moment, if I hadn't seen that bloodstained pillow with my own eyes, and her frock and her arms. She knew that, of course, and—"

"I doubt it," I said.

"Doubt what?" he said, very vexed. "By the Eternal! Doubt what?"

"Everything," I said.

"Will you please listen to me?" he said, adding, "Where was I?"

"No place, much," I told him. "Just believing that you saw a bloodstained pillow, which you did see."

"I did see it," he said, as if I'd said he hadn't. "Of course I saw it. And so I believed her lies. I thought that it was her horror of what Twill had done—or, perhaps, something which he was trying to force her to do—that had made her lose her senses and shoot him. Under these circumstances I felt that, even if the body were found, she should not be held accountable. The murderer was dead. I gave her a chance that she'll wish she had taken when I left that money here for her today."

Brigid made another one of those disgusted, "fisty" utterances.

Adam went right on. "This afternoon, necessarily, I began questioning my conclusions—seriously questioning them. But not until Reggie gave me a bit of information—"

"Reggie?" I said.

"Reggie," he said it over, differently, making it sound dignified. "He happened to mention that when Rosemary went riding on Thursday morning she took a package with her. He thought that she was carrying food, delicacies, to Kent in jail. So he doubted her positive statement that she had not seen Kent in the jail."

"Well, what do you think of that!" I said. But he misunderstood my meaning entirely and answered:

"My first thought was that her leaving the camp with a package might signify that she was carrying food and

water to some hiding-place on the desert. Never mind, I
know without being told that there are no hiding-places
on the desert. I believed that I was sending myself on a
fool's errand when I rode out there alone this afternoon.
As it well might have been, but for the fact that Scamp
ants eat carrion. She made a mistake when she buried that
body not far from a nest of Scamp ants. The wind last
night partly uncovered it. I followed the ants and they led
me straight to the dog with a bullet in its head."

He stopped talking. Brigid said nothing. For some reason the only thing I said was, "Dog!"

"Yes, dog," he started off again. "She shot the dog there
on that pillow Wednesday night, and hid it and came running out to us with her lies. Time was what she was playing
for and we danced to her tune. Twill killed Clyde Shively
and the Judge. He returned today and killed my daughter.
From now on, I am calling the tune."

Brigid opened her mouth and said, "No, I think not.
Because not one word of this crazy theory is true, and I
can prove that it isn't. My own first theory—the one that
I formed without thinking—was just as crazy, though. As
soon as I missed the dog, I thought that he had followed
Twill away because I knew that he wouldn't follow anyone
else. So I thought that Twill had killed the Judge, accidentally, when we heard the shot on Wednesday evening. I
thought that Rosemary and Kent had helped Twill escape,
and—"

"Just a moment, please," Adam said, sounding dangerous. "You missed the dog?"

"Yes. Everyone missed the dog—that is, everyone except you—Mayor Oakman."

"And said nothing about it, of course?"

"I believe that the others thought that the dog's absence was unimportant. I thought that if I were to tell you
that Funny was lost you'd say that it was like a woman to

be fussing over a lost dog at a time like this. Or—well, something of the sort."

"You knew perfectly well," Adam said, "that if you had come to me and told me that you believed Twill was alive, giving me your reasons, I should have thought the information vitally important."

"Yes," Brigid admitted, "I was afraid you might think it was important. It isn't, really. It doesn't make sense. It doesn't answer any of the right questions. If Twill killed the Judge, what has become of the Judge's body? I looked on all the roofs. I took the broken ladder and got to the porch roof here, and then on up to the high roof where I could see all the other roofs."

"So did I," Adam said, much to my surprise. "Very early Thursday morning. Mac and Ernie assisted me."

"But," Brigid went on, "even if we had found the Judge's body—and we haven't, and we can't—how could anyone have helped Twill to escape, in a flash, on Wednesday night? He was a cripple. We began hunting for him almost at once, and in daylight. And why should Twill stop to turn a bloodstained pillowslip wrong side out? And what about the bullet in the wall of Twill's cottage? And why were the pockets of that tan suit empty? And—"

"I haven't the slightest idea what you are talking about," Adam interrupted. "And now, Jeff— Let me see— I had something to tell you. Oh, yes. I sent Ernie off with Mac's horse to pick Mac up and go to Hay Patch. They are there now, seeing to it—unostentatiously—that Kent and that girl don't try escaping again. Lynn MacDonald should arrive at the flying field well before ten o'clock tonight. Mac and Ernie, with Kent and Rosemary, are to meet her in my car and bring her here. She'll want to look over the place, probably, and I thought it would save time to have her listen to that girl's confession at the outset. She'll confess, don't make any mistake about that. And she'll tell us where that murderous scoundrel has gone. She'll assist us in finding him, or—"

"Twill, do you mean?" Brigid asked.

"Most assuredly I mean Twill."

"I found his body early this afternoon when I walked back to camp from the mountain. He is dead. He has been shot below the hollow in his throat—rather far below it, exactly where Rosemary told us that she shot him."

30

"I don't believe you," Adam said, forgetting his streak of politeness.

"I didn't know that you had decided not to prosecute Rosemary when the body was found. I wish you had told me sooner."

"If you have found the body, where is it?"

"I was afraid that you would make serious trouble for Rosemary."

"Answer my question!"

"No, because I am still afraid that you may make trouble for Rosemary."

Adam said to me, "She hasn't found the body."

"I think she has," I said.

"So you, Sheriff of Oakman County—"

Brigid interrupted. "Jeff doesn't know anything about this. If you'll promise me on your Oakman word of honor that you won't make trouble for Rosemary, I'll tell you where the body is."

"I am entering into no pacts," Adam said. "You haven't found Twill's body. If you have, you'll tell soon enough where it is."

"I think not."

"Yes, you will. You'll tell, young lady."

"I doubt it. I've lied, and committed two robberies, and undergone torture and risked my life on the mountain tonight to avoid telling. No, I didn't mind," she added, as if Adam had asked her whether she had minded, and took a roll of bills out of the front of her dress. "These are yours, I think," she said, handing them to him. "I stole them this afternoon."

Adam stuck the bills into his pocket like they were peanuts and he didn't eat peanuts. "I don't believe for one instant that you have found that body," he said. "But, if you have, you will tell us where it is, and before long."

I had been hearing the car coming for quite a while. I thought that Brigid might want to know, so I told her. "The car with the detective is coming right now."

"I don't care," she said, just a little bit like Reggie.

"You will care," Adam said.

"Why?"

"Because you are going to tell her why you came here tonight to use the telephone. You are going to tell her, if you have found Twill's body—though I know you haven't—where it is. You are going to tell her, because she will explain to you that Twill's body is the one thing that can prove that girl wasn't lying, and so keep her out of the penitentiary for from twenty years to life."

Brigid didn't answer.

"Maybe," I said, trying to make peace before the folks came with the detective, "Rosemary shot Twill and the dog both; or, maybe, she shot neither. If Twill killed the Judge there in that cottage, there'd have been—well, plenty of traces of killing without her shooting the dog. And, if Twill didn't kill the Judge, why should she kill the dog? And—"

"In the name of the Everlasting—" Adam murmured, kind of pleadingly.

"And," I said, "I don't much think Brigid was going to telephone. If she was, she was only going to send word to the drummer to keep his shirt on."

Adam slapped his hands flat on the table and stood up by pressing his weight down on them, leaning forward a little. He looked terrible, but before he'd got through moistening his lips, trying to say something, Kent and Rosemary came in the front door, kind of ushering in this Lynn MacDonald. Mac and Ernie followed as if they fairly hated following; and, hovering in the background, was Joe Laud. He told me afterward that Miss MacDonald invited him to come, but he acted all evening like he was wrong about that.

My first idea of Lynn MacDonald was that she was a very good-looking lady in a bad humor. I've always been partial to red hair for ladies. Her red hair wasn't that pretty desert-rock-red that Brigid's was—hers was more the shade of those California Madrona trees' trunks, but it was smooth and pleasing to the eye. She was a little tall for my taste, though neither scrawny nor portly, and she carried herself well, and her clothes became her. Her voice wasn't as sweet-sounding as Rosemary's, but it was better than the average run of voices—clear, and kind of harmonious and well-bred; nothing like you'd expect a detective's voice to be.

The trouble was, that the minute Kent had put through some introductions, she had to begin talking to me as if I was only person in the room.

"Now then," she said, "I have been told . . ." and went on, giving the outlines of the case, just about as I gave them to Brigid on Thursday morning; but making special and extra points of the disappearing bodies and adding Betty-Jean's murder on at the last.

"Yes," I said, when she seemed to me waiting for an answer, "I guess that's about the size of it."

She gave me kind of a queer look, to say the least, and turned to Adam, "And you, Mayor Oakman?" she said. "Do you agree with this?"

"I?" he said, pretending to be surprised at being included in the talk. "I have been listening, intently; but wondering, also, whether you were interested in what you had been told or in the truth concerning what has happened here at Memaloose?"

"In the truth, of course," she answered very pleasantly. "As yet I have talked only with your son, the two deputy sheriffs and the coroner." She looked around for Joe, but he was out on the porch.

"Perhaps, then," Adam said, being suave, "this may interest you. Rosemary Young did not shoot her brother. She shot a small dog, hid it at once, and by means of the bloodstains and her accomplished lying she has managed to confuse us and delay all pursuit of the criminal—he, of course, had killed both Judge Shively and his son— for more than forty-eight hours. I believe that even she thought that her brother would go on his way. He returned and brutally murdered my daughter."

"You have proof of all this?" Miss MacDonald asked, showing interest but no great astonishment.

"Proof? Yes. Yes, of course—absolute proof."

"You have had the blood analysis made?"

"Not as yet. I've had no time. However, I found the dog's body with a bullet in it out on the desert where she buried it."

"But how do you know that it was Rosemary Young who killed the dog and buried it on the desert?"

"She was seen carrying a large package out there."

"You saw her, yourself?"

"No. Reggie Duefife saw her. He doesn't matter. No one else had reason for killing the dog. What else could she have been taking out there?"

From where I was sitting I couldn't see Rosemary, but I'll bet you Mac could. "Well for cripe's sakes!" he said politely but very disgusted. "Can't a girl carry a package any place anymore without having a dead dog in it? First it was a little dog. Now it's a big package. That fat guy, ugh?"

Adam was always a great hand for keeping his temper before strangers, if he wanted to. I was almost proud of the way he stood up and said, sounding kind of like a martyr king, "I apologize for this ribaldry, Miss MacDonald. Perhaps I should warn you that the general tendency here is one of regarding the most bitter catastrophe as mere drollery. The dog's body is in the kitchen. If you will come with me—"

Brigid spoke fast. "Isn't the fact that I found Twill's body, with a wound below the throat where Rosemary told us that it was, more important than Mayor Oakman's finding the dog?"

"Yes, it is," Miss MacDonald said. "Where is the man's body, Mayor Oakman?"

"He doesn't know," Brigid said. "I found it only this afternoon. He has been trying to make me tell where it is, but I won't. You see, he hates Rosemary and he wants to make trouble for her. He really does. She killed her brother accidentally and is heartbroken over it. But I'm afraid that if I tell where the body is, the Mayor will say it was not an accident and have her tried for murder. He is dictator of Oakman County. He could."

Miss MacDonald asked, "But that shooting was entirely accidental, wasn't it?" and everybody in the room, except Adam and Rosemary, said, "Yes," or, "Sure it was," or something on that order.

In a minute even Ernie said, "Yes," and then Adam said, "I am confident that Rosemary did not shoot her brother. However, if the body is found, proving that her story is true, I shall know that the shooting was accidental, and I shall proffer no charges."

"The body is across the lake in the canoe in the boat-house. I'll swim over and push the canoe across," Brigid said, and dropped her dress off at the door.

Very luckily she was wearing her swimming suit under-neath. Everybody got up, just kind of standing around, though, and some were saying one thing and some anoth-er, and the next thing I knew we were all standing on the front porch and she was splashing in the lake.

"We ought not to have let her," I said. "An errand like that. A child like Brigid."

"Couldn't one of the men go, now, to help her?" Miss MacDonald asked.

We all felt sheepish and acted that way. None of us but Kent could swim. I knew why he didn't offer. I had seen Rosemary's face as she had crossed the room to come out on the porch. She was his girl, and he was staying with her where he belonged.

Miss MacDonald led off and, still sheepish, we all fol-lowed her to the lake shore. The stars looked terrible spar-kling so bright in the sky and the lake.

Adam said to me in a low undertone, "Brigid was unfair. I don't hate that girl. I can't. By the Eternal, I hope Brigid is telling the truth. I hope she has found the body. By the Eternal, I do. But it is impossible. That canoe wasn't on the place until Thursday morning. And, since then— No, it can't be."

He was right, it couldn't be. But, like everything else at Memaloose, it was. After Mac and I had waded out and tak-en the canoe from Brigid and dragged it up on shore, there was no more doubt. Miss MacDonald had a flashlight.

I heard Kent trying to keep Rosemary from coming to look, but she came. She didn't take on. She brushed Twill's hair off his forehead a little and stayed kneeling there only a minute or two before she stood up and leaned against Kent.

"He has killed himself," she said. "I never believed that he would. I never did believe him, never all these years when he threatened to kill himself. But, Kent, he has killed himself."

Adam and I had walked off a little piece. He said, and I thought less of him for hours for saying it, "A different story, now that the body has been found."

31

Kent and Rosemary looked as if they were heading straight for the big car.

Adam said to me, "I happened to put the key in my pocket," and, I guess, felt pretty foolish when they sat down on the community house steps without even glancing at the car.

Miss MacDonald spoke to Brigid, "You found the body in the canoe."

It hadn't sounded like a question, but Brigid answered, saying that she had, shortly after twenty minutes past one that afternoon.

"Now then," Miss MacDonald said, getting a little brisk. "I think we must have the canoe taken into one of the houses. Do you agree with me, Coroner?"

Joe said, "I do," like he was getting married again, but I was pretty sure he hadn't heard the question because, when Ernie and Mac picked the canoe up and started carrying it to the nearest cottage, Joe was all taken aback and would have put a stop to it then and there if I hadn't explained things to him in a hurry. I was glad Miss MacDonald had gone on ahead with Adam.

The boys had to put the canoe down on the parlor floor. Miss MacDonald said, then, that she wouldn't need

anyone now but the coroner. Mac and Ernie could take a
hint and glad to, but Adam stuck around.

Since he was staying, I thought I should to save situ-
ations, if possible, so I sat down just inside the breakfast
nook.

I meant to keep well out of the way and I did for a
while. Joe said that rigor was complete. Miss MacDonald
agreed with him. She asked Joe please not to do something—I don't know what to this day—and then Adam
said, "By the Eternal! A thirty-six Colt's with three shots
fired!"

By the time I got over there, she had snapped the
gun shut and was putting it into a little sack thing she'd
brought with her.

"Three shots!" Adam said. "One for Clyde Shively, one
for the old Judge and the last one for himself. That accounts for the shooting Reggie heard here at noon today."

"He could have heard only the one shot—the last one—
today," I said.

Adam didn't answer me. I guess he thought that I ought
to know that one shot would sound like a bombardment
to Reggie, and I did know it. I was a little surprised that
he'd heard even one.

"Miss MacDonald," Adam said, "did Joe Laud tell you
that Clyde Shively had been shot with a thirty-six Colt's?"

"Yes," she said. "I stopped at Ferras and saw the body—
the two bodies—before I came here."

"Half an hour," Joe said, and I didn't know whether he
was apologizing to Adam or boasting.

I went and sat down again. I hadn't been there but a
few minutes when Miss MacDonald snapped her pocket-
book shut and said, "Now then: If you are willing, May-
or Oakman, and if she is able, I should like to talk with
Rosemary Young."

"If *I'm* willing," Adam said.

"It seems rather cruel, I know. But I haven't much time—"

"You haven't," he said.

She gave up talking to him, and no wonder with him answering back like that, making his simple pronouns sound like personal profanity. Outside he stopped to lock the door. I thought that we'd had enough of disappearing bodies, so I mentioned that any key on the place would unlock any door and, if not, either a hairpin or a button-hook would do fine.

Miss MacDonald said I might have one of my deputies watch the cottage, if I liked, and I understood Adam's use of his pronouns; but I said nothing, beyond calling Mac and Ernie over and asking them if they'd mind keeping an eye on the place.

Kent and Rosemary were still sitting on the community house steps. Miss MacDonald sat down opposite them, and I sat on the step below her, beside Brigid. Joe sat next to Kent, and Adam, after he had lighted the porch light, just kind of stood around. Except for Brigid's looking not very suitable in Mac's Sunday coat—he'd put it on to go to Hay Patch—over her swimming suit, we might have been just any nice group of people sitting on the front porch, anywhere, to keep cool.

Miss MacDonald was asking Rosemary if she felt able to answer a few questions, and Kent was objecting like sixty, saying that questions would have to wait, when Adam burst in:

"Did you kill your brother on Wednesday night, or did you shoot the dog and lie to us?"

The words were hardly out of his mouth before she answered, "I shot the dog and lied to you."

"To help Twill escape," Adam asked, "because you knew that he had killed Clyde Shively and Judge Shively?"

"He didn't kill Judge Shively," she said, and I thought she was on the point of saying something else, but Adam wouldn't give her a chance.

"Who did then? Did you?"

Kent flared up something terrible at this, and Miss MacDonald said—I liked it in her, trying to keep peace— "After all, you don't know that Judge Shively has been killed; do you, Mayor Oakman?"

Adam explained to her then about the Judge's age, and his heat prostrations, and his rheumatism, and his cane, and his one pair of glasses. (Seemed that the old gentleman had misplaced them one day and Adam had found him groping around in his cottage hunting for them. He had another pair at home, he said, but had forgotten to bring them.) All this explaining took so long that everybody got restless. I kept hoping that Miss MacDonald would begin talking and put a stop to it, but she didn't. Even after he had stopped on his own hook, she waited a minute before she said:

"This man you call Reggie, who had the Judge's glasses in his pocket, is the man who said that he heard the shooting here at noon today, isn't he?"

Brigid spoke up, but she sounded very small. "I put the glasses in Reggie's pocket," she said.

"You did?" Miss MacDonald asked, but more as if Brigid had said that she'd eaten her dinner with her fingers, or something like that, "Why?"

"I was tidying Twill's cottage and I found them slipped down beside a chair cushion. I didn't know what to do with them. Reggie was near me with a pocket. I didn't have a pocket. I knew that no one could accuse Reggie of any crime, or possibly suspect him of murder."

"Because he is such a good man, is that what you mean?"

"No," Brigid said, and took it back. "Yes—well, Reggie is good enough, I suppose. You'll know when you meet him. It is difficult to explain. But, for one thing, he is so fat—" The poor kid was doing worse and worse. I was glad to have Adam interrupt, but sorry to hear him getting suave.

"May I suggest," he said, "that we leave this subject of Reggie's appearance and go on to matters of more importance? Rosemary, did you see Twill shoot Clyde Shively in the back?"

"No. Twill told me. He thought that the storm would frighten Betty-Jean so he went to her cottage. She wasn't there. She had come to the community house, but Twill didn't know that, so he went to Judge Shively's cottage looking for her. He found Clyde there, drinking, and they quarreled instantly when Twill asked for Betty-Jean. The large revolver was on the table. Twill was incoherent about what happened, but he said that Clyde Shively threatened him. I think, despite the nature of the wound, that Twill shot in self-defense."

"We are not interested in what you think," Adam said. "We want to hear what you know. This shooting was during the thunderstorm, when all the rest of us were here in the community house, wasn't it?"

"Yes."

"I knew it. And then he shot the old Judge, because he had seen the murder. Where did you and your brother dispose of the Judge's body?"

"We didn't dispose of his body. Twill did not kill Judge Shively."

"He did," Adam said. "Whether you know it or not, he killed the old Judge. And he returned this afternoon and killed Betty-Jean—"

"No," Rosemary protested. "I know that he didn't."

"You can't know it. If you do, how do you know it?"

"I know Twill," she said.

"Ah-h-h," Adam dragged it out, making it sound terrible.

Kent stood up. "Come, Rosemary," he said. "We've had enough of this. Please, Rosemary," he urged.

"So you are in on this, too, are you?" Adam asked.

"Very much in on it," Kent said. "Come, Rosemary. Please!"

"No, Kent," she said to him, and then to the rest of us. "Kent doesn't know anything at all about any of this. I lied to him, just as I did to all of you. I'll try to answer your questions, now. But I can't see how anything I may tell you will help you. You have no reasons for believing anything I say."

Miss MacDonald spoke, and it was high time—she certainly was a great one for holding her tongue. "Until tonight you have been trying to help your brother. Now the circumstances are changed."

"That makes no difference," Adam said. "She still has herself to help and, probably, Kent. And the Everlasting alone knows how many others."

All this time Adam had been standing aloof, very prominently, as if he wouldn't run the risk of associating with any of us, even if he got hoarse from hollering the distance. So, when Miss MacDonald stood up right then and walked over to him, I'd an idea maybe she was going to whisper something in his ear. It was a big relief, for a minute, to see the two of them walking away together. Joe got up and tagged after them, but at a distance. His going left me alone with Rosemary and Kent; so, not wishing to butt in with them I moseyed over to where Brigid had moseyed.

"Well," I said, "it is beginning to look as if, maybe, a little something might be going to get cleared up; isn't it?"

"No," she said. "You and I had the right answers for the wrong questions. I think that now we are getting the wrong answers for the wrong questions."

"What do you mean?" I asked.

"I don't know," she said.

As it turned out, much later, the kid was about half right and half wrong, which wasn't so bad at that early stage of the game.

32

I had hoped that Miss MacDonald might ditch Adam somewhere. But in two or three minutes here they came, her heels clicking very firmly, his languishing, Joe trailing after them. Brigid and I went back to the steps and sat down. Mac and Ernie kind of hovered over, standing about where Adam had been standing, just within earshot.

Miss MacDonald asked Rosemary if she would tell all she knew about what happened on Wednesday.

"Yes," Rosemary said and stopped. "He couldn't have done this," she said, next, "if I hadn't given him the revolver."

"Were you in Clyde Shively's cottage after he was killed?" Miss MacDonald asked.

"No. When Twill and I left the community house on Wednesday afternoon we went to Twill's cottage. He showed me a bullet hole in the wall there and said that he had tried to kill himself a few minutes before and had failed. Then he brought the big revolver out of his pocket and said that he wouldn't fail this time. I took the revolver away from him. I asked him where he had got it. He told me from Clyde Shively and then he told me what I have told you about the shooting."

"Your brother had often attempted suicide?" Miss MacDonald asked.

"Yes. I thought that no one knew it."

"I heard you say that he had." All through this Miss MacDonald was as nice as she could be—not sharp, or smart-aleck, or anything like a detective.

"Twill wasn't insincere," Rosemary answered. "But he was super-sensitive and, perhaps, slightly unstable emotionally—sometimes. Only sometimes. His being so brave, usually, made these bad times worse when they came. He was like a person who is agonizingly ill. He found relief in threatening suicide and, occasionally, in attempting it. I thought that he would never really do it. My only excuse is that several times Twill had tried to kill himself when I wasn't with him to stop him, and he never went through with it. Wednesday afternoon, when I took the big revolver away from him I put it aside. But it was right there where he could have taken it up easily any time while we were making our plans. I didn't doubt his intentions for a moment when he asked me to bring it to him, with his other things, so that he could dispose of it far away from camp somewhere."

"Will you tell us about those plans?" Miss MacDonald asked.

"Yes. At first, there in his cottage, Twill kept saying that trying to escape would be useless because a cripple could be traced so easily. I knew that he was right. And then I saw Funny, his little dog, asleep there in the room and I made the plans.

"I thought that if everyone believed that Twill was dead, it would give us hours, at least, before they began hunting for him. It wasn't very difficult to persuade Twill to try it, though he insisted that I should say he had killed himself. When the time came for me to say that, I couldn't—quite. I couldn't seem to say that I was wholly blameless. I felt so much to blame. I had been so engrossed in my own affairs that I hadn't paid enough attention to Twill for weeks.

And, too, he had wanted to confess, or thought that he wanted to, and I wouldn't let him. This sounds foolishly sentimental, doesn't it? I don't know— It did seem cheap for me to step right out from under all the blame. But perhaps these weren't my reasons. Perhaps I merely thought that the way I told it sounded more irrational—made a better story. Or, perhaps, I didn't think. I can't remember. I'm sorry, none of this matters, does it? If you'd ask me questions, I might not get off and talk too much."

"Will you tell us how your brother got away from the camp?"

"He swam to the east end of the lake and crossed it there. I happened to have on a big rubber coat that I'd put on when I was going to ride in the storm. I wore Twill's clothes over my swimming suit. I tied his brace and his shoes to my bathrobe cord and hung it around my neck. The coat was so large that it concealed them very well. I stuck the revolver in my belt, under my arm. I rode to the east end of the lake and across to meet Twill on the north side.

"We had planned that he should walk the four or five miles to the state highway. The foothills would have hidden him after the first half-mile. Going slowly, he could have walked that far easily. We knew that in Nevada the first passing motorist would give him a ride either to Mesquite Forks or Sackawash, possibly farther, where he could go on by train.

"The high fence had been a screen for me. But when I met Twill I found him discouraged and frightened. Reggie had seen him swimming and Twill was sure that all our plans were ruined. I told him that I'd bring his suit back to camp and spread it on the sagebrush in plain sight outside his cottage, and that everyone would think he had returned to camp after Reggie saw him swimming. He thought that no one would notice it, unless I called attention to it, and that that would make things worse. He was determined, then, to come back and confess. We talked a long time. Finally he made me see how dangerous and desperate our plans were—how foolish running away always is.

"And then, when I agreed with him—we are all like this, I think—he changed his mind. He decided to go. He was hopeful. We made other plans about where we were to meet and how we were to keep in touch with each other in the meantime. I wasn't at all afraid to give him the revolver when I left him there. He was eager to live.

"Uncle Adam was by the gate when I rode into camp. The way he told me to stop, that he wanted to talk with me frightened me. I thought that he knew. So, when I found that he wanted to tell me only that Twill and I must leave Memaloose the next day, I acted foolishly. Cried. I can't understand his thinking that my near hysteria was because of what he said—but he did think so.

"As soon as I could get away from him, I went to my cottage to dress. I had scarcely finished dressing when Kent came. He knew at once that something was wrong. I had to tell him that I was unhappy because of the way Uncle Adam had talked to me. And then Kent insisted upon staying with me, making plans for our future, and for Twill's and Betty-Jean's—"

"However," Adam broke in, "you and your brother had made your own plans for Betty-Jean—"

"No, no!" Rosemary protested. "You can't think that, Uncle Adam. We loved Betty-Jean—"

"I don't know what I think," Adam said. "But I know that this story of yours is a lie from start to finish. In the first place, if you and your brother hadn't known that the old Judge was dead, you could have made none of these plans. Suppose you contend that the Judge was not in his cottage when Twill murdered Clyde Shively. Suppose you say that, since we all knew that the old gentleman was planning to surprise us with his son's presence, none of us would go to the cottage until neither of them appeared for dinner. You cannot say that you didn't know the old Judge himself would return to his cottage, shortly, and give the alarm at once when he found his son murdered."

Rosemary said, "Judge Shively had left camp before the storm."

"By the Eternal! That caps the climax. Left camp, you say? Without his glasses, without his cane, without his clothes—for that matter? Do you think that there is no end to our credulity. Lies—lies—"

For once Miss MacDonald stirred herself to slip in a few words edgewise. "I wonder, Mayor Oakman, if you will allow Miss Young to go on with her story? Later we shall take up the question of Judge Shively's leaving camp." She turned to Rosemary, "You were saying—"

"That Twill never, never would kill Betty-Jean. No one can believe that. Even Uncle Adam doesn't really believe it. His killing Clyde Shively was a man's murder—if you will. He had taunted Twill for being a cripple and for daring to love Betty-Jean. Twill went mad. Clyde Shively was drunk. He threatened Twill. I think that Twill shot in self-defense. But, if he didn't, he shot in fury—a man and a drunken wretch. If Uncle Adam hadn't disliked us both, as he did, I'd have begged Twill to stay and stand trial. Anywhere in the world but right here, in this county, I'd have begged Twill to stay."

"Easy talk, now," Adam said. "Big talk. But you wouldn't. If he had stayed, he'd have had as fair a trial here as he could have had in any man's country. We haven't much use for cowards, though, who allow innocent persons to suffer for their crimes."

"You won't believe me," Rosemary said. "But, after I had finally persuaded Kent to go to the community house,

I realized for the first time that some innocent person might be accused. I thought of it because, after Kent had gone, I decided to wait until I knew that he would be with others before I fired the shot. And then I thought that since I wanted to protect Kent, I should want to protect everyone—that I must wait until I knew that you'd all be together for dinner just before eight o'clock."

"You're right," Adam said. "I don't believe you. You didn't wait."

"Possibly you are right," Rosemary answered. "Possibly my reasons for even that short delay were fear when the time came to test my plans and—a very little—my horror of killing anything, even Funny. And of course I didn't wait. I knew that I didn't dare wait.

"I had gone to Twill's cottage and lowered the bed to get the pillow. Twill and I had shut Funny in the kitchen. He always ran and barked on the shore when Twill was swimming. I carried Funny to the pillow and shot him. It seemed not to hurt him. One minute he was alive and then he was dead.

"I had hoped that when the shot was heard people would think it was a firecracker. I had hoped to be able to go to the community house and tell what had happened. I had counted on that much time. But, almost at once, I heard footsteps coming along the walk. I thought that ever so many people were coming to find out about the shooting. I picked Funny up in my arms before I carried him on the pillow to the refrigerator. Then I put the pillow on the floor and ran outside.

"As I ran I tried to revise the other plans I had made about what I should do and say. But when I got outside, I didn't act as I'd planned and my words wouldn't come right. It was easier than I'd thought it could be. All my emotions were true. Only my words were lies. I could allow the shock and the terror that I'd been hiding for hours to come out, insanely. It seemed to that I was insane. I wondered whether I should recover—"

"You had no cause for alarm as to that," Adam said. "You were sufficiently recovered, by the following day, to look me straight in the eye and lie with a proficiency I have never heard equaled by either man or woman. Unless it was by yourself during our later conversation on the subject."

Rosemary said, "It was necessary, then, for you to believe that I was sane."

"I can't understand," Miss MacDonald said, surprising me by speaking, and amazing me because I thought that detectives never admitted not understanding anything, "how you planned to account for the absence of your brother's body."

"I knew that I couldn't," Rosemary answered. "So I didn't try. I hoped for confusion and delay—"

"And got them, by the Everlasting!" Adam said, adding: "But they are likely to be expensive, young woman. Did you ever think of that? You got what you wanted. But in this world we usually pay for what we get."

"I know," Rosemary said. "I thought that I was willing to pay."

33

"But now you've changed your mind?" Adam asked.

"Of course I have. I'd act the same way again, but I hate paying. When Kent was in that hot jail—"

"You didn't care one good red cent. I told you how hot it was, how dangerous—"

"I cared. Kent wasn't my responsibility. Twill was. He always has been. Have you any more questions to ask me, Miss MacDonald?"

"A few more, I'm afraid. You buried the dog's body on the desert?"

"Yes. I took it out there Thursday morning. I could find nothing but a big cooking-spoon to dig with. The handle snapped almost at once. I thought that this didn't matter, because when I had covered the grave over and put some rocks about, I couldn't notice it at all. Footprints don't show on these rocky deserts. I rode out there again this morning; but I hadn't left any landmarks and I couldn't find the place. I didn't dismount to look. I thought that much at least was safe from discovery. I can't understand how the grave was found. I'm sorry. This doesn't matter, of course."

"It does not," Adam said. "Get on to your tale about Judge Shively's leaving camp before the storm."

The way he said that it sounded terrible. I was glad when Rosemary showed more spunk and answered, "Why should I try to help, if you don't believe anything I say?"

I thought that Miss MacDonald would make peace again by telling Rosemary that she believed her word for word. To my horror, she asked another question, and not quite so pleasantly, either.

"Do you know, positively, that Judge Shively left the camp before the storm?"

"No, I don't," Rosemary answered. "I know that Clyde Shively told Twill that the tourists who had brought him— Clyde Shively, that is—to camp had returned to bring him a piece of luggage that he had forgotten in their car. And that the Judge had decided to ride into Ferras with them."

"And that is a likely story, isn't it?" Adam said. "What about his clothes? What about his glasses?"

"It is possible," Rosemary answered, "that Clyde Shively may have brought some extra things of his father's with him. He might easily have brought the extra glasses. I've wondered, too, if these tourists might have kidnaped the Judge, or—"

"Worse and worse," Adam said. "You're getting in too deep, now."

"No," Rosemary said. "It has to be thought out. The wind lasted at least ten minutes, I'm sure, before the rain came. Betty-Jean said that she was afraid of the wind, so I think it was during that time that she telephoned to the Judge. We know that the Judge was planning to surprise us all by bringing his son to the dinner party. He might have wanted to go to Ferras to get balloons, or snappers, or something he thought would add to the gaiety of the party. He may have planned to pay the tourists to bring him back to camp. When the cloudburst came, the car couldn't return. It seems unlikely that the Judge would simply ride away with the tourists. Something must have happened. Kidnaping doesn't seem probable. None of this seems very probable. But something of the sort is possible. And nothing is as impossible as thinking that the Judge has simply vanished."

Adam admitted, I liked it in him, "If a car was here during the windstorm and before the rain began, the Judge could have gone away in it, either dead or alive."

Brigid spoke up. "That Clyde Shively was a thorough rotter," she said. "Probably he killed his father and got these persons in the car to take the body away."

"Or," Adam said, "possibly Rosemary Young and her brother paid these people to take the body away."

"Rosemary was in the community house from before the storm started until it had almost cleared," Brigid said, adding, very saucy: "And shouldn't you think that if they were sending one body away, they'd send both bodies? Or should you—think?"

I thought it was high time Miss MacDonald said something. Not she. She sat there listening so hard you could almost hear her doing it.

"On the other hand," Adam answered Brigid's remarks, "if Clyde Shively killed his father, and a car was leaving here, why should he send the body away and stay here himself?"

"Thousands of reasons," Brigid answered, and if she hadn't been talking too much I might have been a little proud of her. "If he came here planning to kill his father—and his bringing the revolver points to that—he probably didn't come with tourists at all. He probably came with persons who were helping him. He stayed here to tell us, as he told Twill, that his father had gone to Ferras with some tourists. Later, he'd write notes to be found here and there, demanding ransom money. Later still, he'd be the one to carry the ransom money to the kidnapers. Probably even then he would have returned here, freeing himself of all blame, before he rejoined his accomplices weeks later."

Joe said, "Yeah, but why would he have to rejoin them at all?" I don't know, but it seems to me, yet, that Joe was right about that.

Mac said, "A high power car could have made it around the mountain, easy, after the wind began but before the cloudburst. But if he'd used his gun, would you think he'd be sitting with it there on the table? Come to think of it, wouldn't somebody have heard the shot, any time except when it was thundering?"

"There are ways of killing besides shooting," Brigid said, and Adam said, "There are—indeed."

Maybe Miss MacDonald was trying only to change a sad subject, but she sounded as if she was after something when she asked Rosemary: "Did your brother tell you to say that you saw Judge Shively and his son alive together at four o'clock?"

Rosemary waited so long to answer that when she finally said, "Yes," it sounded too important.

"Do you know why he asked you to say that?"

"No, I don't. I thought at the time that he must have some reason for it. But we were so hurried, so frightened—"

"He had a very good reason for it," Adam interrupted, and waited for somebody to ask him what the reason was. Nobody did so. Miss MacDonald went on talking to Rosemary.

"After Wednesday, did you ride again to the place where you had left your brother, across the lake?"

"I wanted to," Rosemary answered, "but I didn't. I was afraid that I might be seen going there. I should have gone. That was another of my mistakes."

"Four o'clock," Adam said, telling whether he was asked to or not. "After the storm was over. Twill Young killed both Judge Shively and Clyde Shively. If they were seen alive at four o'clock he would have an alibi, of sorts, for himself."

Joe said, "What did he kill himself for, then, if he'd set his alibi?"

To this day I think that Miss MacDonald spoke more from surprise at Joe—she being unacquainted with him—than from any wish to give us information. "But, Coroner," she said, "you know that Twill Young was not a suicide, that he was murdered there in the canoe. I thought we were agreed on that."

"What's that?" Adam asked, and kept asking, like Reggie, over and over. "What's that? What's that?"

Joe started explaining. "He didn't kill himself, because no man can shoot himself in the back—"

"He was shot below the throat," Brigid said. "I saw it "

"The upper lobe of the left lung," Miss MacDonald said.

Joe hadn't stopped talking, but I'd stopped listening for a minute. "So you see," Joe was going on, "he couldn't shoot himself twice, once in the back and once in the lung—let alone kill himself twice. Once, yes. Twice, no."

Adam began saying "Twice?" just the way he had been saying, "What's that?" I couldn't blame him. I was so mixed up myself that I went clear off thinking about the pearl-handled revolver that had been shot twice, while Miss MacDonald was explaining, much better than Joe had explained, that Twill had been shot twice—once in the back and once in the lungs.

"Incredible," Adam said, adding. "Impossible."

"Suicide is impossible," Miss MacDonald said. "The nature of the wounds and the position of the body positively preclude suicide."

"But the gun was right there in the canoe," Adam said.

"Yes," she said. "He was killed in the canoe. The revolver was put under his body after the murder."

Adam said, "Then two persons were murdered here this afternoon?"

"Yes," Miss MacDonald said.

Adam didn't say anything more. Nobody said anything. We were all stunned dumb. I'll bet you that even Mrs. Duefife wouldn't have said anything if she had been there.

Kent and Rosemary got up and went to the big car and sat in it. If Kent had been afraid that Miss MacDonald was going on into what might have been called the gory details concerning the canoe, he needn't have worried. It was almost unwomanly the way that Scotch-Irish detective always stopped talking long before it was necessary. Finally who should take a notion to break the silence but Joe Laud, remarking:

"According to my count that makes four.

"Murders," he volunteered, when nobody asked him what he was counting. "Four murders. Two here on Wednesday. Two here this afternoon. Four murders. No suicides. Two by two. I mean, if you think of it that way, that's what you think. That everybody on this place is getting murdered two by two. Or in pairs. It ought to be put a stop to. It looks awful," he said, and added: "Present company always excepted. Not counting the dog. He makes five."

I couldn't have been glad, but I wasn't sorry when the phone bell started ringing right then. I got up and went in to answer it, taking hold of Brigid on my way and kind of drawing her along with me.

"Brigid, honey," I whispered, when I'd got her inside the room, "whatever you do stick to your story about a man, two horses and a hammer."

"I will not," she said, backing off like I was contaminating. "Not now. But what did I tell you?"

"When? Which time?" I asked. "You mean about the extra luggage?"

"No. I told you that we were getting the wrong answers to the wrong questions. I said that things were not getting cleared up; didn't I?"

"Yes, but how do you know?" I said.

"I don't know," she said. "But I think Miss MacDonald does," and went scooting outside again before I stop her.

34

The phone was Shorty of course. I told him what to tell the drummer. After that I sat there alone deducing and deducing for quite a while.

A lot of things I hadn't understood very well began to shape into sense, but that didn't make me feel any better. I understood why Brigid had been carrying on the way she had, but I doubted like thunder that anybody else would understand. It looked to me like she had done a terrible amount of good lying at a terrible bad time. I found myself getting scared. Being scared made me mad, and being mad made me more scared. I thought about O'Dell, gallyhooting around back East drinking tea with carefree editors. I decided that I'd just let that young man in on the fact that his only daughter had bitten off from here to hades more than I knew how to chew.

I disguised the wording of my wire by calling Brigid one of the hundred or so nicknames that her papa calls her in private. It seemed, at first, that I'd picked the wrong name because when Curly Merts—the telegrapher operator at the depot—read the wire back to me over the phone: ("Simon Legree accused of four murders and two robberies. Come pronto. Wire advice. Jefferson Davis Johnson.") what did Curly up and say, but, "O. K., Little Eva."

Come to find out, it didn't matter, though, because
Curly thought I meant Adam by "Simon Legree." I was
glad to leave it at that, and I went outside again feeling
some better and a little smart on account of having added
the robberies to make it sound stronger.

Just as I'd feared, Miss MacDonald had managed to get
Brigid alone with her on the porch and was leading her on
to talk too much. Kent and Rosemary were still in the big
car, and Joe—it was just like him—was there too, sitting
in the back seat. Adam was with Mac and Ernie, milling
around in front of the cottage where Twill's body was. I
sized it up that I wasn't wanted on the porch, but I wanted
to be there, so I sat down easy trying to look absent.

Brigid was telling Miss MacDonald what had gone on
in the community house during that Wednesday afternoon
before the trouble started, and Miss MacDonald was dis-
playing quite a bit of housekeeping curiosity about there
being only one pineapple to make the pudding and it getting eaten, when Adam started hollering at me. He had
hollered nine or ten times before Miss MacDonald told me
that Mayor Oakman was calling me.

I hate being hollered at. I wanted to be nice to Adam,
but I couldn't help asking him, when he came to meet me,
why he had to be always hollering at me all the time.

"During the entire course of my wretched and harassed
life," he said, "I have never once hollered at you. Please let
that pass. I shall consider that you have flatly contradicted
me, as usual, and get on with what I have to say.

"Two persons were murdered here today. Twill shot
Clyde Shively. We believe, because there is nothing else
to believe, that the old Judge was either taken away from
camp or left on his own accord before the cloudburst on
Wednesday afternoon. Now, if Twill did return to camp
and murder Betty-Jean—"

"I don't believe he did, Adam," I said. "Do you?"

"No, damn it," he said. "I don't. I never have."

"You said you believed it. You said it I don't know how many times to everybody."

"What else was there to think? I had to believe it. I couldn't allow my senseless intuitions to rule my reason, could I? Where was I? What was I talking about when you contradicted me?"

"I didn't contradict you," I said. "I don't know what you were talking about, but I think you were getting ready to talk about who murdered Twill, if he did kill Betty-Jean, which you are pretty certain he didn't—but I don't know."

"Very well," he said, like something—I don't know what—was all settled. "Do you know why none of us took any action, whatever, today when Brigid O'Dell told us of seeing a man here in camp with horses?"

"No," I said.

"I presume," he said, "that it was because we knew she could not have seen Clyde Shively. But, as someone suggested, she could have seen a man who resembled Clyde Shively."

"No," I said. "I guess she didn't."

I knew that the time had come to make a clean breast of it to Adam. I thought that I might be going to need his help for Brigid before long. But I wanted to tell him in a nice way and I couldn't think of a nice way.

"You mean," he said, "that her entire story was a lie? That she saw no one here? I've had that feeling from the first. However, spoiled and precocious as she is, I think that she wouldn't lie for the simple love of lying. That she would need some real or fancied necessity—"

"Yes, you bet," I said, jumping at the chance to agree with him. "She had a fine necessity. She saw you—"

"Saw who?" he said.

"You," I said, and was going on to explain but he had stopped and had sat down on the stoop of the cottage there.

When I sat down beside him, "I? Me?" he said, and finding that neither of them suited, he began rolling his head in his hands and sounding exactly like Rimrock. "Insane. Riding two horses and leading a hammer. No. I'm insane. She's insane. You're insane—"

I couldn't let that go on. I decided that I'd have to tell him the facts and hope against hope that he wouldn't ask me how I'd come by them. They were correct, as it was proved afterward; but I had an evil foreboding of how he'd act if he knew that I was giving him mere deductions right then.

"Listen here, Adam," I said. "When Brigid got back to camp this afternoon she saw the canoe—"

"The canoe?"

"Yes, the canoe floating on the lake with something in it. She put on her swimming suit and swam out to it, the poor kid. It must have been a sickening shock to her, finding Twill's body there like—well, like it was, you know. How she screwed up her pluck to push the canoe back to the boathouse landing and drag it into the boathouse as far as she could, I can't figure. But she did. And then she phoned for me to come and bring Kent—"

"I've been meaning all day to ask you," he interrupted, "by whose orders and by what right you took Kent out of jail."

"Oh, well," I said, but very weakly, I'm afraid, "if that's the way you feel about it, to hades with the job."

"Good boy, Jeff," he said. "Go on. Go on. Can't you stick to your subject? Brigid telephoned to you—"

"But you got the word first. So, when she ran out to meet Kent and me she saw you coming instead. Like sixty. She thought that she daren't tell you about finding the body. She feared you'd make trouble for Rosemary.

"So to avoid all other trouble, and give her time to be alone with Kent and see about disposing of the body, she did the only sensible thing to do—she just up and lost consciousness until she heard that Doc Sprague was coming. Then she had to lose her memory.

"No, but she was doing her level best," I said, in answer to what Adam said then. I can't be repeating all the interruptions he made while I was giving him these facts. It wouldn't do. He didn't mean most of them, so I'll omit them all.

"She is a good girl," I said. "She was trying only to do good. I suppose you'd like it better if she tattled all the time the way Reggie does? You hate people who stick up for their friends?

"Of course little Betty-Jean was her friend," I said. "And when the terrible news came about her, Brigid nearly went crazy. I know because I saw her.

"She did not," I said, answering him again. "But one of the reasons Brigid nearly went crazy was because she did wonder, just for a minute or two in there, if Rosemary—well, had done just right about everything.

"I know some things without being told," I said. "And, maybe, I was wondering something the same myself. But as soon as Rosemary walked in, and we could look at her, and hear her talking, Brigid and I both knew that we had wronged her something terrible. And Brigid went back, stronger than ever because she'd been unjust to Rosemary, to trying to help her.

"No," I said, answering him. "The next thing was that Kent, unthinkingly of course, began questioning Rosemary out in public about her not telling that she had been for a ride that morning. Brigid took a notion—the poor kid was so upset—that Kent was throwing off on Rosemary. Brigid has always thought a lot of Kent. So she decided that if she couldn't count on him she couldn't count on anybody and she made up her mind right then to go it alone.

"She did not," I said, again answering him. "But she may have had some childish notion that now, since things had got so terribly bad, she shouldn't ask anybody, even me, to lend a hand—implicating themselves and all that. It would be just exactly like her.

"That's not true," I interrupted. "She gave it back to you, didn't she? I told her myself that the roll of money was on the kitchen table. She borrowed a little of it, just the same as she borrowed the drummer's car. She had to, so that she could come over here tonight to get in touch with the Killaky boys and pay them to take the body away somewhere. She knew she'd be too noticeable driving a strange car into Nameless, so she had to run the chance of phoning them from here.

"It was not," I said, when he got through. "And what would she swim in but her swimming suit. She had her dress on over it, didn't she?"

"Leaving the matter of her costume," he said, "which, by the way, I did not mention. Have you finished your story?"

"No," I said, trying to think of something else to say.

"Exactly as I thought," he said. "I have been patient. I have listened, quietly, to this endless rigmarole, only to find that there is and can be no explanation for that fantastic, unnecessary story that she told of seeing Clyde Shively, alive, riding here on the place, leading a horse, carrying a hammer—"

"Hold on," I said. "Unnecessary? You were fixing to send Rosemary to jail because she was the only person on the place who could ride the only horse on the place. One more horse was an absolute necessity. Brigid put it in, and then she put in the other horse, the man and the hammer for good measure. I guess she thought she ought to. She's nice that way."

Adam got right up and began leaving me. There was something about his gait—kind of a cross between a dog

trot and a hippety-hop—that I mistrusted. It was too spry.
He was up to something, I knew; so I followed him as fast
as I could.

He stopped in front of the community house where
Rosemary, Kent and Joe were still sitting in the big car, to
ask where Miss MacDonald was.

Joe said he thought she'd left camp. Kent said that she
and Brigid had gone into the community house, so we
went in and located them in the kitchen.

As we had walked across the living room I'd heard Brigid saying, "Yes, I am sure, Miss MacDonald. I closed the
gate when I came into camp, and I didn't open it later. I
suppose any gate might possibly swing open by itself, but
there wasn't any wind." So it was some discouraging, when
we got to the kitchen, to find both ladies talking about
food again.

Adam said, behind his hand to me, "Women! Cooking
recipes!" But I guess Miss MacDonald's hearing was sharp,
too, for she spoke right up:

"I was wondering, Mayor Oakman, why you insisted
that your daughter should give such a long, elaborate dinner for an invalid who, as I understand it, had a train trip
ahead of him?"

"Apparently," Adam said, "your experience with slight
heat indispositions has been limited. As for the menu,
I prefer simplicity in all things. I merely requested my
daughter to give a small dinner in honor of our guest.
Nothing had been done for him in the way of hospitality
since he came to camp. Now, if I may, I should like to
present to you some important evidence that has just now
been brought to my attention."

"Yes?" Miss MacDonald said, sounding exactly as if
she was hurriedly answering a noisy telephone on a busy
morning.

"I presume you have been told," Adam said, "that a man was seen here this afternoon, riding a horse, leading another horse—"

Brigid spoke up, not saucy, just imparting information. "I've told Miss MacDonald that I lied about all that," she said.

"I am sorry—" Adam began; to this day I don't know what he would have said if Miss MacDonald hadn't interrupted.

"That's quite all right. Don't apologize—"

"I was not apologizing," Adam said, and kind of paused to pick his words, so Miss MacDonald didn't exactly interrupt when she asked:

"Does the gate out there often swing open by itself?"

"I don't know. Possibly, if it has been carelessly closed."

Brigid was frowning at me and motioning toward the door with her head. She knew as well as I did that no power could get Adam away from there if he didn't want to go. I did the best I could. I went outside and sat down on the front steps making myself a good excuse for him to come out if he wanted to. But when he came he was tagging Miss MacDonald and Brigid.

"Where are you going, Adam?" I said, hoping to detain him; but he didn't answer.

Brigid told me that they were going to Judge Shively's cottage. I thought she was hinting for me to come with them and take care of Adam; and I might have gone, though I didn't much want to, if the phone hadn't begun ringing again.

It was Shorty. Seemed the drummer hadn't had his shirt on for quite a while, and Shorty was at his wit's end. He offered to let me talk to the drummer, but I didn't wish to. I went outside again and sat down on the steps.

In about fifteen or twenty minutes, more or less, Miss MacDonald, Brigid and Adam came along, walking rapidly.

I hated stopping them to mention the drummer's car, but
Shorty had been my friend for thirty years.

Adam said by the Eternal this drummer's car had been
haunting him like an evil echo for hours and hours and
what about it anyway.

I told him again, and as nice as I knew how, that Brigid
had asked Shorty, and then borrowed the car. But no, he
had to start another furor.

Forgetting all his afternoon promises about never letting the dear little girl out of his sight again, he began by
ordering Brigid to drive that car straight back to the hotel
then and there. I said I wouldn't have that. Brigid said
never mind she wouldn't think of such a thing, and offered
as an excuse that she was afraid. Maybe she shouldn't have
said that, since we all knew better. But I guess she thought
that one excuse was as good as another, as Joe said about
his different wives.

I offered to go with Brigid. Adam told me to stop inter-
fering and called Joe over from the big car and ordered
him to drive the drummer's car back to Ferras and then to
return at once to Memaloose with the hearse for the body.

Joe said he couldn't drive the drummer's car and yawned,
covering it very politely with his fingers.

Adam said Brigid could do the driving. Joe said not
with him she couldn't, because it was against his principles; adding that every man ought to have some principles,
and that he wouldn't bring the hearse around Tumboldt at
night, anyhow, even if he or others didn't have any.

Brigid said, "Ouch, Joe!"

Joe said, "Pardon me." He had stepped on Brigid's foot
while leaving.

Miss MacDonald said that she'd be through with her
work there at camp very soon and that then she'd drive
the car back to the Ferras Hotel. Adam said that was nonsense. She said not at all, that she was going to spend the

266 KAY CLEAVER STRAHAN

night in Ferras so that she could make an early start for San Francisco (she called it that because she lived there) by plane in the morning. So, if someone would direct her to Twill Young's cottage, she would go on with her work.

I jumped up in a hurry and offered to take her there. Adam hadn't got much said except, "By the Eternal!" when we started out. But his voice came booming after us objecting to everything: to her spending the night in Ferras; to her going to 'Frisco; to her accepting the job in the first place; to her leaving it now, and several other things.

Apologizing for your friends is terrible, but finally I had to. "Mayor Oakman," I said, "is all upset. He's not at himself. You know—what he has been through today, and all."

"Surely," she said. "I understand. But I hope he won't be troublesome about my leaving."

"No, no," I said. "Not the Mayor. As soon as he thinks it over, he'll want you to do whatever you want to do. He's the greatest one you ever saw," I told her, "for wanting other people to do as they please."

"Really?" she said, as she unlocked Twill's cottage with a key of her own. "Thank you," she said next, I'm not sure what for, and then, "You needn't wait."

I went back to the community house and sat down beside Adam on the steps. "I'm afraid," I said to him, "that I'm repeating something I'm not supposed to. But I was asked, in my capacity as sheriff, to assist in getting everybody away from here without any fuss—just making it appear a matter of impulse. You see, as long as this big crowd sticks here, a certain person won't have a chance in the world of catching the criminal."

"Irreproachable logic," he said. "If we all leave Memaloose, and the criminals—this is not the work of one person, single-handed—should return for any reason, they could come and go without any fuss and impulsively, as you say."

I never claimed to be a good liar, but I was very humiliated at finding myself such a bad one. "I gave you credit for gumption enough to know that Mac and Ernie and I are staying here," I said.

"If you boys stay, I stay," he said.

I was all tired out. I thought that Adam and I both would be better off if we had our night's rest. "The only thing is," I said, "that I figured she wanted a chance to consult you alone over in the hotel where there'd be no fear of eavesdroppers. All this talk about leaving for 'Frisco early tomorrow," I said, "could be done to throw others off the scent."

After saying a few words, Adam went on, "There's the woman of it for you! Why couldn't she have told me this, frankly, herself? It serves me right for engaging her. I knew better. Watch me spike her guns." (If I'd known that these were the last remarks Adam was going to make to me for months to come, I might have treasured them more; or, again, I might not have.)

I watched the gun-spiking. It went off fine, if I do say it myself. I'll bet you no lady was ever more surprised than Miss MacDonald was when she came back before long fearing trouble and found, instead, the folks all ready and waiting to go. Adam, Kent, Rosemary and Joe went in the big car. Brigid and Miss MacDonald followed in the drummer's car. Mac and Ernie and I stayed at Memaloose. The boys went to a cottage, but I dozed in the community house hoping to hear from O'Dell.

It seems funny that even being waked up out of a sound sleep would make me forget entirely that he was crazy, but it did. Curly had to read the message to me four or five times before I could believe my ears. What O'Dell, the doggone fool, had wired in answer to my desperation was as follows:

PLEASE TENDER SIMON LEGREE MY
HEARTIEST CONGRATULATIONS.
FONDLY YOURS, ELIZA AND THE
INFANT ON THE ICE.

35

Joe brought the hearse over again about eight o'clock the following morning. He said that Kent had come with him to take Acrasia to Hay Patch, but had ridden her right off without waiting to say so much as "Good morning" to the boys and me. Joe said, too, that Miss MacDonald, Brigid and Adam had stayed in Ferras all night and that Adam and Miss MacDonald had left at six a.m. that morning by aeroplane for parts unknown. I guess nobody could blame me for thinking that Joe had everything all wrong as usual.

The boys and I let Joe and his hearse get a good long head start and then we left. Joe had brought over a new padlock for the gate; so Mac locked it when we had driven out and said, when he got in my car again:

"After death the doctor," adding, "What I'd like to know is why in blue blazes that gate wasn't kept locked all the time."

"Being so well up on your adages," I told him, "you should remember the one about no use in locking the barn door after the horse has fled. That's what we all thought until yesterday evening."

"Not me," Mac said. "I didn't think the horse had fled. I thought he was shot. I thought sure this Twill guy had bumped off both the Shivelys and that the pretty girl had killed him by accident like she told us."

Ernie spoke. "Sure," he said. "That's what I think yet. I mean, part of it is what I think yet."

"Yeah, but you can't," Mac argued.

"I ain't so sure she shot that dog," Ernie said.

"Who do you think did shoot it, then?" Mac asked. "It was shot all right. I saw it myself."

"I don't know who shot it"—Ernie gave me kind of a sidewise glance—"but Oakman—well, he found it. Seemed that there was something about Oakman's stepping into his own footprints, or somebody else's out by the gate that night. I don't know."

"But the pretty girl confessed right out to shooting the dog," Mac said.

"I know," Ernie said. "She confessed to shooting her brother, too. Oakman's got a good-sized foot on him. But, speaking of confessing. Some women are great hands for it. My wife, Ellie, is. She'll confess to everything the kids do, from taking money out of my pants pockets to heaving rocks through the neighbors' windows."

"The pretty girl ain't even married," Mac pointed out, some shocked sounding.

"I heard she was going to be," Ernie said.

"What's he getting at, do you know, Jeff?" Mac asked.

"I don't think he knows," I said.

Mac asked, "Do you, Ernie?"

Ernie didn't answer.

"Kent was locked up in jail, wasn't he?" Mac kept it, insisting.

"What are you asking me for?" Ernie said.

"I wasn't," Mac said. "I was asking Jeff."

"What are you asking him for?" Ernie said.

Mac gave up at that, of course. I was glad of it. I was sick of the whole subject. Ernie had talked himself out for a month, so nothing much more was said. In town I dropped the boys off at their places and went on to the hotel.

Bert Thalen, the day clerk, came to the door to meet me bursting with bad news.

"Oakman and the lady detective skipped out by plane this morning," he said. "Some think he's paying plenty for the ride. Good-looking dame, at that."

I hate a man who can't stand up for his friends. And, to make it official, I told him that I knew for a fact that they had gone to track down the criminals and that arrests would be made within twenty-four hours.

"Awful disgraceful, ain't it?" Bert said. "Joe's got three bodies over to his place now. Some say there's several others missing. Joe won't have room for them, if they find them. Did you ever hear of such a thing? You can't blame Brigid O'Dell for being scared to go on to Hay Patch. She's stopping here. Locked in room three. She said to tell you. Some think that Oakman might—"

I'd been counting ten. If I'd counted twenty I'll bet I'd have knocked him for a goal. But Bert is a nice fellow, in his way, so I just gave him some advice, for his own good, and went on upstairs to Brigid's room.

She opened the door looking terrible but kind of cute in bright blue pajamas and holding a yellow paper in her hand.

"St. Dennis is intuitive," she said, while she was locking the door again. "I got this from him this morning. I wouldn't go down to answer the telephone so Curly brought it over to me from the station. Curly is sweet."

I took the paper and read, written in pencil:

"Pineapple Supreme.
"Freckles.
"Black teeth."

I found me a chair to sit down.

"You're reading the wrong side," she said. "That's my list. Clues. New ones. Turn it over."

I turned it over and read, *Crambe repetita.* I took Latin in high school. I thought I'd forgotten the doggone stuff. But I hadn't, though right then I wished I had.

After a while, noting that she was still talking, I said, "What?"

"'What?'" she said, very vexed. "I knew you weren't listening. How much did you hear? Where did you leave off listening?"

"At your papa's message. At the cabbage," I said, adding, "Warmed over."

"No," she said. "It means any unnecessary repetition. I just told you. St. Dennis and I use it instead of saying that we are fond of each other. He has sensed that something is wrong and has sent me this to remind me that he likes me and is standing by if I need him. And I do." To my horror she began crying a little. "I do need him. I want terribly to send him a telegram saying that I have a slight earache."

"Oh, dear me!" I said, sounding exactly like Reggie and not caring. "What next? What next? When did it start aching, honey?"

"It doesn't ache," she said. "But he'd come by plane. He's been silly about my ears ever since that mastoid performance."

"I should hope so," I said. "I'll run right down and get the wire off for you."

"Don't you dare! I wouldn't worry him like that for anything. But I'll tell you something I do want you to do for me, Jeff. I sneaked in here last night, telling only Kent and Rosemary. So if you'll find that revolting, hypocritical, quarrelsome old—"

"Adam left town early this morning," I told her. "He went with Miss MacDonald in the plane."

She stopped crying with a scared expression. "But why on earth? She knew that he had a hand in all this. Is she trying to set some trap for him? But he wouldn't walk into it, or—"

"Trap?" I said, sounding this time like a frog.

"Don't look that way, Jeff," she said. "I'm sorry. I suppose that no one could believe, really, that Mayor Oakman murdered anyone—that is, on purpose. But I do think that he had some slick plan and that it all got away from him and that these terrible things happened instead. I'm sure Miss MacDonald thinks so too."

"Did she tell you that? When you were riding over here together last night?"

"Not she. She doesn't tell. She asks. But all the same—"

"Crazy as hades," I said, with relief.

"I am not. Coming back from Judge Shively's cottage last night she managed to make Mayor Oakman confess that he had written to the Judge, without letting any of us know, and asked him to come to Memaloose."

"That's not a confession," I said. "That's an invitation."

"All the same, he hated admitting it. And he hated admitting that he had told the Judge that Betty-Jean was in love with a worthless, crippled, penniless boy, younger than she was, and had asked the old gentleman to come and see whether he could break off the affair."

"Adam was never a great one for telling about his little dodges," I said.

"You don't understand," she said. "I think that Miss MacDonald was making a connection between the Judge's coming here and his leaving."

"At that," I said, "there was a connection. There always is. If a visitor comes to a place he generally goes. Coming, going. To and fro."

"Look at it this way, Jeff," she said. "Do you mind? Early Wednesday morning, say, before anything had happened, the cloudburst, the murder, the disappearances, the one thing that made Wednesday different from other days at Memaloose was that Judge Shively was planning to leave there that evening."

"Murdering practically everybody on the place wouldn't detain the old gentleman," I said, adding: "Anyway, it didn't."

"No," she said. "It didn't. He has gone—somewhere."

"With tourists," I said. "Riding off at leisure before any of the trouble could have started."

"If those tourists, as you call them, came to return a piece of luggage to Clyde Shively—then where is that extra piece of luggage?"

More to change the subject than anything else, I asked: "What did you and Miss MacDonald and Adam find when you were in the old Judge's cottage last night?"

"Mayor Oakman and I weren't in it," she said. "When we got to the front door, Miss MacDonald asked if we'd mind letting her go in alone, first, for a few minutes. Even he could scarcely refuse that, though it made him furious. He and I stayed outside. When she finally came out she said that she wanted to go on to Twill's cottage. But before she spoke to us, she heard him raving and roaring at me, and I'm glad of it.

"No. Nothing that mattered at all," she said, answering my questions. "I considered him maniacal, as I told him, just before I put my fingers in my ears. He was holding my wrists and shouting at me when Miss MacDonald came out of the cottage. He didn't see her and I didn't warn him. I was glad to have her get an impression of the handsome Mayor's more informal manners. Now don't start scolding. Come on. We're going to Memaloose."

"Hay Patch," I corrected her.

"Memaloose."

"Adam's not at Hay Patch now," I told her, thinking she had forgotten.

"See that door?" she said.

I did. It was the size of a door, square in front of me, and it led into the next room.

"I lay there on that dirty carpet last night," she said, "with my ear to that crack underneath for an hour or more. Miss MacDonald and Mayor Oakman were talking in that room. I couldn't hear anything that she said, but of course he roared now and then. The first thing that I heard him say was, 'Pineapple Supreme!' He said it as if he were going to be sick, right there."

"She shouldn't have brought up the subject of cooking recipes," I said.

"Miss MacDonald is not silly. If she seemed so, she did it on purpose. I rather thought she overdid it—but maybe not. He'd be easier to deal with if he thought she was a fool. At any rate, the next thing he said that I could hear, was, 'Freckles,' and, oh, so condescendingly!"

"Nobody could say 'freckles' condescendingly," I told her.

"I suppose he was talking about mine. Finally, and the last thing I heard him say, was 'Black teeth.'"

"He couldn't have said 'black teeth,'" I began.

"Why not? I've just said it. You just said it. Why couldn't he say it?"

"Oh, well, he must have said 'back feet,' speaking of the dog, or 'back East,' or—"

"He said, 'Black teeth.' His enunciation is excellent. Doubtless he took lessons in public speaking before he went to the Senate. Do you know, Jeff, that is just what he is, himself. One long public speech for any occasion. Sorry. Come on, Angel, we're going to Memaloose."

"No," I said. "Why? What for?"

"Maybe we can get ourselves killed and land all cool and cozy in St. Dennis's cosmic spaces."

"Shame on you," I said. "And I'm not going to take you to Memaloose, Brigid. You needn't beg. I won't do it."

"When I came into camp yesterday," she said, "I closed the gate. When I went out to it again to look for you and Kent and saw Mayor Oakman coming, instead, the gate was wide open. That was about two o'clock I think. I was swimming, pushing the canoe across the lake. Afterward I was in the community house telephoning. I couldn't have seen anyone coming in or leaving during any of that time. Do you think someone did come in and go again, leaving the gate open? Or do you think that the gate swung open by itself?"

"Gates can and do," I said.

"Yes. But they can't and don't murder people. Come on, darling, let's go to Memaloose and have a look at that gate and—other things."

Looking at the gate was useless. We opened it and shut it and pushed it a little and didn't push it, and finally decided that, if the catch wasn't on it—and Brigid could not remember for certain whether she'd caught it or not—it might have swung open by itself, or that, maybe, it might not have swung open.

Looking at everything else at Memaloose was worse than useless. Brigid gazed at the lake, sprawling there with the old bruised calico hills upside down in it, and shivered. "If I hadn't taken the canoe back to the boathouse on Thursday, for no reason except that it made me jittery floating empty out there, Twill couldn't have come across the lake in it yesterday."

"Black wreath," I said, thinking about Joe's old hearse crawling up and down that road in the dogged sunshine. "Maybe Adam said 'black wreath.' Something will have to be done about a lot of funerals."

"He said, 'black teeth.' Before that he said, 'pineapple supreme' and 'freckles.'"

"Could it be barely possible," I asked, "that poison was found in that pineapple pudding?"

"No," she said, "because there wasn't any pineapple pudding. And no one was poisoned. Turn here, please, Jeff, and drive to Judge Shively's cottage. I want to go there first."

I stopped the car. "Brigid," I said, "I won't have it. I won't think of letting you snoop around down there in that cottage. I've got to put a stop to this some place. Don't beg. I won't do it."

36

White feathers were drifting around in the bedroom of the Judge's cottage like cotton drifts lazy through the air in Arizona. It was a queer thing that I should have noticed the butcher knife lying on the floor there before I noticed the feather pillow beside it, cut wide open.

"Fools!" Brigid said, meaning us. "Something was hidden in this pillow," she went on, sitting down beside it and stirring the feathers until she sneezed. "Why didn't we think of that? Miss MacDonald must have thought of it the moment I told her about the slip's being changed. She's cut it open and taken whatever was in it. Yes, see here, Jeff. This end of the pillow is sewed up with long stitches. Silk thread. Wasn't there a little sewing-kit in that bag of Clyde Shively's? Never mind I'll look later. No woman would sew a pillow with silk thread."

"If it was the first that came to hand?" I suggested.

"It wouldn't be."

"I'd hardly think a man would sew it at all."

"Yes, if he'd hidden something in it. These pillowslips fit tightly—see here? When he pulled the pillow out the slip turned wrong side out. He sewed the pillow up and put his seam down at the closed end of the slip where it wouldn't show. Now what could he have hidden in that pillow?"

"Who?" I asked.

"It must have been something small and light. The pillow wasn't heavy when I was handling it, and it didn't bulge."

"Some rare and precious jewel or gem, I suppose," I said. "Come on now, Brigid; let's get out of here."

"I'll bet that it was something Clyde Shively brought with him."

"The papers," I said.

"What papers?"

"The papers that always go with murders," I told her, and picked some feathers out of her hair.

"Don't," she said. "Miss MacDonald wasn't carrying anything but her big handbag when she came out of here, last night," she went on. "I'm going to look around."

There was nothing for it but to wait while she rummaged through the whole cottage, poking her fingers into every crick and cranny and turning things upside-down. In the little grip she found the sewing-kit with tan cotton and white silk thread in it. She said that the white silk thread was the one used to sew up the pillow. Beyond this single deduction she got nothing for all her trouble, but she made a lot of disorder for me to tidy up again.

She thought I needn't bother so much; but I went right ahead so she helped and hung the clothes up, and I put the small grip back in the big one and stood them in the closet where they belonged, and did my best to leave things exactly as we had found them.

"You think that Miss MacDonald and Mayor Oakman will be returning before long, don't you?" she asked.

"I shouldn't be surprised," I said.

"I should," she said, and went flipping out-of-doors when I was trying to brush her off.

As I feared, she was at the wheel of my car and I just had time to jump on the running board before she headed it straight for Twill's cottage. When we got there instead of going into the cottage, as I had also feared, she went into the garage and, as I'd never even thought of fearing, walked directly to another valise that was standing in there, and opened it.

Anybody would think that a man's capacity for being horrified would give out, in time. After living through three certain murders, none of them nice, and one doubtful murder with the body missing, why I should all but keel over because Brigid opened that valise, in a businesslike way, and dragged out another bloodstained pillow and something else white and fluffy, I don't know. Too many valises, too many pillows, too many bloodstains, too much Brigid being businesslike and knowing where to find things, something made me feel the need of air. I stepped outside and got some, in gasps.

It wasn't long before she came out of the garage, still being businesslike by brushing her hands off in a kind of finished though finicky way. "What's the matter with you now?" she asked, as if different things were always the matter with me.

"How did you know that grip was in Twill's garage?" I asked.

"I put it there," she said.

"You did not," I said. "Don't say such a thing."

"But I did. When I tidied Twill's cottage, Wednesday night, I put the pillow that was on the floor and Rosemary's frock in that suitcase and set it out in the garage. I didn't know what else to do with them. I told Miss Mac-Donald where they were. She has cut a piece out of that pillowslip, and out of the front of Rosemary's frock and taken them with her. The bloodstains, you know."

I still didn't feel so very good, but I stood up and began trying to pick a few more feathers out of Brigid's hair.

"Won't you please leave my hair alone," she said, "and listen? If Miss MacDonald believed that Rosemary killed the dog, why should she take the samples of blood to have them analyzed?"

"A matter of routine," I said. It just came to me, and it sounded fine, but Brigid said, only, "Yes—maybe," and folded her legs under her and sat down on them.

"Miss MacDonald's taking those bloodstained samples," she said next, "looks as if she thought that there might be a doubt as to whether Rosemary killed Funny on the pillow. But if Rosemary didn't shoot Funny, then who did shoot him, and why?"

"What does the dog matter, now?" I asked.

"Somebody shot him, for some reason."

"Rosemary shot him, for a good reason," I said.

"When I found Twill's body in the canoe," she said, "I only glanced at it—you know why. But I did see the wound. Could it be coincidence that whoever shot Twill shot him where Rosemary said she had shot him? No—I rather think that gate must have swung open."

"Let's go take another look at it," I said, and offered to help her up.

"What's that all over your fingers?" she asked.

"You left that iodine bottle uncorked in that bathroom back there," I told her.

"Sorry," she said. "It was such a tiny bottle. You must have spilled it all. But that doesn't look like iodine on your hand."

"It said iodine on the label," I said. "I spilled it all."

"Jeff, are my freckles that color?"

I looked at my fingers. "They are not," I said. "This stuff is a dull dirty brown. Your freckles are ornamental—kind of gleaming and gay."

"Sweet!" she said. One thing that made her so likable was her way of saying things.

"I thought we were going to look at the gate, honey?" I tried coaxing her.

"About Funny," she answered, not budging. "We have only Mayor Oakman's word for it, really, that he found him out there on the deserts."

"No," I reminded her. "Rosemary told all about burying him out there. And if I ever heard the truth I heard her telling it last night."

"I thought on Wednesday night that if I ever heard the truth I heard Rosemary telling it."

"She had to help Twill, then," I said. "He was her younger brother and she loved him. You can't blame her for that. Ladies should—" I was going on to say that they should understand each other when it came to things like that, but she interrupted so saucy that she threw me off.

"Lie?" she said.

"Love," I said.

"Not necessarily," she said. "All right, Jeff. If you're determined to leave here, I'll go. But do stop picking at me. Let me brush you off. You look as if you'd sat in those feathers."

We had a nice quiet trip on the way back; both of us, I guess, were sick of talking. We were driving into Ferras before she said:

"There weren't so many of us who heard Rosemary say that she had shot Twill rather far below the throat."

"Eavesdroppers might have been around, for all we know, after the dark shut down. And word gets passed around. It's surprising."

"There weren't many of us in camp yesterday afternoon, either," she said.

"Nobody has any way in the world of knowing who was or wasn't in that camp yesterday afternoon," I told her. "The gate was open, the deserts were free to be ridden, or the lake to be swum."

"I swam. Everyone knows it. I told lies all afternoon. I'm the only one who has freckles. Wouldn't it be distressing for St. Dennis?"

"For a girl of your age," I said, "you do get the craziest ideas of anybody I ever knew. In the first place, you were on the mountain at five minutes to twelve when Reggie heard the shooting."

"Reggie was frightened out of his wits. Any clever lawyer could discredit his testimony. Probably he could be proved moronic. You know, none of us ever paid any attention to anything he said—"

"But you are going to pay attention to something I'm going to say, right now," I told her. "Nobody would even think of accusing you of any wrongdoing—let alone murder. It's like you said about Reggie—it couldn't be done. So don't you put the idea into peoples' minds. Listen, honey: You aren't going to be nervous and scared and lose your sleep and get sick, are you?"

"No. Not really. I'd hate it for St. Dennis. I'd probably be acquitted. But trials aren't nice."

"Put it out of your mind right now," I begged. "Promise me that you won't give it another thought. Go on, promise. Please, honey."

"I'll try," she said. "Don't you worry about it, either, Jeff."

I tried not to; but it wasn't so easy with three funerals to attend and nothing to do but think during the services. Not that Kent didn't arrange the funerals fine, having them dignified, short and private. Just that everything was terrible.

Sunday morning all the hired help except Jeremiah left Hay Patch.

Monday morning Mrs. Duefife opened a bank account at the Ferras Bank with one of Kent's checks made out to her. The word went around town like wildfire—the amount being given at everything from a thousand dollars up to a quarter of a million. I have never heard the truth of the matter.

Monday, after the last funeral, Mrs. Duefife and Reggie departed for back East. The town was at the depot to see them off. Reggie kept dropping pennies in the slot machine, getting gum and chocolate out, until the train came. Remarks were made that this seemed very unfeeling so soon after a funeral.

Wednesday afternoon I got an airmail letter from Adam. It was posted from Pasadena. It said:

"Dear Jeff: Among ants, the males have the keenest eyesight, the females less keen, and the workers, though they have the best brains, are very often blind. You are a hard-working man, Jeff.

"Judge Shively has been found. He is dead and buried. A man who gave his name as D. R. Reorjeod was responsible for all the crimes at Memaloose. We discovered him barely in time to get a complete confession before he died from self-administered poison. The authorities here agree with me that further investigation, or publicity, will be unnecessary. The name you will note is difficult to pronounce, and I may have spelled it incorrectly

"I have telephoned to Kent giving him full instructions as to funerals, weddings, endowments and any other events that may be necessary during my absence. I am leaving for an extended trip through the Orient—perhaps. Affectionately and faithfully, your friend, Adam Oakman."

My first idea was to destroy that letter pronto. Then I decided that I should show it to Brigid first to make her stop worrying. She had gone to Hay Patch to keep folks from saying she was afraid to go, so I lit right out with it.

"Sounds like a Mex name to me," I said, after she had read the letter but while she was still saying nothing.

"Or Chinese?" she asked.

"Oh, well," I admitted, "if a person likes reading backward, it might come out something like Doe, J., Roe, R., bad men, both of them. I'm sure glad they have finally self-administered poison. Look at the work it is going to save county sheriffs—"

"It isn't funny," she kind of burst out. "It is rotten. That is what it is. I thought that MacDonald woman was honest—really honest. Do you think Mayor Oakman meant for you to decode this thing?"

"Maybe. He told me once he was always deciding that I was a fool and then changing his mind. He claimed it kept him apologizing."

"Why didn't he tell you straight out then?"

"He never tells things straight out," I said. "He's a millionaire."

After a while she said, "Nice what money can avoid doing, isn't it?"

37

I knew that Adam, the old codger, hadn't gone for an extended trip anywhere that would keep him long away from Oakman County. I'd given him a month. But he stayed away three months, so that his friends could decide that he had skipped the country for sure, and I could be kept on edge denying it and meeting all trains from the South.

At that it was luck, as much as anything else, that took me to the depot the night he got in on twenty-one from back East, waving and hollering at me, before the porter even got the step put down, about how was I and how was everybody.

"Fine," I kept telling him, "Fine!" And "Fine!" he kept saying when he got off the train, duded up fit to kill, and I asked him how he was. "Fine!"

"Ferras looks fine to me," he said next. "How has it been getting along without a mayor?"

"Fine!" I said.

"While I think of it," he said after a minute, "I've all sorts of messages for you from Kent and Rosemary. I saw them off for Europe last month. Honeymoon. She's a good girl, Jeff—intelligent and not bad-looking. The boy could have fared worse for a wife. But why don't you tell me some news? How is everybody? How's Jeremiah? How's Hay Patch?"

"Fine!" I said. We were in my car riding to Hay Patch by that time. "They say Jeremiah likes being lonesome."

"Tell me," he said, "how are the O'Dells? And Mac and Ernie? And Shorty, and Bert, and Slim and Taylor? Is Goldfield Red's garage paying any better? And say, how is Doctor Sprague? And Joe? Are the Penroys getting along all right? Has Rimrock drunk himself to death yet?"

"If you mean James Kelly," I said, "he is now a converted church member who hasn't touched a drop for three months."

"Well," he said, but kind of taken aback. "I'm glad to hear that. Have they been having revival meetings here in town?"

"No," I said. "There was a spelling bee at the schoolhouse the other night, but Rimrock didn't go. He's been opposing education here lately."

"How's Lang?" he asked, "and Timmy Monk, and Iverson?"

"Fine," I said.

When we let ourselves into the front hall at Hay Patch, Jeremiah was tiptoeing downstairs in his nightshirt, wearing a boxing glove and carrying a baseball bat. When he saw Adam he sat right down on the steps and began sobbing to shake the rafters with joy.

"Here's a homecoming," Adam said to me as he picked up the bat that came bumping down the stairs, "that I call a homecoming."

It took him quite a while to let Jeremiah welcome him and get him back to bed again; but, finally, Adam and I were free to go to the kitchen and rustle ourselves something to eat.

We talked about this and that until, "Well, Jeff," Adam said, offhandedly, when we were finishing up, "I suppose you have been able to satisfy Oakman County's curiosity concerning the Memaloose tragedies?"

"Only moderately," I said. "I could have wished you hadn't skipped the country when you did."

"I see," he said. "So they think that I'm the murderer; is that it?"

"Some of the crazy ones," I told him.

"O'Dell?" he asked, but sharp and fast.

"No, no," I said, stalling for time. "No, not O'Dell."

The trouble was that O'Dell wouldn't look at things right. He swore that he was going to tell Adam, when he got a chance, because he was sick and tired of Adam's thinking that he could get away with murder and make fools out of everybody all the time. So I had decided long ago to kind of take the edge off of it, if I could, by telling Adam first myself.

"Gratifying," he said, but kind of smirking.

"You bet," I said. "Another gratifying thing is that O'Dell is like Brigid, nice about keeping secrets."

Adam cocked his head and looked at me with that queer, pausing look that folks generally use only when they think that they've broken a tooth or swallowed a bone.

I knew that I had to tell him, so I did. "Adam," I said, O'Dell has figured out who the criminal was over at Memaloose. He may spring it on you, so I think you ought to know that he knows."

"He doesn't know. He can't know. But if he is actually making definite accusations, I'll—"

"No, he isn't," I said. "Brigid and he and I know. We haven't let it go any further, and we won't."

"Who is O'Dell accusing?" Adam asked, getting very hard.

There was nothing for it but finishing what I'd started. I hated it like thunder, but I told him.

He leaned back in his chair and heaved a long relaxing sigh. For a minute I could feel it doing me as much good as it was doing him.

"Jeff," he said, then, "you are the best friend I have on earth. I am telling you the truth, with our friendship as a pledge, when I say that my little daughter, Betty-Jean, is as innocent as a baby; that never in her poor little life did she do so much as think of a crime—much less commit one. As for O'Dell and his 'figuring,' I'll— By the Eternal! Is this your idea of a joke, Jeff? Even O'Dell can't be as crazy as that. Didn't anyone tell him that Betty-Jean was herself a victim of the murderous fiend? Are you and he trying to force me to disclose the identity of the real criminal? You can't do it. Or is O'Dell hoping to assure himself of my silence regarding his own daughter's deplorable behavior during those frightful days at Memaloose? In either case, it is sheer maliciousness—dirty slander. But I know how to deal with it. I've dealt with it in the past, and—"

"Hold on now, Adam," I said. "Hold on. Brigid went through a lot. You've got to remember that. O'Dell had a right to be interested. I think it is pretty white of him to say nothing—"

"You do; do you? 'White of him' to blacken my little daughter's name, after her death? Of course he's saying nothing. He wouldn't dare. He hasn't a shred of evidence."

"He has a lot of what he thinks is evidence," I said, and thought I'd better be going.

In the hall Adam began giving me messages to take to the O'Dells. It was quite a few minutes before he begged my pardon and said that maybe I was right. Maybe he shouldn't condemn a man and run him out of the county without hearing his side of the story. We went into the front parlor and I began explaining.

"O'Dell did take kind of a crazy starting point," I admitted. "He said that no woman who was a rotten bridge player and a good cook would sit playing bridge all afternoon when she was giving a company dinner. He said that Betty-Jean had begun her dinner by one o'clock and

by nature she'd have fussed with it all afternoon. He said
nothing much but murder would keep a good cook from
preparing her dessert—Pineapple Supreme this was—and
getting it into the freezing trays on a hot day like that day
was. He said she stayed tight in the living room because
she was determined to have the bridge game, with three
people, for her alibi. She never stepped out of there for a
minute all afternoon."

"However," Adam said, "she did have the alibi. A perfect one, as you have just explained."

"No. She came in during the worst of the storm, scared
to death—"

"Of the wind and the thunder," Adam said very sadly.

"O'Dell said likely she was afraid of storms and Twill
knew it. So he ran to her cottage to keep her company. Not
finding her there, he went to the Judge's cottage, arriving
just in time to see her kill Clyde Shively, or to know for
sure she'd done it."

Adam asked, "And her motive for killing an old friend?"

"O'Dell thought maybe they weren't so friendly. But
they'd known each other before. Likely he threatened to
tell something on her—something in her past life that she
didn't want known. She had been in the plot with him, to
begin with, but—"

"What 'plot'?"

"That's thickening. But, after she got here, she found
herself well fixed with a rich papa and everything nice.
She wanted Clyde Shively out of the way. If you'd told her
you were sending for the Judge—"

"Now that you mention the Judge?" Adam said, making
it a very sarcastic question.

"I'm coming to that. After she had shot Clyde Shively,
she threw herself on Twill's mercy. He loved her. He promised to help her. He sent her to the community house on
the run to set an alibi for herself. O'Dell thinks her saying

that she had telephoned to the Judge, during the storm, was her own idea. But not so smart as it seems, because likely she had telephoned when the storm began, and was just saying so."

"We return," Adam said, "at last to the Judge?"

"In the meantime," I said, "Twill, left alone there with the dead man, began looking around to see what could be done. Twill wasn't so anxious to come right out and take the blame for shooting a man in the back. The boy was young and in love. But pretty soon his being in love was the worst of it.

"O'Dell says it is easy to imagine the boy alone there in the cottage, scared, trying to make some plans, beginning to find the Judge's belongings around, and beginning to wonder where was the Judge, anyway. He found his glasses, and his cane, and his broad brimmed hat that shaded his face, and his clothes. Maybe first, maybe last, he found a white wig.

"Probably he didn't notice that Clyde Shively had black on his teeth, from where he'd pulled bits of tape off that had made them look ugly and missing. Probably he didn't notice that the brown age spots on his hands—you called them 'freckles'—would wash off. But he remembered how the old Judge had been practically in hiding in the cottage next door to Betty-Jean's for three days, showing himself only in darkened rooms. Maybe he remembered that Betty-Jean hadn't wanted to give the dinner party that night, but that you had insisted—as Miss MacDonald took pains to find out. Maybe he thought of Betty-Jean s ordering candles for the lights that evening. Anyway, whatever he thought, or found, some time in there it dawned on him for certain that old Judge Shively and his son Clyde Shively were one and the same person. After that, anything he thought was enough to drive him crazy. He knew that Betty-

Jean and this fellow must have been in cahoots, at best or worst, about something none too good.

"But he stuck to his promise to help her. He ripped the pillow open and hid the white wig, and maybe other things used for disguising, in it and sewed it up again with the thread he found, likely, when he was hunting for other things that had to be hidden. I guess, unless Lynn MacDonald has told what was in the pillow, exactly, we'll never know. Shively's being around Hollywood and having to do with actors, some, would have helped him with the tricks of fixing up for an old man."

"May I call your attention to the fact," Adam said, "that the things you are choosing to call 'disguises' were not hidden? You may invent a pillowful of wigs and costumes. The facts are that the cane, the hat, the old gentleman's clothes were all in plain sight there in his cottage."

"What on earth could Twill have done with them? Rosemary couldn't take a trunk with her. Canes and clothes and so on weren't easy to get rid of over at Memaloose. We were kind of bothered about the glasses; but we decided that he must have forgotten to put them in the pillow before he sewed it up—or maybe didn't find them until the last thing. Anyway, he must have stuck them in his pocket and forgot them. When he took his clothes off to go in swimming they could have dropped there in the chair seat where Brigid found them."

"Guess work! 'Maybe,' and 'probably'!"

"O'Dell thought that, after Twill had finally finished hiding things (the wall bed was the only place he could put the body where it might not be seen if somebody should look in the window—or under the bed in the other room, and that would have been worse) and got outside again, he decided that none of it was any use. So he probably wrote a note, saying that he had killed Clyde Shively—"

"A note? I was not aware that any note was found?"

"There wasn't. Being fact and not fiction, O'Dell says, either Rosemary or Twill actually succeeded in getting that note teetotally destroyed, instead of leaving it around for Will Cuppy to quote."

"Ah," Adam said. "A humorist enters. I see that we are now approaching the amusing aspects of the tragedies. Jeff, if this is your whimsical idea of a capital joke will you desist?"

"It isn't," I said. "But I'd just as soon desist. I'd sooner."

"Go on."

"After Twill wrote the note, the poor boy took a shot at himself there in his cottage. But, as Rosemary thought, he didn't want to kill himself. He didn't want to at all. So it was easy for him to decide that he'd better fix things a little safer for Betty-Jean before he tried another shot.

"He went to the community house and said he'd seen the Judge and his son just then, well after three o'clock. Betty-Jean had been in that room since before three, with the rest of you. She'd been getting along pretty well. So why, as Brigid said, should she wait until Twill had set her alibi for her and all, to get scared silly and go to pieces?"

"Why indeed? You weren't there. I was. My word should be as good as that—"

I interrupted in a hurry. "What scared Betty-Jean was that she knew Twill couldn't have seen both men. And she knew that he wasn't putting on, either. That he was cold furious. Probably he'd just been sorry for her when she'd left him at the cottage. She went to pieces by insisting on leaving, then and there. Twill saved her once—pushed her by main force back into the room. After he'd gone you saved her by refusing to let her leave the house—"

"This entire tale," Adam said, "is not only false, it is also dangerous and bad."

"There is that," I confessed, "about murders and the folks who do them, as a rule."

"And those who gossip about them, and make false accusations?"

"That's bad, too," I said. "O'Dell thought that Betty-Jean's saying all the time that Twill didn't do it, and couldn't on account of being a cripple, and so putting the idea of his doing it into all our minds, and starting us figuring how he could maybe have done it, was pretty mean. Poor judgment, too. Aiming at being very foxy and overshooting the mark."

"It takes a vicious imagination," Adam stated, "to turn loyalty into a crime."

"That's why O'Dell couldn't find it in his heart to blame Brigid much, or Rosemary at all," I said. "And of course the story that Rosemary finally told Miss MacDonald was true from start to finish as she knew it. She believed that she was telling the truth then, word for word."

"Granted," Adam said. "But for any of this fantastic theory of O'Dell's to be even slightly plausible, he should have to say that Betty-Jean's death was a suicide. It was not."

"He knows that," I said. "He knows she was killed."

"We have then another killer? A second one?"

"Yes," I said. "And almost another murder."

"There was but one murderer," he said. "Go on."

"After you and Miss MacDonald left, that morning," I told him, "I went back to Memaloose for another look around. Brigid went with me. In the Judge's cottage she found that the one small grip we thought Clyde Shively had brought with him fitted with room to spare into the big Gladstone valise that the old gentleman—as we supposed—had brought with him. Fact is, she found the little one put inside the big one and thought that Miss

MacDonald must have done it. Brigid didn't know why. I thought nothing of it, when I put them back in the closet that way. O'Dell figured that his bringing one grip inside the other, and a dudish suit of clothes, certainly looked as if he'd planned to come to Memaloose as an old man and make his getaway as an able-bodied young fellow. Why should he bother with all that, unless he had something afoot?"

"Why indeed?" Adam said. "That is, why should he bother with a third piece of luggage when he had the other two pieces?"

"Those were supposed to belong to the old Judge. They'd been seen and were going to be left some place to be found. Besides, he brought a six gun with him. He'd probably been told that was the make of gun generally carried in these parts. Well, didn't he come planning to kill somebody? Maybe, the young man you wrote and said that Betty-Jean was in love with? That is, supposing he was in love with her himself and pretty jealous? Or, maybe, you?"

"Originally, I believe," he said, "that was my own suggestion? I think I remember telling you that I should have been the victim."

"You were right, for once," I said. "He'd have had a fine chance to make away with you, if you'd started driving him over to the train that night. Suppose he knew that you'd left Betty-Jean a nice piece of money?"

"This makes a story," Adam said. "That is, it does as you tell it, disregarding point after point that can't be disregarded. For example, if Betty-Jean had been even slightly or unwillingly implicated in any of this, do you think that she would have urged me to get a criminologist on the case?"

"O'Dell says that few people in times of danger are consistently dull. He said that Betty-Jean was pretty

bright several times. One of them was when she wanted the
detective. She thought that you wouldn't engage a man
from L. A. or a woman from anywhere. She was wrong
about that. But she was right about thinking that you'd
phone to the lawyer when she gave you his card."

"She did not give me the lawyer's card or mention him
to me, ever."

"O'Dell figured," I said, "that when you and Miss Mac-
Donald traced that telephone number in L. A., you'd find
a vacant apartment and the janitor would tell you that a
man moved in there for a few weeks but had moved out
again, leaving no address."

"I'm sorry, Jeff," Adam said. "I shouldn't have allowed
you to go on and on with this. My brief association with
Lynn MacDonald must have infected me with a germ of
her gruesome curiosity. This structure of O'Dell's falls to
pieces, doesn't it, when I tell you that we found Judge
Shively's body in Pasadena and that he had been murdered?"

"I'm sorry, too," I said. "But you see O'Dell thought
that this Clyde Shively, before he ever came up to Memaloose, had killed his father, and got away with it, and told
around that the old gentleman had gone to Nevada. It
wouldn't have done to have the Judge living where folks
might find him when they started hunting for him."

"The imagination of a pen-pusher!" Adam said, like
he was grieving over it. "Go on, since you insist. If there
should be even one small detail to which O'Dell confesses
the least uncertainty, I should be particularly interested in
hearing of it—for a change."

"The chief one is," I said, "why in thunder Twill came
back to camp. O'Dell thinks that the boy got cold feet,
knowing how easy a cripple would be to trace. But he says
that nobler motives—giving himself up and saving either

Betty-Jean or Rosemary, or both if they happened to be in trouble, could be considered by those looking for sentiment. O'Dell says Twill's coming back when only the two girls and Reggie were on the place seems to favor the fear theory.

"If he'd been hiding in the boathouse across the lake, say, he'd have known when we all left that morning. Then he might have waited until noon, when he knew Reggie would be in some kitchen at the back of the camp, eating his lunch. Twill thought sure that the girls would help him. Maybe hide him on the place until they could get a car for him to leave in. Something like that. Like I told you, O'Dell couldn't be positive.

"But he was certain that Betty-Jean saw Twill coming in the canoe across the lake. She knew that Rosemary was out riding and that Reggie was eating somewhere. Maybe she thought that Reggie didn't matter, because he was in love with her and wouldn't tell on her. Or, maybe, she didn't do much thinking. The shock of seeing Twill, when she really believed that Rosemary had killed him—"

"Stop right there!" Adam ordered. "It can't be possible that you are going on to accuse Betty-Jean of killing Twill—the boy she loved?"

"Some of us wondered how much she loved him," I was bound to say. "How much she could love anybody? We're pretty sure that she didn't trust him; that she believed he'd tell on her to save himself, if he needed to, the same as she'd have told on anybody to save herself, if she could. O'Dell says that loving requires intelligence. He didn't think Betty-Jean had much of that—none to spare. Her shooting Twill twice—believing that the second wound would make folks think that Rosemary had shot him, like she told us. And then, to cap the climax, sticking that gun away under him there in the canoe—"

"Ah! The revolver. May I ask how Betty-Jean came into possession of it?"

"Likely she met him on the shore and got into the canoe with him, begging him like everything to go away again. Likely he refused. Being sweethearts, she probably cuddled up while she was coaxing him to go. Maybe she felt the gun in his pocket. Maybe she swiped it. Twill was the one living person who knew her secret. Shooting is quicker than thinking and it is pretty certain she didn't do much thinking. She shot, twice.

"But, back in her cottage, she had plenty of time to realize what a foolhardy thing she'd done. Or, maybe, she didn't realize it even then, until she peeked out of her front window and saw Brigid swimming to the canoe. Desperation and vanity—'the inviolable vanity of complete ignorance,' O'Dell called it—explain what she did next.

"Acrasia was in the shelter. Maybe Betty-Jean had seen Rosemary riding her in at one o'clock, bareback, as easy as sitting in a merry-go-round. If not, she'd seen her doing it time and again. Betty-Jean, knowing nothing whatever of horses, thought that if Rosemary could, why couldn't she?"

"Speaking of complete ignorance," Adam said, "if O'Dell knew anything of that horse he'd know that Betty-Jean could never have bridled her. Even Kent and. Rosemary had some difficulty in doing so."

"Yes. We thought that was the reason Rosemary left the bridle on her when she was planning to start for Hay Patch in an hour or so. But Acrasia was a little tamed to ladies, on account of Rosemary's riding her so much, so by hook or crook, Betty-Jean managed to mount her. O'Dell thinks that Betty-Jean believed she could ride right down to California and get with her friends. He says the most remarkable thing is that the horse carried her even a quarter of a mile before throwing her.

"Mac and Ernie showed O'Dell the exact place. There are mean rocks there, same as everywhere on these deserts. O'Dell though that Betty-Jean hit her head on a bad jutting one there, and rolled on down into the gully. Acrasia—the second killer—lit out for Memaloose and her shady shelter again."

"Where she removed her own bridle?"

"Do you remember it being off her, when you came in?"

"I do not. Of course I don't. I was completely occupied with that—"

"Neither do I remember about the bridle," I confessed. "And neither did Brigid. But I do remember that when you stopped Kent and me, after we came in my car, Kent jumped right on Acrasia and rode down to Rosemary's cottage. So the bridle had to be on then. And that means that Acrasia had it on when we came in."

"I don't remember Kent's riding down to Rosemary's," Adam said.

"You were all excited. He did. And when he came to the community house after you'd phoned him, you reproved him for having his mind on horses. And that is a kind of excuse—the only one we can think of, for our being so dull that day. The boys, all of us, including even Joe and Doc Sprague knew horses—some. We couldn't imagine even a tenderfoot trying to ride Acrasia bareback. She was the only horse on the place. Murder was heavy on all our minds. And lost bodies. So, when the boys found Betty-Jean out there all of us kept right on thinking of murder. I've wondered if I'd left Dollar on the place, instead of riding her off on Thursday, what might have happened then?"

"Why do you wonder what might have happened," Adam asked, "instead of wondering what did happen? Why do you cling to this fantastic story of O'Dell s, forgetting what I told you at the outset of all this, with our friendship for a pledge? I told you the truth, Jeff, when I told you that my little daughter, Betty-Jean, was as innocent as a baby. I'll add that she did not attempt to ride Acrasia. That she was not thrown from her. I'll add that she is as guiltless as O'Dell's own daughter, Brigid. Perhaps more so. Though I can't see that Brigid's behavior did any real harm, other than shortening my own lifetime by perhaps a score of years."

I thought of telling him that there was still another theory, more mine than O'Dell's, only I thought that he was sick of theories. I knew I was, and of the sound of my own voice. For quite a while I'd been reminding myself of Mrs. Duefife. Still, I did keep on thinking of my own theory, very much surprised that I had been right and O'Dell wrong, until I noticed Adam counting on his fingers.

"Kent and Rosemary," he was saying. "The two O'Dells, you, myself—"

"Reggie and Mrs. Duefife," I helped him out. "But O'Dell was back East at the time."

"What I was wondering," he said, "was whether a secret shared by half a dozen persons could remain a secret? At any rate, I cannot have you and the O'Dell's accusing—"

"Nobody is accusing," I said.

"You are accusing. Of course you are accusing. What is all this theorizing but direct accusation? But, strangely enough, despite the fact that O'Dell started from a false premise and so reached a false conclusion, some of his reasoning happens to be fairly exact.

"When Lynn MacDonald came to Memaloose that night she had seen Clyde Shively's body, at Joe's, and she had noted the traces of recent disguise that you mentioned. She told no one but me—not even Joe—so how O'Dell got hold of the idea I can't fathom. However, so far at least he was right.

"This Clyde Shively was a rascal of the worst sort. Blackmailing backwash from Hollywood. He was older

than we supposed—death made him look younger. He had
been a no-good, wastrel son in the Shively household when
my wife went to them and when little Betty-Jean was born.
All these years, undoubtedly, he meant to use his knowledge as a means of getting money from me. He, and not
the Judge, wrote the letters to me telling me of Betty-Jean.
Had I decided to go to Pasadena, he certainly would have
had arrangements made for greeting me in the old family
home there. Hail and Farewell!

"O'Dell happened to be right, also, about Clyde Shively's murdering his father and telling the old man's few
remaining friends that he had gone to Nevada. The Judge
had been blind and childish for years. It wasn't hard, we
presume, to remove all signs of identification and take the
poor old man out in a small yacht at night and drown him
in the bay there. Lynn MacDonald and I traced the body
through the unidentified persons who had been brought
to the morgue.

"Clyde Shively himself, when he was pretending to be
his father at Memaloose, gave me the lawyer's card. The
lawyer—that is, the supposed lawyer—was an accomplice.
We found an empty apartment when we went to see him.
We still hope to find him, though as yet we have been un-
successful.

"Lynn MacDonald thought that this prearrangement
a spurious lawyer definitely settled the fact that Shively
intended to commit some crime at Memaloose and effect
his escape by means of his disguises. That is—a decrepit
old man would be missing, and sought. A dapper middle-
aged man, somewhat on the youngish side, would be
quietly going his way.

"It would seem that I was, probably at least, the intended victim. What his exact plans were, we shall never
know. He brought the Colt's revolver with him. But the

situation here shaped itself excellently for him. The Tumboldt Mountain Road, for example. Knock me in the head,
change his clothes and run the car overboard. Then, walk
a few miles to Ferras and take the train. An automobile
accident, when and if found. Or, kill me and drop me over
and proceed with the car—"

"There's your plot," I said, or tried to say. But, "I'm
talking now," he said, and added, kind of worriedly,
"Where was I?"

I felt like saying, "At the bottom of Dead Man's Hook,"
but I didn't. I knew that if I did, he'd accuse me of something; so I just said I didn't know.

"At any rate," he said, "when Miss MacDonald came
to Memaloose that night, after stopping at Joe's in Ferras, she was all but convinced that Rosemary's story was a
lie. She reached this conclusion by an astonishingly simple
method. It seems odd, now, that none of us thought of it.
She merely premised that bodies could not disappear in a
trice. Since they could not, they had not. So she believed
that Twill had shot Clyde Shively—who she was certain was
also Judge Shively—and had escaped; Twill that is, with
Rosemary's help. She had even asked Ernie—she took quite
a liking to Ernie, by the way, for some reason—whether
there was a dog, or a cat, or some small animal on the place.

"Finding Twill's body, recently murdered, changed her
opinion as to Twill's being the criminal. She chose to say
that finding Twill's body 'simplified' the entire affair. An
affectation, of course. As was her way of repeating, 'But
what can't be, isn't.' The childishness of that remark made
it exceptionally irksome to me."

"Before we get clear off the subject," I said, "if Miss
MacDonald believed Rosemary's story about killing the
dog, why in thunder did she take the bloodstained things
away with her to have them analyzed?"

"A matter of strict routine, I was told," he said. It gave me a queer, eerie feeling. As if an old ghost had come creeping up and pinned a medal on my chest.

"Proof," he was going right along, "was her pet obsession. By the way, she made out quite a case against Kent—supposing it had been possible for him to get out of jail—and, also, a case against our Reggie. Reggie, it seemed had no alibis and did have motives—of sorts. She did this—outlined the theoretical cases, that is—in order to show me what unproved evidence could be made to do.

"In fairness, though, and I am a fair man, Jeff, I suppose I must grant that, though she took infinite pains to prove her evidence, her reasoning, step by step, paralleled O'Dell's. Yes, to all intents and purposes, it was precisely the same as O'Dell's. With the somewhat important exception that her reasoning led her to the right criminal."

"Who was?" I asked, just to please him.

"A doll-faced moving-picture extra named, absurdly, Iris Fields. She was Clyde Shively's wife. He married her a year ago. She has led him a merry chase, we gathered. He was insanely jealous of her. But they needed money—preferably much; if not, as much as they could get. So she came here pretending to be my little daughter, Betty-Jean, who died when she was five years old."

"That was what I kind of thought," I said, "that she wasn't your daughter. But O'Dell said that while in fiction she couldn't be, in fact she almost assuredly was. Some of us who could remember thought that she looked like your wife."

"She looked like all the snub-nosed, big-eyed blondes in the world," he said. "O'Dell should have known that no daughter of mine could have been as damn dull as she was."

"Pretty good actress, though," I said. "Most of the time."

"And, perhaps," he said, "at least part of the time, a woman with a few good instincts? I've wondered, Jeff, if her first crime—her killing Clyde Shively that night, might have been committed to save my life?"

"O'Dell kind of thought you'd wonder that," I said. "But he didn't take a bit of stock in the idea."

Adam gave me a very queer long look. "O'Dell," he said, and sighed, "is crazy."

"He has to be," I said. "That's how he makes his living."

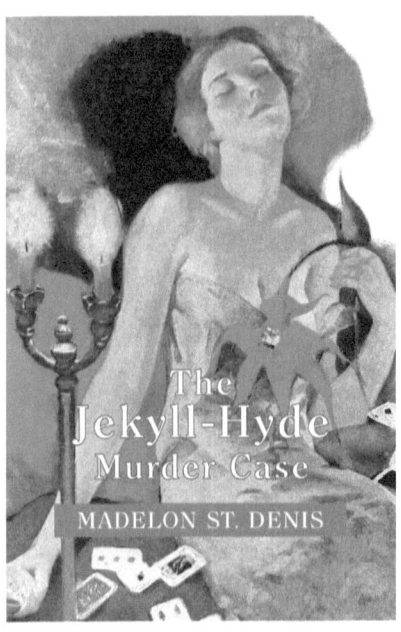

Coachwhip Publications

CoachwhipBooks.com

I'll Hate Myself in the Morning

Murder on the Left Bank

Elliot Paul

THE BAND PLAYED
MURDER
EDITH HOWIE

CRY MURDER
EDITH HOWIE

NO FACE TO
MURDER
EDITH HOWIE

Coachwhip Publications
CoachwhipBooks.com

Coachwhip Publications
CoachwhipBooks.com

WHISPER
MURDER!

VERA KELSEY

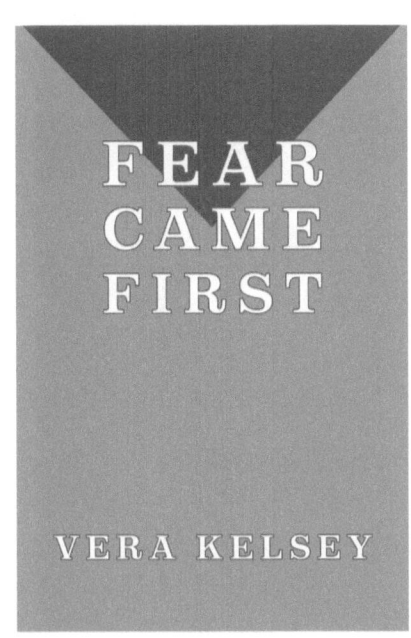

FEAR
CAME
FIRST

VERA KELSEY

LATE
for the
FUNERAL

Douglas and Dorothy
Stapleton

The Railroad
Murder Case
R. M. LAURENSON

Coachwhip Publications

CoachwhipBooks.com

Coachwhip Publications

CoachwhipBooks.com

MURDER
À LA RICHELIEU
THE ADELAIDE ADAMS MYSTERIES
ANITA BLACKMON

**THERE IS
NO RETURN**
THE ADELAIDE ADAMS MYSTERIES
ANITA BLACKMON

THE CRIME,
THE PLACE,
AND THE GIRL

DOUGLAS AND
DOROTHY STAPLETON

CRIME IN
CORN-WEATHER

MARY MEIGS ATWATER

Coachwhip Publications
CoachwhipBooks.com

Jack Dolph

MURDER MAKES THE MARE GO

THE CASEBOOK OF
MR. CARRINGTON
SIMON
CARRINGTON'S CASES
J. STORER CLOUSTON

THE
DARTMOUTH
MURDERS

THE
WAILING ROCK
MURDERS

CLIFFORD
ORR

HIDE AND GO SEEK
with, GOING TO ST. IVES

HOTEL

COLVER HARRIS

Coachwhip Publications

CoachwhipBooks.com

The Hollow Tree Mystery

MADELON ST. DENIS

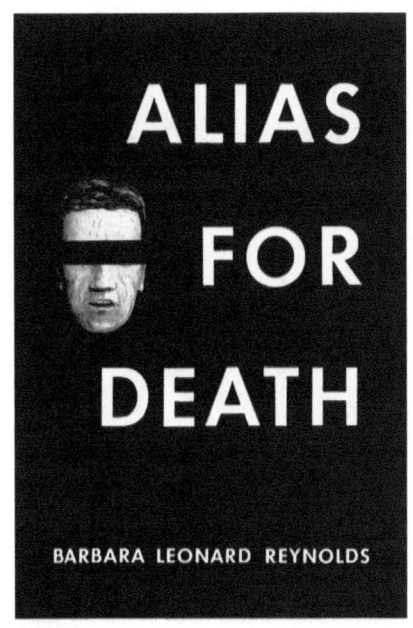

ALIAS FOR DEATH

BARBARA LEONARD REYNOLDS

VULTURES IN THE SKY

A HUGH RENNERT MYSTERY

TODD DOWNING

SAMUEL ROGERS

YOU'LL BE SORRY!

YOU LEAVE ME COLD!

Coachwhip Publications

CoachwhipBooks.com

THE
SLEEPING CAT

Isabel Ostrander

Scarecrow
EATON K. GOLDTHWAITE

TYLINE PERRY

THE OWNER
LIES DEAD

PATTERN
IN BLACK
AND RED

FARADAY KEENE

Coachwhip Publications

CoachwhipBooks.com

THE
SARA ELIZABETH
MASON
MYSTERIES

MURDER RENTS A ROOM

THE CRIMSON FEATHER

DEAD
WEIGHT

ADDISON
SIMMONS

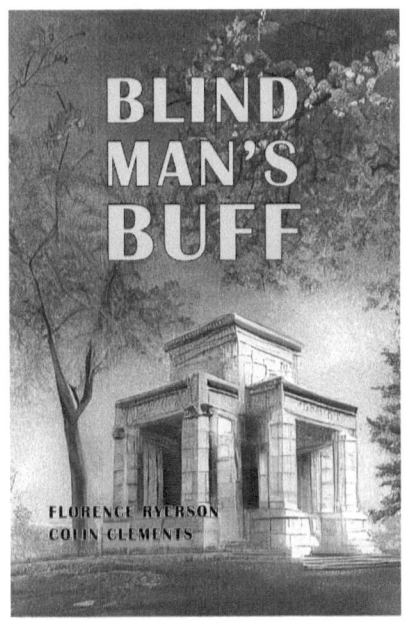

BLIND
MAN'S
BUFF

FLORENCE RYERSON
COLIN CLEMENTS

VIRGINIA RATH

THE ANGER
OF THE BELLS

Coachwhip Publications

CoachwhipBooks.com

www.ingramcontent.com/pod-product-compliance
Lightning Source LLC
Chambersburg PA
CBHW030341020726
47493CB00003B/628